LONESOME RIDGE

More from Maisey Yates

LONESOME RIDGE

MAISEY YATES

KENSINGTON
PUBLISHING CORP.

kensingtonbooks.com

KENSINGTON BOOKS are published by

Kensington Publishing Corp.
900 Third Avenue
New York, NY 10022

All Kensington titles, imprints, and distributed lines are available at special quantity discounts for bulk purchases for sales promotion, premiums, fund-raising, educational, or institutional use.

Special book excerpts or customized printings can also be created to fit specific needs. For details, write or phone the office of the Kensington Sales Manager: Kensington Publishing Corp., 900 Third Avenue, New York, NY 10022. Attn. Sales Department. Phone: 1-800-221-2647.

KENSINGTON and the K with book logo Reg. US Pat. & TM Off.

ISBN: 978-1-4967-5350-2
ISBN: 978-1-4967-5351-9 (ebook)

First Kensington Trade Paperback Printing: March 2026

10 9 8 7 6 5 4 3 2 1

Printed in the United States of America

The authorized representative in the EU for product safety and compliance
is eucomply OU, Parnu mnt 139b-14, Apt 123
Tallinn, Berlin 11317, hello@eucompliancepartner.com

To the wild ones

Chapter 1

I never was a lady, but now I think I've gone too far.

—Belle Martin's Diary, July 1865

Jessie Jane Hancock was the proud owner of a whole collection of toxic traits.

Generally, she found them to be a good time at the very least. But currently, her desperate need to climb impossible mountains was eating at her. Making her life downright miserable, in fact.

So miserable that she got distracted and did something she rarely ever did: Jessie Jane missed a trick. Which was how she found herself tumbling off her horse face-first into the arena dirt.

"Whoa there."

She popped up and looked across the arena at her older brother West, who was not on his way to help her up. Instead, he was sitting there on the back of his horse, his arms crossed across his broad chest as he stared at her.

"Thanks for the help," she groused as she stood up and hauled herself up onto her own mount.

West only looked at her, the maddening fool. "If you fall off the horse, you have to get back on again. No one can do it for you."

"Well, aren't you a big old Magic Eight Ball."

"I've been called a lot of things, Jess, but rarely that."

"*Rarely* isn't *never*, West."

She was supposed to be rehearsing a new routine for this summer's opening of Butch Hancock's Wild West Show. Instead, she was stewing. About the upcoming mayoral election. The thing was, everyone hated the current mayor.

Well. That wasn't true; Danielle had been elected. But she was a mean girl. She had been a mean girl in high school, and she was mean now. She had very notoriously stolen the town librarian's fiancé—though Jessie Jane definitely believed that the man in question needed to be held equally accountable. But the man in question was basically a turnip with testicles. So she gave him less credit for the seduction because he was an idiot.

Danielle wasn't an idiot. For all that she was an awful human being.

Rustler Mountain was a small town nestled in the southern Oregon mountains only eight miles from the California border. It had a rich gold rush history, and was steeped in the myth and legend of the Wild West. The Hancock family had made money off that myth and legend for years.

With their reputation, there was nothing else to do but lean into it.

In Rustler Mountain, things were black and white. It was as simple as good guys and bad guys. Some of the town was descended from lawmen, while other folks . . . Well, they were outlaws.

The Wilder family being the most notorious of the outlaws, given that back in the late 1800s Austin Wilder had been shot dead in the main street of Rustler Mountain by Sheriff Lee Talbot. So when, one hundred and fifty years later, a Talbot and a Wilder had married, the narrative of the town had been suddenly disrupted.

It was like a mountain that had stood unchanging for centuries had suddenly ruptured, reordering the landscape around it.

Those clearly defined lines weren't so cleanly delineated anymore.

There had been big pushes to correct some of the misinformation that had stood as history for well over a century, and as the local narrative changed, so did some of the ways that the whole town worked.

She couldn't lie—it was a little bit annoying to have more of the nice townies in her favorite bar on the weekends. But it was also nice to have some more locals showing up to the Wild West Show.

The Hancocks' show, which featured historical reenactments and trick riding, along with rodeo events, was extremely popular with neighboring communities, but was often wasted on their own. But again, that had to do with the reputation of the Hancock family.

A reputation that rarely bothered her. Except now . . .

"I can hear you thinking."

"I doubt it. I assume deep thoughts operate at a frequency you can't actually hear."

West snorted. "If only. But unfortunately, I know you too well."

"That viper is running *unopposed*."

"The viper?"

"Danielle LeFevre. There is no other mayoral candidate, and just three days left to declare."

"Not your problem."

"It's everyone's problem. You know that noise ordinance she's been amping for is going to affect us—which isn't even fair. Her parking permit stuff is outrageous, and she's misallocating funds—you can be sure of that. She wants to gut funding for the Historical Society, and she's now reversing her stance on the new plaques in town saying we're . . . revising history or something when you know it was about correcting lies and making sure people know the truth about the history of this place."

"I agree with you. She sucks. But why you?" West asked.

She didn't answer that question directly. "I just can't understand why no one else is running against her."

"They aren't dying to be in charge of a town with under two thousand people so they can lord their supposed authority over everyone around them?"

"All right. When you put it like that."

"Danielle isn't your problem. She's just going to do what she's going to do. Spend money on silly trips that probably should've gone to patch cracks in the sidewalk. End up stealing the librarian's fiancé, which I wouldn't even kick up a fuss about except that he has the same name as her brother."

Jessie made a face. "Ugh."

"But hey," West continued, "our ancestors were full-on betrayers and murderers."

"Not *all* of them. Just *one* of them was."

"One of them was a courtesan."

"You say that like it's a bad thing." Jessie Jane grinned widely at her brother.

"No, I didn't. I'm just pointing it out."

"If something is in demand, it's a smart business decision to go into that business. And I think we know what sells. Always," she pointed out.

"I'm certainly not dragging the great and glorious Belle Martin. Not for any reason at all. My point is, we have an eclectic history."

"Sure."

And that history pretty much never included walking the straight and narrow. Oh sure, they were on the up and up with the Wild West Show. But Jessie couldn't deny that she had some side hustles that were a little less than scrupulous. Her farrier business, on the other hand, was totally scrupulous.

And anyway, regarding the gambling, it was her opinion that if people wanted to bet their hard-earned money on horse races, fistfights, and football games, it wasn't her job to talk them out of it. And she made a little bit of cash whenever she talked them into it.

She was good at explaining a position. Holding it.

If she knew one thing, it was that she was . . . Well, one of her friends in high school had said that she should start a cult. Because for all that she was rough around the edges, she had a way with people.

A hard-earned way.

Not with everybody, though. Flynn Wilder came to mind. He was not charmed by her. Not at all. Annoying, because he was a sexy bastard. Another unclimbable mountain, but one that Jessie had long ago accepted she would never scale. There were a lot of handsome men. If she wanted to hook up, she could just . . . pick one of them. She didn't need to borrow trouble with a Wilder.

But what a spectacle it would be . . .

"You're literally scheming," West said.

"I'm not *scheming*." West continued to treat her to the patented hard glare that many women about town called *sexy* and she called *annoying*. "Okay. I'm lightly scheming. It's a mild scheme. But it will probably never make it out of the scheming phase."

He lifted his brows. "And if it does?"

"At that point it will become a *plot*," she explained.

"Tell me more."

"If we execute it, then it's a crusade. Maybe even a quest."

"We?"

Jessie looked out at the mountains, at the jagged line where the pine trees met the wide blue sky. "Don't worry. I'm not going to involve you in anything. Yet."

"What I would like to involve you in is a perfectly executed trick-riding routine where you don't break your neck."

"I can do that."

She urged her horse forward, but she couldn't keep the idea from turning in her head, over and over again.

She had lied to her brother. This was more than just a scheme. More than a plot.

She had a feeling that before the day was out, it was, indeed, going to become a quest.

And when Jessie Jane Hancock went on a quest, she didn't come back home empty-handed.

Flynn Wilder was happy that his brothers were happy. He really was. But there was some complexity to that happiness on his end.

Austin and Carson being happily hitched changed the dynamics at the family ranch. It was all good. Of course it was.

It was only that it meant things were different. They didn't all go down to The Watering Hole in a big group anymore. Most days it was just Dalton, his lifelong best friend, and his younger sister Cassidy. And he was getting a little tired of Cassidy hanging out with them.

She had a crush on Dalton, and everybody knew it. It was damn near embarrassing to witness. He never wanted to say anything about it, but it wasn't like Dalton didn't know. It was impossible to not know.

Though he was pretty sure Cassidy didn't know, or rather, she pretended not to know.

"Your sister's a nice girl," Dalton had said just the other day. "But I have literally known her since she was a snot-eating child."

"She was nine when she moved here. She wasn't exactly a snot-eating child."

He wasn't sure if calling what Cassidy had done "moving here" was the correct choice of words. She had been abandoned by her mother at Christmas, brought to live at the Wilder Ranch when she had never met her father's side of the family.

He was well aware of the complexities of family issues. He might have different ones from his younger sister, but he had plenty.

Hell, they all did, really. His older brothers were actually his half brothers. Their mother had taken off when they were young. His mother lived in town but . . .

She'd married into a real family. The right one. All respectable and rich, and definitely nothing to do with their dad and his bad reputation and all of his issues.

Flynn had gone to visit his mom, even though his dad had primary custody.

She had always made the custody arrangement out to be a kindness. She had wanted Flynn to stay with his brothers. But . . . after his dad had died, when he was still a young teenager, she hadn't rushed to get him.

He had continued to see her on some holidays. Sometimes over the summer.

When his grandpa, James Parker, had died, he'd left Flynn Lonesome Ridge, a rocky, nearly inhospitable mountaintop where Flynn had had a house built. He hadn't seen the point of turning down this acknowledgment from his mother that he was connected to her family.

But he had always been a Wilder. That was the thing.

No one thought of him as part of his mother's new family, and certainly not his stepfather's family.

Not even now that his half sister was the mayor.

She was also a deeply unpleasant human being, so he basically wanted nothing to do with her. It went both ways. Fine with him.

His younger half brother, Mike, was a douchebag who sold insurance. Yeah. He was happy with their lack of interaction. He knew he made Mike and Danielle uncomfortable, and that was wild to him, because he didn't make *anybody* uncomfortable. The Wilder family outlaw reputation had been difficult for Carson and Austin. Flynn had sunk right into it. Maybe it was because he had a whole other respectable family to rebel against. Maybe that made being an outlaw feel good.

He had actual enemies to flaunt his bad boy reputation at.

Sometimes he could see the envy in Mike's eyes. Back when they'd been kids. When Flynn had ridden up to school on his motorcycle, or on the back of his horse. When some aspect of his unconventional upbringing had been on show.

Yeah. Because what teenage boy wanted to try to live up to the insurance sales legacy of Mike's father? Especially when his half brother was getting to smoke, drink, and have all the sex he wanted?

Flynn had *lived* for that. For being the envy and outrage of his maternal relatives.

The truth was, he still did.

But right now, he wasn't looking for envy and outrage. He was looking for a cold drink, and maybe an easy lay. That was the other problem with Cassidy tagging along. It made things a little awkward.

Mostly because she wasn't doing the same thing. She was always outside the action, and he had a feeling it was her crush that kept her like a vestal virgin.

He wanted to tell her to knock it off. To go find some guy besides Dalton and have a good time, for God's sake. Life was too short to moon after people who didn't want you around. He was intimately acquainted with that truth.

But he couldn't say so to Cassidy. Well. He could. He just wasn't going to. Because while he wanted to give her advice, he also figured her pride was an important piece of this equation. He would never do anything to injure her pride.

Because that was another thing he knew as an unwanted child. It took a lot to build damaged pride up. He had found it in claiming his connection to the Wilder family. And he knew that Cassidy had done the same. But sometimes he could still see the little girl who had been left on their doorstep at Christmas. He never wanted her to be hurt.

"What are we drinking tonight?" Cassidy asked as they walked into The Watering Hole. It was a dive. And he loved it. The place was grimy in all the best ways. The neon sign out front made it clear exactly what kind of establishment it was. And if that didn't tell you, the line of motorcycles parked by the curb ought to give you another hint. If you still didn't catch the drift, walking in and actually seeing who populated the place would do it.

Of course, the vibe was a little bit watered down now. Austin had married Millie Talbot, the town librarian, daughter of the former sheriff, descendent of the actual sheriff who had killed the first Austin Wilder in a shoot-out in the 1800s.

Millie liked to come to the bar now. And sometimes she brought her friends. Who had then started bringing their friends. They clustered about like anthropologists observing a society they didn't belong to.

Granted, their presence had freshened up the dating pool. Of course, he used the term *dating* loosely.

"Why don't you choose tonight's drink, Cass?"

Cassidy's eyes widened with glee. "Really?"

"Sure," Dalton said.

Cassidy practically skipped over to the bar, and Flynn and Dalton exchanged a glance. But they didn't say anything. Flynn had only had a couple of conversations with Dalton about her crush. Anything more felt disloyal.

Flynn scanned the crowd, looking to see if any of the women caught his eye.

"Redhead," said Dalton.

Flynn glanced in the direction his friend was looking and nodded. She was pretty. Not really what he was looking for right now. *What* are *you looking for?*

Well. That was an interesting question.

There was a restlessness inside him. It had something to do with his brothers getting married. He knew that. This feeling that the band was breaking up. That they weren't just outlaws riding endlessly into the sunset. His brothers were grown men now with *responsibilities.* Austin was a father now.

He had a feeling Perry and Carson wouldn't waste a whole lot of time before having babies.

It made him feel . . . Well, like the ridiculous youngest brother that he was.

And then the door opened. He saw the crowd's reaction to whoever it was before he turned to look.

His heart slammed against his rib cage, and all his blood rushed south of his belt buckle. There she was. Long brown hair cascading over her shoulders, tight black tank top showing off her incredible rack. Her jeans were bedazzled, those rhinestones flashing as her hips moved.

Jessie Jane Hancock.

The woman drove him nuts. In all the ways a woman possibly could.

"*Damn,*" Dalton said.

"Yep," Flynn said, gritting his back teeth.

He couldn't even deny his attraction with a snarky comment. Because she was looking so fine, it would be a criminal lie to pretend otherwise.

Jessie's eyes scanned the room. And when her gaze landed on him, he felt it. But what shocked him more than anything was that she began to walk toward him, those glittering blue eyes laser focused.

It was like an electrical current arced between them, and he found himself taking a step toward her.

"Well, howdy, Flynn Wilder," she said. "Fancy meeting you here."

"I'd ask what a girl like you is doing in a place like this, but this is exactly where a man goes to find a girl like you."

"Touché. Usually when I'm looking for a man like you, I go to the streets."

"Careful," he said. "Perilously close to calling yourself a lady of the night there."

"Oh, if I intended to say that, I would."

They regarded each other for a moment. Sometimes he wondered whether they were closer to a fistfight or fucking against the nearest wall.

He didn't hit women.

So in truth, it could only be the one thing. On this, he had to congratulate himself for his self-control. Despite all the years and all the sparks, he'd never once made a move on her.

"I have no doubt. I'm not going to bet on any team, buy a piece of land from you, or invest in something, so if this is a scheme . . ."

"That's funny. My brother said that I was scheming earlier today."

Well, he didn't like her brother either.

"Are you?"

One of her brows lifted, and her pink lips curved into a smile. "Maybe. And believe me when I say, you're going to want in on this."

"I doubt it."

"You don't know what I have to say yet."

"Well, let's see. You are Butch Hancock's great-great-great-great-great-great-granddaughter. And he betrayed my just as many times great-grandfather. Historically, alliances between the Wilders and the Hancocks don't really work out."

"Well, I promise I won't frame you for murder." She smiled, and right then he was actually certain that she *would* frame him for murder if the need arose. Because that innocent smile was a lie. There was nothing innocent about Jessie Jane. The trouble was, that was exactly why she appealed to him so much.

"I'll make sure I have an alibi if we should ever speak again."

"Just give me thirty seconds," she said.

He looked toward the bar. Cassidy was on her way back with the drinks. "I'm about to have a drink."

"Thirty seconds. Just step outside with me."

She wanted to step outside? Now his curiosity was aroused as well. He held a finger up, caught Cassidy's gaze, and mouthed *One second.*

Then he followed Jessie Jane out of the bar and into the warm evening. The pink sign with the buxom cowgirl leading her horse to water cast an electric glow over her. The truth was, Jessie Jane could be the cowgirl on that sign.

Hell, maybe somewhere inside his imagination she was.

Though he preferred not to acknowledge that she lived anywhere in his imagination.

He and Jessie circled each other. They both frequented this bar. He'd watched her leave with a man on any number of occasions, and she'd most certainly watched him leave with a woman. They never left with each other.

Except . . . they just had.

Not really, though. He was going to go back inside. Any minute now.

"It's an election year," she said.

"Oh, I am well aware." He couldn't walk past a well-manicured lawn without seeing a sign that had his half sister's overly smiley face on it.

"No one has declared that they're running against Danielle. There are three days left to enter the race and, well . . . I'm going to run for mayor."

He stared at Jessie Jane, and he couldn't help himself. He laughed. He laughed as if it was the funniest goddamned joke he'd ever heard in his life. Because it was.

"You," he said when he finally caught his breath.

"Yes, me."

"What's your ticket? The yellow-bellied coward and dissolute gambler ticket?"

"I don't think anyone could accuse me of being a yellow-bellied coward. Don't confuse me with an unfortunate man in my lineage. And I won't confuse you with yours."

"Everybody else does."

"I didn't mean Austin Wilder. I meant *Mike*."

She made such a regretful, scornful face that he couldn't help but laugh again.

"Fair enough."

"I thought you would be interested, since I imagine you don't exactly love watching Danielle flex her influence all over town."

"You don't know anything about me or my relationship with my mother's family."

"I know that you consider your half sister your mother's family."

"You don't know anything else."

"I pay attention, Flynn. I'm not blind to the dynamics."

"Well, good for you. What's a little family dysfunction?"

"Nothing. Hell, in my family it's fun. But what do you think about the outlaws staging a takeover of the town?"

"I'm not following you."

"I want *you* to be my first man."

"What?"

"This town loves drama. People love that more than heroes; they love it more than sinners. And you know what they really, really want? A good old-fashioned showdown."

"I don't . . ."

"Outlaws versus lawmen. Jessie Jane Hancock, many times great-granddaughter of Butch Hancock the traitor, engaged to marry Flynn Wilder, running against Danielle, who is engaged to be married to your sister-in-law's ex-fiancé. That's not just drama; that's a whole soap opera. And you and I are going to be the stars."

Chapter 2

When I was little, I used to dream of wearing fancy dresses. I wanted to be like one of the ladies who walked by Ma and me where we sat, waiting for a man to come and pick Ma up for the evening, so that in the morning we could buy food. I didn't understand then that a girl like me would never be a lady, no matter how fancy the dress.

—Belle Martin's Diary, August 1865

"You've *got* to be kidding me," Flynn said, looking her up and down as if she was a crazy person.

"Is it painful being that much of a cliché?" Jessie could definitely understand why Flynn was reacting this way, but she wasn't going to give him the satisfaction of pretending she understood, even for a moment.

Because why shouldn't she be mayor? That was the energy she was carrying herself with. If there was one thing she had learned at a very early age, it was that you had to fake it until you made it. You could never show that you were vulnerable, that you cared too much, that your feelings could be hurt.

When she was small, she had wanted nothing more than to be like all the other girls in her class. She'd wanted to have the same jelly bracelets, and the same kinds of rubber bands in her hair. She didn't want to go to school with her mom's hand-me-downs from the eighties combined with whatever random shit they could pick up at a thrift store.

She hadn't wanted to bring any friends back home to the collection of campers and trailers where her family lived beside the Wild West Show. It was like living at a circus combined with a carnival, and although her parents had always been loving, involved people, they had also always been . . . unconventional. And for a good long while, Jessie had ached to be normal. To be included.

To get invited to a birthday party at one of the houses in the new gated community in town, where the houses were designed to look like historic homes, but were filled with all the modern conveniences. Once, she had been invited, and she had been amazed at how organized the house was. How much food was in the pantry.

How much space there was.

And the air-conditioning . . . Yeah. That had been pretty amazing.

But she must've done something to make it weird, because she had never been invited back again.

Her childhood had been crushing humiliation after crushing humiliation. She didn't like to think about the time her mom had sprayed glitter all over her hair to cover up the fact that she had lice.

Worse than the glitter, which had been weird, was the fact that the front desk lady had been immediately suspicious. And had searched Jessie's hair.

And then sent her home so she didn't spread lice to anybody else.

One of the boys had started calling her *Contagion* after that.

Thinking of it made her skin crawl now, and it wasn't the memory of the lice that did it.

But middle school had been the turning point. Where she had realized that if she acted perfectly okay with her own company, people would be a lot more interested in her. Interested in figuring out why.

She had started to imitate her dad, who conducted himself with cocksure confidence in all things. Wearing his fringe jacket, with his handlebar mustache, he was an eccentric. A cheerful con man. Mind you, the Wild West business was mostly legitimate, but were the games weighted in favor of the house? Maybe.

Still, her dad had a booming voice, grand gestures, and a larger-than-life personality that drew people to him. Even people who would normally avoid folks like the Hancock family were enticed by her father. Against their will, sometimes.

She had started carrying herself the same way. Dressing nothing like anyone else. Walking to the beat of her own drum. And she noticed that the more she didn't try to fit in, the more people wanted to know why she didn't care.

And the more she convinced herself she didn't care, the more confident she became.

Which meant she wasn't going to respond to Flynn's shock now. "I'd be great for the job," she said.

He stared at her. She had the uncomfortable feeling that he was looking down through layers of carefully crafted confidence. That he could see the Jessie Jane that had come before the one who stood before him now, and she didn't like his penetrating gaze. Not one bit. It was one of the many things she didn't love about Flynn.

Flynn cocked a brow. "I have seen no evidence of that."

"Because you don't actually know me, Flynn. You come into my bar—"

"It's *not* your bar."

"Gus and I have an understanding. He doesn't mind if I hang out and collect bets. It pays the bills."

"Butch Hancock's Wild West Show doesn't pay the bills?"

"Not all of them."

She had a horrible, tight feeling in her chest as Flynn looked at her. This was the problem. She didn't care what anyone thought of her. That was a carefully crafted mantra she repeated every day.

She didn't care. Fuck everyone.

And the more she thought that, the more she carried herself with that air, the better people responded to her. It was the damnedest thing. *Caring* didn't get you anywhere. The less hungry she was, the more magnetic, the more charming people found her.

Flynn's eyes seemed to cut straight through her.

No. She didn't care what he thought. He sucked.

Well. He didn't totally suck. She needed his help. And if he totally sucked, she wouldn't seek out his help. Not at all.

"Trust me on this," she said. "People like *me*. They like *you*. *We* don't like each other, but that is one of life's great mysteries."

He stared at her still, those uncompromising green eyes making her heart flutter.

Maybe it wasn't so much a mystery why they didn't like each other. No. She suppressed that thought.

"Walk me through this," he said. "Danielle is descended from politically active people in this town."

"So are you," she said.

He huffed a laugh. "You know that part of my bloodline has never counted for much of anything. I'm a Wilder through and through."

"I do know that," she said. "And here's what I think: I think the average person in this town is actually tired of the status quo. I think they're tired of . . . this narrative. Aren't you?"

"No. The present narrative gets me laid. That's actually all I care about, Jessie."

She ground her teeth together, holding back what she really wanted to say. Holding back a reply that was going to get them both in trouble. "Well, *I'm* tired of it. Danielle is no good, that's the thing. She's petty, and she wastes the town's money. She hurt your sister-in-law, she's hurting my family business with her new anti-noise ordinances, and suggesting a dining tax for people who want to eat here is ridiculous."

"Yeah. It is. It's also a town filled with cowboys and ranchers and people who have nothing to do with the tourism circus."

"I know," she said. "But she also wants to gut the historic society, the library, she wants to go back on the plaque changes. It's not just your outlaw angle that I'm after. You've got the rancher angle too. Together we are as local as it gets. And we have a different perspective from Danielle's."

"Your family also has a reputation for scamming people. You yourself spend a good amount of time right here, parting fools from their money."

"A bet is a bet. I also have connections with a lot of people in town."

"*Connections?* Is that what the kids are calling it these days?"

"Well," she said, feeling her temper ignite. "Even if that is what the kids are calling it these days, between the two of us . . ."

"Point taken."

"Come on. You have nothing to lose."

"I don't have to marry you, do I?" he asked. He sounded so horrified by the thought, it was almost funny.

"No. It's going to start tonight. We're going to make everybody think that you and I hooked up. And from this point on, we'll be totally inseparable."

"That is insane," he said.

"Maybe. Maybe it is. But maybe it's genius. We will be the subject of so much gossip, *so* much gossip. People are going to be fascinated. Everyone knows we don't like each other. A Wilder and a Hancock? Becoming physically and emotionally intimate? Insanity. Me running for mayor, double insanity."

He stared at her for a long moment. "I don't know whether I'm terrified of you or in awe of you, because this is starting to make sense."

There was that cult leader skill set shining through.

"You know I'm right. People are tired of Danielle and her minions. Hell, half of the town isn't even going to bother to vote, or they're going to write in *Austin Wilder*. Not your brother, the dead one. Because they're just so bored. So let's make them not bored."

"Am I actually helping you execute some evil, maniacal supervillain plan to take over the world?"

She crossed her arms. "Rustler Mountain isn't the world."

"Maybe not. But I'm a little bit nervous about helping you ascend to power."

"I have good intentions. I . . ." She ignored the strange hitch in her chest. "I care about this town, okay? Or at least I care about my ability to exist here. And what I want to do is going to help preserve small business, and not just small businesses my friends own."

"And what about the ranchers?"

"You have my ear. If there are town policies that are problematic for ranchers, you let me know. I'll help." She smiled, that slow way that men always responded to.

"Why do I feel like I'm making a crossroads deal with a literal demon?"

"You might well be, Flynn Wilder, but if you are, then so am I."

He seemed to consider that. "All right. So all we have to do is . . . leave together."

"Yep."

"You're sort of ruining my evening, Jessie."

"Sorry."

She noted that he didn't ask if she was going to make it up to him. The very idea made her feel hot and sweaty and panicky, and those were three things that she never, ever showed.

Jessie Jane Hancock was cool as a cucumber at all times. Completely unflappable.

Maybe if she kept telling herself that, she would start to feel it again.

"I can tell Cassidy and Dalton the truth, right? Because they're not going to believe . . ."

She lifted a brow. "They won't?"

She was banking on the fact that his family must have noticed there was . . .

There was *something* between her and Flynn. Always. She could never decide if it was dislike or something a whole lot sparkier.

Maybe it was both.

But she found that pondering the mysteries of the universe never got her anywhere. It was best if she acted like she knew everything. It made other people think they were confused. Made them question themselves instead of her.

"Fine. Fine. We'll discuss the details later."

"You should buy me a drink," she said.

He took a step toward her. "Sure."

And then he did something that made her feel like her skin was on fire.

He put his arm around her waist as if she belonged to him, and started to propel her back into the bar.

His brain was screaming that this was the worst idea in the entire world. The worst idea *anyone* had *ever* had. Yet, for some reason, he was going along with it.

He had to admit that the idea of messing with Danielle's life appealed to him. Messing with her family's sense of power, comfort, and superiority. Oh, it really, *really* appealed to him.

If he helped Jessie Jane beat Danielle in the race . . .

Oh, the LeFevre family would be just furious. They'd melt down. They would have lost their seat of power in the community for the first time in generations, and he would feel . . . *better*.

Better than *them*.

They had always thought they were so much better than Flynn Wilder.

His mother, Connie, had married Don LeFevre when Flynn was two; before that her last name was Parker. The Parker family had often held political positions in town, but they'd been a mixed bag.

His grandfather had been a great man. James Parker had served Rustler Mountain as mayor with total integrity. In Flynn's opinion, Danielle made a mockery of their grandfather's legacy.

Jessie Jane was correct. His mother's family went around acting as if they were the good people. While they stabbed people in the back. He knew for a fact that Mike was skimming money off the payments for those insurance policies. He knew that Danielle was lining her pockets with town money. People didn't see it, because this town was so . . .

So damned narrow-minded about whom they labeled good and whom they labeled bad.

He didn't have patience for it anymore.

Normally, he didn't fight it. Normally, he just leaned into it. But hell . . . Jessie had served him this opportunity on a platter, and he wasn't above taking it. Except the problem was, now he had Jessie

Jane pressed up against the side of his body. Now he could feel her curves. The roundness of her hips, those firm breasts, pressed up against his chest. He was no green, inexperienced boy, but she was making him feel a touch out of control.

He walked up to the bar, past Cassidy and Dalton, who was busy chatting up the redhead, while Cassidy looked like a sad puppy. "Gus," he said. "Can I get a drink for the lady?"

"*Lady*," she said. "What an upgrade."

"Well. A man can admit when he's made a mistake."

"*Can* he?" she asked, lifting a brow.

Her hair slid over her shoulder, a glimmering river of chestnut gold.

God, she was so hot.

He had to remember that this was a game, and not in fact a pickup.

He could've asked. He could have asked her if maybe . . . since they were pretending, there was some merit in not pretending. But that was another thing he just flat out refused to do. Because there was tension between them, and he was absolutely certain that she felt it too. He would be damned if he'd be the first one to acknowledge it. He would be absolutely damned.

Which meant he wouldn't even ask.

"And what would the lady like?" Gus asked with far too much mirth in his voice.

"I *am* a lady, Gus," she said. "And I would like a motherfucking beer."

She looked at Flynn and smiled. He smiled back. And then he became aware of his sister's presence. "Hey," she said.

"Hey yourself," he said.

"Are you and Jessie *hanging out* tonight?" Cassidy looked at him far too meaningfully. If he were actually picking Jessie up, and if she weren't . . . well, her, Cassidy would have likely messed this whole thing up. His little sister really was a menace.

"*Maybe*," he said.

She grinned. "Okay. I need to call Austin—he owes me money."

Cassidy walked away, and he stared after her, his jaw practically on the floor.

Jessie nearly howled. "Does your family bet on . . . *Seriously?*"

"It's news to me," he said. "They never told me that they had a bet going."

"How wholesome."

"Yeah. Well, my family never claimed to be wholesome. But you realize this is going to cause issues for me."

"Look, if you need to tell your family, that's fine. But keep it on the down-low. We can't have everybody knowing. West will know. I mean, he would never believe . . . Sorry, but my brother is not taking bets on us."

"Yeah. Well. The only bet I have that concerns West is whether or not Carson would punch him if he had to interact with him again."

"Why?"

"Didn't you hear about the whole thing where Perry went on a date with him?"

Jessie Jane blinked. "No."

"Yeah. They kissed, in this very bar. Carson took a dim view."

Carson Wilder and Perry Bramble had been best friends since they were children and had spent most of their adult lives trying to outrun their attraction to each other. They had stopped running about a year ago. But there had been a lot of drama on the way there, and West had gotten tangled up in it.

Jessie put her hand on her chest. "Well. I'm a little bit offended that West didn't tell me about that. He knows I love drama."

"You clearly do. *You clearly do.*" Gus slid a beer across the bar, and Jessie grabbed it, nodding, before taking a sip. "Drink quickly," he said.

She looked at him out of the corner of her eye. "Feeling impatient, cowboy?"

"Very," he said.

He was gratified when he saw color rise in her cheeks. She wasn't unaffected by this. By him. By them.

She swallowed the beer down. "All right, Wilder. Let's get out of here."

And then she grabbed him by the collar of his shirt and pulled him toward her.

He chuckled, grabbed her hand and twisted it behind her back, pulling her body up against him.

And he was almost sure he was going to die of heat stroke. But he didn't let her see that. "Behave yourself," he said, their faces a scant inch apart.

Fistfight. Fuck. The jury was out.

"Well," she said, and her voice was breathless, as he had never heard her sound before.

"Do you need me to be the designated driver?"

"Yeah. I can pick my truck up in town tomorrow."

"Perfect."

He released his hold on her but then took her hand in his. He turned toward Dalton and tipped his hat. Dalton was staring at him, his mouth open. Cassidy was in the corner, texting wildly.

Dalton probably had a ride home with the redhead, and Cassidy was going to have to get a rideshare. But then, that was sort of the way these things went. And by the time he was out on the street with Jessie, he wasn't thinking about them anyway. His body was on high alert, his heart pounding hard, and he had to keep on reminding himself that he wasn't actually taking Jessie Jane home. He was just . . . taking her home.

He was still holding her hand, conscious of how soft her skin was. That surprised him, considering she was such a devoted horse-woman. He had expected her to have some calluses. When he had thought about it. Which was a couple of different times.

Just a couple.

"I can take you back to your place, but it might be beneficial for us to meet up in town tomorrow morning."

"Hey, whose scheme is this?" she asked.

"It's yours. But you roped me into this, so now I'm going to be mouthy."

"Lord. I should've enlisted Cassidy to pretend to be my girlfriend. She's probably less of a hassle than you."

"She isn't. On that you can trust me."

"Anyway," Jessie said, "I do agree. I think we should be seen having coffee together tomorrow, and then in the afternoon I'm going to file the paperwork to enter the mayor's race. And I'm going to have to . . . I'm going to have to set up a social media page, but I'll start with the Wild West Show's page, and I'll do a live video."

"Wow. You have to actually . . . do things like that."

"I'm great with people, Flynn," she said, her voice sounding overly cheery.

"I've heard that."

They were still holding hands. As soon as they got far enough down the block, he let go of her. "I'm just right there," he said.

She began to walk a little faster ahead of him. Then she opened the truck door and climbed inside. He hadn't bothered to lock it; there was no reason to in Rustler Mountain. He was the trouble. And these days, he caused a lot less trouble.

Back in their teen years, he and his siblings had been hellions. Until Cassidy had shown up.

He opened the driver's side and got in, jamming his key into the ignition and turning it over. "I live like twenty-five minutes out of town," he said.

"I don't live any closer," she said.

"Right. I forgot. You still live up at the Wild West Show."

She shifted beside him, and he tried to ignore the movement of her body. Tried to ignore how aware he was of her.

"Why wouldn't I? That's my family property."

"Didn't y'all end up with that land because you scammed some guy back in the day?"

"That tale has been greatly exaggerated," she said, sniffing. "My great-great-great-grandfather engaged in a *couple* of dowsing scams.

I can't deny that. Absolutely occurred. But the thing is, he actually ended up finding water, and the guy who owned the property was so grateful he wound up leaving it to him when he died. So nobody really got scammed. He was an old man who lived by himself. He didn't have anyone else to leave the land to."

Flynn couldn't even really be scornful. Considering how he had ended up with *his* property. They both had property thanks to an old man who had decided to leave it to them for some reason or another.

"Have you been up to Lonesome Ridge?"

"No. That's your place?" she asked.

"Yep. I own most of the mountaintop. That's actually why I started ranching elk. Because they do better on the mountain than cows."

"How does that . . . ? I mean, how is that even going? It's such a weird thing."

"Yeah. It's kind of a weird thing. But my brother has cows, a lot of people have cows. I wanted to do something of my own, something that didn't compete, but that still . . . Ranching is in my blood. Some of my blood, anyway."

"Did you scam anybody to get the land?" she asked.

"Kind of. My grandpa Parker was maybe the only person in the world who thought I was decent. Might have been a scam to let him think so."

"Right."

He had rarely heard Jessie Jane at a loss for words, but she seemed to be now. Granted, he had never really been with her when she wasn't in public. This was the first time he'd ever been alone with her. His muscles went tight, his blood hot.

"So," she said, her breath hissing through her teeth, "you have an extra bedroom, right?"

"Yes," he said.

"I'm *not* having sex with you," she said.

His neck practically popped as he whipped his head around to look at her. "I didn't ask you to."

"Well, a woman can't be too careful," she said, resting her hands on her knees. "Because men make assumptions. And I don't have any interest in getting tangled up in your assumptions."

"I didn't make any *assumptions*," he said.

"I can't bank on that. You know what they say about assuming."

"It makes an ass out of you and me?" He was beginning to wonder if this entire scheme was going to make an ass out of both of them.

"That is correct. That's what they say."

"Right. Well. No danger of me coming on to you, Jessie Jane. If I was going to do it, I could've done it anytime over the past . . . I don't know, decade?"

"I guess so," she said. "But you know, you might not go out of your way to get, like, a frozen pizza, but if it's available, it's what you'll eat."

"Are you comparing yourself to shitty pizza?"

"Sort of. Not exactly."

Silence settled between them. "If I want a woman, she doesn't need to ask for clarification. She knows."

It sounded good, but it was a lie. Because he wanted her. But he didn't want to want her, and he was going to go ahead and claim what mattered. Because he was never going to do anything about it. At this point, his pride was tangled up in that shit.

And her making assumptions about the fact that he might . . .

"I've never had to do anything underhanded to get a woman into my bed, Jessie Jane Hancock. And you ought to know that."

"Yeah. I've watched you walk out of the bar with a whole parade of women, so there is that."

"Right. The thing is, you don't really know me."

"You don't know me either. And why would you? Our families are mortal enemies and all of that."

"Yeah. Well. It's going to be interesting to see what Austin thinks about all this. I'm going to have to level with him."

"He'll understand," Jessie said. "I'm sure he will."

"You don't know him either," Flynn said. "You really have no idea what my brother would understand or not."

"I guess I don't, but I do know that your relationship with Danielle is complicated."

"I don't know that I would call it complicated. I would call it nonexistent. When we were kids, we were forced to interact sometimes, and every so often my mom manages to guilt me into going to an Easter brunch or something. But I'm never sure why she wants me there. It has something to do with her own guilt, I think."

"Yeah. I don't know. For dirtbags, my parents are pretty great."

That was funny. He had never given it much thought, but the Hancock family was close. Not just the siblings, like the Wilders, but the parents. They seemed to be a united group, and that was something he didn't know anything about.

His dad had been all right. Just irresponsible as hell. And then he had gone and gotten himself killed being a dick driving drunk on his motorcycle.

"Nice for you. My dad was lousy at picking partners to have babies with. And he never really grew up himself."

"Yeah. I know. I mean, everybody knows. It's kind of town lore."

"Just like you guys, I guess. And all the fables about you cheating people out of their land."

"The way I see it," she said, "we get talked about an awful lot, and it's not for anything we choose to be talked about. I actually run a lot of the Wild West Show. I do a lot of the paperwork, the marketing, all that stuff. I manage the budget. West is great. He has an eye for showmanship. Like my dad. He does insane tricks. Totally fearless. But he can't complete a piece of paperwork without getting distracted. He wants to do things. He doesn't want to organize them. My dad is the same. The place was a mess before I took over. I'm good at organizing. I know that I could do a good job for the town. I'm actually great with money. Why do you think I make it hand over fist with all that gambling stuff? I can read the odds."

"And you want to be known on your own terms," he said. He could actually understand that. This little gambit wasn't going to do the same for him, but it was going to take down his mother's family a peg, so there was that.

"Yeah. I want to be known on my own terms, I guess."

"I get it."

He had a feeling that was as close as he was ever going to get to understanding Jessie.

He took a sharp left turn, pulling off the paved, curving road onto the dirt driveway that led up to Lonesome Ridge. His ranch was right on the border between Oregon and California, with some of his pastureland straying over into what he considered to be enemy territory.

But the view was fantastic. The road wound up and around, but in the darkness, the vista of trees and lake below was invisible.

"Like, no offense," she said, "but do women honestly go home with you? Because it seems dumb. Like you might be a serial killer."

"Typically we get a room in town," he said. "But I'm not going to spend the money when I'm not getting laid."

She huffed. "Well, that would've been very showy, though."

"We don't want to be *too* showy. I don't want this to look like just another hookup, right? This is supposed to look like the beginning of a relationship. Which . . . I've never actually had before, so that should be interesting."

She huffed out a laugh. "That makes two of us."

They pulled up to the house, and he felt a surge of pride, which he suppressed, allowing it to turn into annoyance. Because he didn't want to wonder what Jessie would think of the place. He had been working on it pretty intensely ever since he'd moved in five years ago. It was done now, a fully remodeled log cabin with a rustic exterior and a modern interior.

It was actually the perfect sort of place for a man who wanted to start a family. Alas, he was not that man. The only people who had been up here were his family and his friend Dalton.

"Nice place," she said.

And he suppressed the satisfaction her praise created in him.

He got out of the truck, and so did she, following him up the wooden steps to the front door. He opened it and gestured inside.

"Not locked?"

"Up here?"

"Fair. I always lock my trailer door because we have a lot of different people working at the Wild West Show. Though I confess I am more likely to lock it if I'm inside than when I leave it."

"Fair enough."

She looked a little bit lost, standing there in her jeans and tank top. He had the uncomfortable thought that she would probably take her jeans off when she went to bed and just wear a pair of panties and that tank top. The mental image just about undid him. He also felt that he had betrayed her by imagining it, since he had told her in no uncertain terms that he didn't want her, and here he was, lusting after her.

She didn't look like herself just then. She looked younger. Vulnerable. He didn't think he had ever seen her look vulnerable. Gone was the bravado she'd displayed outside the bar. "Come on now, let's not build any suspense. You can sleep upstairs. There are two rooms in the loft, mine is down here. You have a lock on the door."

"I know I don't need it," she said, starting up the stairs at a clip, as if she was desperate to get away from him no matter what she said.

"But go ahead and use it," he said.

Her eyes widened fractionally; then she turned and made her way up the stairs. He heard a door close behind her.

He let out a long, hard breath and went into his bedroom, closing the door firmly behind him. And locking it.

He took his phone out of his pocket and turned it over. He had a text from his older brother. Because of course he did. Oh, Austin. The man just couldn't help himself.

What the fuck?

Not what you think. I'll explain tomorrow. In person.

See that you do.

It's possible you're going to hear a whole lot of rumors before I
see you, so you're going to have to keep your shit together.

And with that, he turned his phone to Do Not Disturb. Austin
could have his say, but it was going to have to be tomorrow.

What Flynn needed right now was a cold shower and a good
night's sleep.

But he didn't get a good night's sleep. Instead, he lay there awake
all night wondering what the hell he had gotten himself into.

Chapter 3

I have to write down these stories, because I have no one to tell them to. Ma is dead now, and the girls all have sad stories—mine isn't any worse or better. None of the men want to talk at all.

—Belle Martin's Diary, September 1865

When Jessie Jane woke up the next morning and looked up at the unfamiliar ceiling, she was more than a little bit confused. She didn't *do* unfamiliar ceilings. She didn't do beds that weren't her own.

She *really* didn't do walks of shame or anything even close.

And she didn't . . .

Well, for heaven's sake, if she finally had, she would remember.

But no, there were no memories of anything sultry. Of course, then the real memories came back. Her leaving The Watering Hole with Flynn.

An immediate shiver went through her entire body.

Flynn Wilder.

What a problem.

But he had agreed to help her. *And* she had gone home with him. For the express purpose of starting some rumors.

She got out of bed, still dressed from the night before, because the idea of taking her clothes off in Flynn's house had been unthinkable.

In fact, walking out of the bedroom felt a little bit impossible too. But she managed to do it anyway. Because that was what she did. She didn't do shame; she didn't do embarrassment. She did the hard things, the kick-ass things, the things other people were too afraid to do.

Because she was Jessie Jane Hancock, dammit. Descendent of Butch Hancock the Traitor.

Yippy-ki-yay.

"Morning," she called out. "I don't want to go catching you in a state of undress."

"No worries."

The voice that came up the stairs was still gravelly from sleep, and she shivered just slightly. It was so weird to see him in this totally different context. To be alone with him. No, she wasn't going to think of it that way. They were business partners. That was the thing.

"Should I pay you for this?"

She spoke as she was going down the stairs, and when the words exited her mouth, Flynn stepped in front of the landing. He was wearing blue jeans and a tight black T-shirt, and she almost would have preferred if he were in a state of undress, because then she could have at least been annoyed. Instead, he just had bare feet. And for some reason that was . . . intimate in a way she didn't want to think about.

"Excuse me?" He sounded like a scandalized maiden.

"I just realized that maybe *vengeance* isn't appropriate compensation," she said.

"Oh no," he said, smiling slowly. "It is. I've had time to think about it."

"Have you?"

"I sure as hell didn't sleep. Not pondering the implications of all of this. Come and grab some coffee."

"I thought we were going to have coffee in town."

"I need a pre-coffee before we get to the performative coffee."

She shrugged. But she stayed where she was in the middle of the staircase.

"I'm not going to bite you," he said, crossing his arms over his broad chest.

She blinked. "I know that."

Then she began to make her way down the stairs, careful to skirt him like a particularly skittish cat as she walked into the room that he had just come out of.

The kitchen was nice. Natural stone and raw wood cabinets. It was very upscale, but very Flynn all at the same time.

"Wow," she said.

"You like it?"

"Yes. It's . . . beautiful."

"Thanks. I did most of the work myself." He paused for a second. "My brother Carson helped with a lot of it. He's great at woodworking and things like that."

"You're obviously not too bad at it either."

"Not too bad. I try to make myself useful where I can."

"You don't really give off that vibe. Useful."

He shrugged. "I like to have fun. But you know, most of my life I was having fun at other people's expense."

"Explain that."

He turned away from her and opened one of the cabinets, taking out a gray stoneware mug and setting it heavily on the counter. He poured a cup of coffee from a stainless steel carafe and slid the mug toward her. "Cream?"

"Please," she said.

"Anyway. You know reputation is such an important thing to Danielle, to Michael. To . . . Mom. And so I always took a lot of joy in not caring about it. The things that always bothered my oldest brother . . . they've never bothered me."

"Well, it may surprise you to learn that my family has never cared about our outlaw reputation."

"You've built an entire business off it."

"Damn straight."

"But it seems sort of out of step with your wanting to be mayor."

He could have slapped her and it would've been less painful. How did he manage to hit her insecurities right on target? She couldn't quite understand that. His intuition was unerring in so many ways.

"What I don't like is a lack of fairness."

"I wouldn't think an outlaw would care about fairness."

"That's not true. Anyway, I'm not an outlaw. To be clear."

"I get that. But I just meant . . . You're sort of like a Western carnie."

A crack of laughter escaped her lips. "You're actually not the first person to say that."

She ignored the fact that the description made her skin feel too tight. She just laughed. Because what she had learned was as long as she could laugh at herself, and her family, at their exploits, then no one could hurt her.

Not even Flynn Wilder.

But for the first time, she wondered how hard he had taken words like that. Because she knew what it was like to have the town look down on her while the Hancocks rallied together as a family, them against the world. Flynn was looked down on by his own family. And that seemed . . . altogether unfair.

"How old were you when your mom left?"

"Oh. Not quite two?" He shrugged. "Honestly, I don't remember being emotionally scarred by it. I had my dad. I had Austin, Carson. It was good. We were able to run around and do whatever we wanted."

"Did you always visit your mom?"

"Yeah. Pretty much. Holidays and birthdays. She wasn't single very long. Even though my dad never talked about it, and I've definitely never had the discussion with my mom, my assumption has always been that she left him for Don."

"You don't seem very bothered by it." But what Jessie knew for sure was that just because somebody pretended not to be bothered by something, that did not mean they were actually unbothered.

"What's the point of being bothered by it? Like I said: I want to have fun. And I would rather be me than my insurance salesman brother, I'll tell you that right now."

"Right."

"Anyway," he continued, "they're just . . . Last time I was over there, you know, Danielle was talking about how Rustler Mountain is too rough and she wants to deemphasize the Western element. She wants it to be more like Bend."

"She didn't say that!" Jessie shrieked.

"She did. She wants it to be cuter. She wants it to be a tourist attraction for the right kind of people, who want to do wine tastings and go on curated hikes."

"I have no issue with wine tastings but like . . . we're Rustler Mountain. We're the Wild West. We're not curated, and I fear half the people in town are the wrong kind of people as far as she's concerned."

"Why do you care so much about that?"

"There's just a point where you just can't let the mean girls win anymore." And that was as deep as she was getting. "I don't need you to understand me. I just need you to be my arm candy."

He raised his brows. "*Arm candy.* Tell me truly, Jessie, did you really choose me because you think I'm hot?"

She did her best not to stare at his green eyes, perfectly formed jawline dusted with golden stubble, or aquiline nose. She'd read that adjective in a romance novel once and had looked it up. Aquiline could be kind of an unflattering term, she supposed, but it perfectly described his strong, straight nose, which balanced perfectly with his sculpted cheekbones and . . .

She cleared her throat.

"Sure, you're hot," she did her very best not to react at all as she said that. "But what I really like is how obnoxious you are."

She took a sip of her coffee and looked over the rim of the mug, realizing too late that was a grave error. Because when their eyes met, she felt as if she'd been struck by a bolt of lightning.

"Do you have any business in town today?" she asked, trying not to choke on her coffee.

"None other than delivering you back to your truck."

"Great. That's . . . fine."

They finished their coffee in silence. "Let's go down to Scally-wags," he said.

"Sure."

It was her favorite coffee place in town. There were three of them, but Scallywag's had baked goods, and she *did* like baked goods. Not that she often got herself a little treat, but when she did, she preferred it to be from there.

They regarded each other for a moment in the silence of the kitchen. She made the first move toward the front door.

"Hang on a minute," he said, and she heard the sound of his keys scraping across the counter as he followed her out of the kitchen and toward the door.

She was already getting into the truck by the time he closed the distance between them. She didn't like that feeling of tension in her chest. That feeling of tension in his kitchen. And she wanted to get as far away from it as possible.

Because there was no call for anything like that. None whatsoever.

She was buckling her seat belt by the time he got in and started the engine.

"Thanks for the coffee," she said as they began to back out of his driveway.

"You're welcome," he said. "You know you're going to have to act less like you want to claw my eyes out when I get near you if you think that we're actually going to pull this off."

She winced. She didn't think she had been that obvious. Anyway, she didn't want to claw his eyes out. That was the trouble. She had never really known what she wanted from Flynn.

Well, realistically, she knew she was attracted to him.

It was a problem. He made her feel all small and delicate, and even though she wasn't very tall, she never felt delicate. But he was just so big and so muscular and so god damn manly.

She didn't have to live in that space, though.

Usually, men didn't ruffle her. They were so basic. They paid her a whole lot of attention, especially because they assumed she was easy, based on her friendly demeanor and, well, her clothes. In fact, they spread plenty of rumors that she was, because none of them wanted to feel left out.

Oh, Jessie Jane? Yeah, I totally hit that too.

Idiots.

She didn't care. But when it came to Flynn, she felt that awful, hot, shameful caring settle in her gut. It was half of why he was a problem, and being in proximity to him like this made it feel like an even bigger problem.

"I don't actually want to claw your eyes out," she said, because it was the truth.

"You don't?"

"Nope. You're giving yourself a lot more credit than you ought to. I find you mildly irritating at worst *and* best, Flynn. Otherwise, I mostly don't think about you at all."

That was a lie. She thought about him quite a lot.

For the first time, she wondered if she'd chosen him because he was the best person for the job, or because he was the first person she had thought of.

What if she had partnered up with somebody who had a better reputation?

No. That actually wouldn't have worked. If she'd chosen someone with a better reputation, she'd be running the risk of two things:

He'd be too good to get involved in something like this, or he'd be so much shadier than she could ever be.

She wanted a known quantity.

Because, yeah, Flynn was shameless. He was a womanizer. He had a reputation for running wild around town. But he was open about all that. There were no surprises to be had with Flynn Wilder, and that suited her.

Nothing more.

"You sure do know how to flatter a man's ego."

"Weirdly, I actually don't care about flattering men's egos. They can rot in hell for all I care."

"Bitter."

"Realistic."

When the road transitioned from gravel to pavement, she looked out at the view from her window. It was beautiful. All pine trees and the sparkling blue of the lake below.

"It's a beautiful drive," she said.

"Yeah. It's a nice drive out to the Wild West Show too. I was glad we got to go last year. You know, before that, Austin wouldn't let us."

"Are you serious?"

"Not really. Mostly because if Austin ever tried to outright tell me what to do, I would tell him where to shove it. But he would never have approved, no. When you asked Carson to fix your wagon . . ." He paused for a moment. "You didn't have a *thing* with my brother, did you?"

She nearly howled in shock. "What?"

"Well, last year when you came to him and asked him to help restore the wagon, we kind of thought maybe you were . . . trying to pick him up. And I know he and Perry hooked up sometime after that but—"

"I *never* hooked up with your brother," she said. "Good God."

The idea had never even occurred to her. Carson Wilder was a decent man but he . . .

He did not make her skin feel like it was too tight. He didn't make her feel like she was overheating.

Only *Flynn* Wilder did that. She hated to admit it, even to herself. But it was true.

She was unlikely to ever act on the feelings Flynn aroused inside her.

The idea of acting on some kind of sexual impulse with a man she wasn't into was . . . Nope.

If there was one thing Jessie didn't do, it was vulnerability. In the past, she had cared too much. She had tried to make herself be what other people wanted her to be, needed her to be.

And she just wasn't going to do it anymore.

She didn't like looking as if she didn't know what she was doing. As if she wasn't on top of absolutely everything.

"Then what was that?"

"A request for your brother's good restoration work. The end. As for the show, I was being neighborly because he agreed to help fix our wagon. Also, I genuinely wanted you all to see it. We've never been what you thought we were, you know. It wasn't like we were gleefully profiting from your family tragedy."

"You kind of do, though."

"We aren't gleeful, though."

"That's beside the point, Jess," he said.

"Just because we do a reenactment of the death of your ancestor? It's not like you *knew* him."

"Fair. But my brother takes the murder of the first Austin Wilder very personally. Maybe because they share the same name."

"Well, that is also not my fault. Yes, my family was involved in all of that, and I know that Butch Hancock betrayed Austin, but . . . there's nothing I can do about it. We might as well make some money. And anyway, Wild West shows are supposed to sensationalize history. They're not supposed to be one hundred percent accurate. I get that your brother has a stick up his butt about that. But I *like* the sensational. I feel there's room for legends that are bigger than Big Sky Country, and tall tales taller than the mountains."

It was possible some of that speech was in the intro to the Wild West Show. But hey, if it was effective, why not use it?

"You really are a showman," he said.

She was. She had been trained by the best. Her dad was magnetic when he stood out there in his fringe jacket and cowboy hat telling stories and introducing each act. He wasn't totally wrong when he called it a carnival. Or maybe even more accurately, a Western Circus. The result if a rodeo and a circus had a baby.

"It's my job. And I'm going to take that experience and make it work in this mayoral race."

"Are you going to have time to do the Wild West Show and run the town?"

"It's not like it's a full-time job."

He laughed. "Yeah. I mean, I know that the mayor has to keep their day job when they take on this position. But your day job is a little bit unconventional."

"This *town* is unconventional. Which goes back to my original intent. This place is so much cooler than we're treating it. It's been sanitized and watered down and given over to people like *Danielle*. I refuse to allow that to stand."

Her impassioned speech ended right as they rolled into town, where all the perfectly preserved brick buildings glowed in the early morning sun. An American flag waved merrily from the pole mounted on the front of the old hotel, and Scallywag Coffee was a little aqua beacon at the end of the street beckoning weary travelers to come in and grab some caffeine.

Flynn managed to find a parking space right in front of the building, and she waited in her seat until he came around and opened the door for her.

"My lady," he said, extending his hand.

She was reluctant to touch him again, but she knew she couldn't get around it. So she reached out and took his hand, and she smiled. Because she refused to appear uncomfortable, to him, to anyone.

The minute his skin touched hers, she felt heat rush through her.

Her heart began to beat hard as he pulled her out of the truck, and she stumbled forward, falling against his chest, bracing her hand on his shoulder, and regretting it instantly, because he was so solid. So hot and hard.

Without her permission, her fingers curled, just slightly, gathering up a little bit of his T-shirt fabric and skimming over all those muscles.

She gasped and straightened.

"Steady there," he said, his eyes dipping down to her lips for a second, and she felt an arrow of reaction pierce that place between her thighs she thought far too much about in his presence.

She cleared her throat.

"What kind of coffee do you like?" she asked, because she needed something to say.

"Well, this morning I had my coffee black, but I would actually like a latte now."

"I didn't realize that cowboys drank lattes."

"Cowboys that are secure in their masculinity can drink whatever they like. And I'm good."

She snorted a laugh. He opened up the white door, which had a raccoon decal on the window, and held it for her.

She cleared her throat. "You *do* know how to treat a lady."

And he didn't even make a joke about her not being a lady as they walked in and found at least ten pairs of eyes glued to them.

Oh yes. They were definitely going to be gossip. Most definitely.

She couldn't get used to the way he held her hand as they walked up to the counter. She felt as if her skin was on fire. So she just tried her best to stare straight ahead as if she was focusing on the menu. She had a feeling she was holding her head at a weird angle, like she was trying to put some distance between him and her, which was not what she should be doing. She didn't know how to do this. And suddenly, she questioned herself, because this was a whole lot of things she didn't know how to do.

Usually, she was very good at faking it. It was how she navigated the world.

But this was a lot more faking it than normal.

"I'll have a latte," he said. "And whatever she would like."

"The Milky Way, please," she said, just choosing something on the menu that sounded decent, and she liked the Milky Way candy bar, so surely it would be all right. She didn't go out for coffee routinely. The Wild West Show made very good money these days, but her family had never changed the way they lived.

"Two cinnamon rolls too," he said.

Jessie was so used to pinching pennies that she just did it as a matter of course.

This felt extravagant in ways she really wasn't used to.

He paid for the coffee, and she knew it was just part of the performance; then they moved away from the register to wait for their drinks.

"You can go have a seat," he said.

She nodded and realized that she was probably requiring a little bit more direction than he expected. Shouldn't she know all the steps of a one-night stand?

The Jessie Jane that everybody *assumed* she was certainly would.

Well, maybe not. Maybe she never stayed the whole night or something.

He came to the table a few minutes later with their coffee and the warmed-up cinnamon rolls.

She dug into the treat with great enthusiasm.

Then she took a sip of her mocha and moaned. It was delicious. A Milky Way bar was made of chocolate and caramel, so she assumed the drink had the same ingredients, but the coffee and rich, frothy milk made it even better than a candy bar.

"Good?"

She didn't care if he saw how much she was enjoying her drink. It would've embarrassed her when she was a kid. Because it betrayed how foreign such luxury was to her.

She wasn't embarrassed now.

"Yeah. It's great. I don't come here very often. And when I do, basically I get a regular coffee. This is a treat."

"Well. Glad to treat you."

"Yeah."

"I'm going to have to go up to visit my brother after this. He's going to have questions."

She wrinkled her nose. "Funny. Well, my brother is probably going to have some questions too. Normally, he stays out of my business, and I stay out of his."

"What's that like? My brothers are always in my business. My sister is even more in my business."

Jessie chuckled. "That's nice, isn't it?"

"It can be. But you know, we raised Cassidy, basically. Well, Carson and Austin more than me. But she came to live at the ranch when she was just nine, and Dad was already dead so . . . it was up to us. Three idiots and a little girl."

She had never really given a lot of thought to that part of his life.

He had been pretty young when his dad had died. And he would've been young when Cassidy came to live with them.

"That's when we cleaned our act up a little bit," he said. "For her."

"That's . . . that's nice."

"I guess so. We try, anyway."

"Well, I guess that just leaves one question," she said, looking down at her cinnamon roll, then gathering all her bravery to look up at him. "Do you want to go steady, Flynn Wilder?"

"I want nothing more," he responded. And then he grinned. She thought she might die. She thought she was going to pass out. She had never been on the receiving end of his smile. Not like this. Full watt, less than a foot away from her.

No wonder women fell at his feet. No wonder they could scarcely handle themselves around him.

"Great," she said.

And then she speared the remaining third of her cinnamon roll with her fork, taking a bite that was far too big and chewing it so long, it meant that she didn't have to think of anything else to say.

"Better go," she said, snagging her coffee. "I have to get back to the property. I didn't tell West where I was going. Or that I was going to be gone all night."

"I thought he's not usually up in your business."

She did not tell him that this time was different because she was never gone all night. Instead, she pivoted. "Sure. But we're working on a new routine. So he'll be expecting me."

Her parents wouldn't wonder. They'd just assume she was out having lots of fun. Good for her. West, though, he had more opinions.

Though the main thing was that she really needed a break from Flynn Wilder.

"You could just text him," he pointed out.

"I could. But he never answers my texts. My brother's phone is exclusively used for receiving texts from women who want to sleep with him."

Flynn snorted. "He must be busy."

"Waaaay busier than I would like to acknowledge."

He stood up and took their dishes to the trash can, held the door open for her while she walked past him. "You don't have to walk me back to my truck."

"I do."

"Really?"

"For God's sake, what kind of men do you usually hook up with? You've got to walk a lady back to her vehicle."

"Amazing. Now that I've pretend-slept with you, I'm a lady."

"Yeah, I have that effect."

She rolled her eyes, and was grateful when he didn't grab her hand again.

When they got to the truck, her heart stalled out for a moment. She wondered if he was going to do something crazy, like kiss her.

Eventually he was going to have to.

She opened up the truck door and climbed in quickly. "I'm going to the courthouse to file the paperwork, and then I'm going to make my announcement later today."

"Do I need to stand behind you like a silent, dutiful partner?"

"No. But . . . we'll have to get some signs made. And get them put up around town."

"Are you going to ask me to recruit my family?"

"I might."

He shook his head. "All right. Well . . . You know, I don't have your number."

"Your brother does," she said, smiling.

On that note, she started the engine of the truck and slammed the driver's side door shut. And then she took her first full breath since first encountering Flynn the night before.

As schemes went, this was going to be a wild ride.

Chapter 4

I was too young when I learned my first lesson about men—but that's how the world is. My ma wasn't in, so he offered me a coin to please him, but it wasn't an offer. In the end I had a coin pressed to my palm and knowledge I couldn't give back. I held the coin tight in my palm like the weight of it would overtake the weight of what had happened. I wanted to learn to hold a coin so tightly in my hand that my payment couldn't be taken from me. I wanted to at least hold that.

—Belle Martin's Diary, November 1865

He texted Austin as soon as Jessie drove away, because he wasn't going to stand there looking after her with longing or something.

He did *not* long for her.

His brother responded immediately. **Just dropped Millie off at the library. Taking Emma to the park.**

Well, an opportunity to see his niece was always welcome. If he was going to get a lecture, he might as well do it while a baby was giggling in the background. He might not be able to see a future with a wife and kids for him, but that didn't mean he didn't like kids. It was a particularly special thing to see his brother be a dad, to see Austin have something so . . . he was tempted to call it normal, but that made it sound common, and it was anything but.

They were the product of a home that had been broken multiple times during the course of their childhood. Flynn didn't take love, marriage, or family for granted.

It was one reason he wanted to steer clear of them himself.

But Austin deserved the world, and thank God, he'd gotten it.

Meet you there.

Flynn started to walk down the block past the historic shops, heading to the little square that contained a gazebo, a stretch of green grass, and a small play structure. He knew that Emma would be on the swings the entire time they were there.

As he saw Austin approaching from the opposite direction, he couldn't help but smile. His big, burly brother had a baby strapped in a front pack on his chest, a white cowboy hat on his head.

He could remember feeling so lost when their dad died. He'd been fifteen, and Austin and Carson were the adults left to care for him most of the time.

He could still remember his mom, in her fancy kitchen with the bright white countertops and tall, dark cabinets. She couldn't even reach the second shelf. Those cabinets were for looks; they weren't for use. The way she'd made him a hot chocolate and stood on the other side of the island while he sat there, feeling certain he would do something to mess up the pristine space. Like maybe the Wilder in him would leave an impression on the chairs that couldn't be erased.

He could still remember her look of . . . sadness, concern, worry. *You don't want to leave your dad's, do you?*

Worried, he'd realized later, that he'd say he did want to leave the ranch, that he wanted to come live with her.

He'd never lived with her full time. It had always been sporadic, joint custody with no real schedule. He'd tried, for a time, to see if anything he did affected her willingness to have him around. If he was extra good, would he get a Christmas invite? If he was naughty, would he be left out of the Fourth of July barbecue? But there never seemed to be any rhyme or reason to his mother's decisions.

Nothing he did—good or bad—changed the situation with his mom at all.

No, I want to stay at the ranch.

He really had. He couldn't imagine losing his dad and then losing the place he called home on top of it, trying to live in that house where he always felt he might break something.

Then Cassidy got dropped on their doorstep at Christmastime, and suddenly, he had someone to care for too.

Austin, though, was the reason they'd all made it. Austin was his hero, even if he'd never actually said those words to his oldest brother.

He deserved the world.

Flynn lifted his hand and waved, but Austin did *not* wave back, which was how he knew he was in some kind of trouble.

Austin didn't wait for them to get close before he shouted, "Really?"

He closed the distance between him and his older brother before he said anything. "What did you hear?"

"Cassidy said that you took Jessie Jane Hancock home."

He met Austin's judgmental gaze. "I did."

"Why?"

"You ask the right questions. It's not what you think. And you know what, Austin, if it was, it wouldn't be any of your business. You are a married man, a *New York Times* best-selling author with a movie in the works, and you don't need to be up in my sex life. You've corrected the historical record in your book. You can let your issue with the Hancocks go."

Austin appeared to be going over the list of things that Flynn had just said to see whether he could dispute any of them. Flynn knew that Austin was sort of uncomfortable with the level of success he was enjoying from the book he'd written about their ancestor Austin Wilder's life and death. He and his wife, Millie, the town librarian, had discovered that Butch Hancock and the sheriff of that era had colluded to frame the Wilders for murders they hadn't committed. Austin's brothers were tried and convicted and hanged publicly. Austin himself was shot in the street.

Flynn's older brother had always suspected that their ancestor hadn't been a murderer. That their family had never been as bad as they'd been accused of being. Outlaws, certainly, but not cold-blooded murderers. It had eaten at him because he blamed the town's unfair treatment of them on that historical lie.

His brother hated the Hancock family, not just because Butch Hancock had set up Austin Wilder and his gang, but because the Hancocks had gone on to profit off a tall-tale version of it.

Austin had disproved the lie, but his brother was the kind of man to hold a grudge. Not just against the man who had betrayed his five-times great-grandfather, but against his descendants. Which included Jessie Jane.

"What are you doing, if you're not hooking up with her?"

"Pretending to hook up with her."

"Again, why?"

"Hey, Bug," Flynn said, looking at his niece and tapping the end of her nose with his finger. She giggled in her sweet baby way. "Let me swing my niece."

"Fine," Austin said, beginning to unstrap the front pack. He worked Emma out of the device and handed her to Flynn. Flynn carried her on his hip, then put her in the little bucket swing, pulling it just slightly and letting it sway while she laughed and laughed.

"What's the deal?"

"We're going to pretend to date. As a little PR stunt to help her campaign for mayor."

"You have *got* to be kidding me," Austin said. "She's running for mayor, and you're helping her?"

"Yes, I am. Because otherwise Danielle will run unopposed. And you know what, I'm kind of tired of the family that hates me being in charge of the place I live."

Austin let out a long sigh. "I get that, I guess."

"I'd have thought you'd be into defeating Danielle no matter what. Not only has she been a pain in my butt, but she was responsible for hurting your wife."

He lifted a shoulder. "Yeah, but she liberated Millie from that asshole she was planning to marry instead of me, so I can't say I'm *mad* mad about it."

"Sure, but Danielle is in a position of power in our community, and Millie's ex is our first man."

He rolled his eyes. "Yeah, okay, when you put it like that. But don't pretend this isn't a little about you taking petty revenge on your family."

"Sure."

"It's going to piss your mom off."

"Yep," he said, grinning. "It will also piss off her husband, and their other son, the one they actually love. So I guess if you want to call that petty, go right ahead. I personally . . . I'm just going to go ahead and call it justice. And that's why Jessie's doing it. Justice for all of us. You felt driven to clear the record about Austin Wilder, while she feels driven to change the whole power structure of this town."

Maybe he was overstating it, maybe he was giving a little too much credence to the purity of Jessie's motives, but hell, anything was better than the continued reign of his maternal family. And repeating their motives back to Austin, he believed that there was good in Jessie's plans even if he didn't have a personal stake in the election.

It was more than just poking at his family, though that was a nice bonus. It was the potential to shift the whole vibe of this place. He liked that idea. Because the town had been divided into the good guys and the bad guys for way too long. It was about time the outlaws had a say in how things ran.

In truth, as founding families, the Wilders and the Hancocks had always had a certain amount of power on the city council, but it was a formality more than a reality. Because their outlaw reputation had hung over the families the whole time. They hadn't bothered to participate for years, not until Austin had agreed to help Millie get funding for Gold Rush Days in exchange for some information he needed for his book. That had ended in the two of them getting married, and Austin changing the historical record forever.

"You opened the door, big brother. She wants to walk through it. I respect that."

Austin looked uneasy. "It's just . . . her family . . ."

He raised his brows. "Are you really discriminating against people who get treated the same way we do?"

"I'm *not*. It's just . . . William Hancock is a glorified con man."

"I think he prefers *carnie*."

"Whatever. You know what he's like. And you know what West is like."

"He's an asshole. Hell, come to that, Jessie kind of is too. I don't know if she can win. But you know, she's pretty damned convincing. Even though I really don't like her, she brought me around to her way of thinking in about fifteen minutes flat."

"Because she's going up against people that you don't like. Not everybody here has a personal vendetta against Danielle."

"Fair enough. But maybe enough of them do. Or maybe enough of them are just tired of the way things work. Jessie's a wild card."

"My wife is going to enjoy this way too much."

"You think so?"

"Yes. Millie is a secret anarchist."

Flynn laughed. "It's actually not that secret. She's a little contrarian. But I feel like librarians usually are." He paused for a second. "Are you . . . are you uncomfortable with this because it relates to the Millie/Michael-who-is-not-my-brother/Danielle thing?"

Austin made a huffing sound. "I . . . no. I'm not . . . no."

"You are a little bit."

"No. I don't think Millie cares about that anymore."

"I know she doesn't," Flynn said. "Though it doesn't mean she wouldn't enjoy seeing Danielle and Michael endure a little hardship."

"It's not about Millie. I just . . . I want you to be careful," Austin said. "Because playing with the Hancocks feels a lot like playing with fire. Maybe you think that's small minded of me or something. I like to think of it as taking the appropriate amount of caution."

He huffed a laugh. "What exactly do you think I'm vulnerable to?"

"There's always been something between the two of you."

"There has not been. Nothing that I don't feel for any number of women. Jessie's hot—I'm not disputing that. But the idea that I'm vulnerable to her in some specific way is ridiculous."

"I'm your older brother. It's my job to look out for you."

"You're not *that* much older than me."

"I'm older enough," Austin said.

He paused for a long moment, and his eyes rested on Emma.

"The thing is, life has been pretty brutal to all of us. Carson and I experienced one kind of parental abandonment. You . . . Your mom left, but she was still here. I don't know how you dealt with that. I got to pretend that my mother never existed. Hell, I guess even Cassidy got to do that. She moved in with us, not knowing us, which was its own whole drama, but her mom wasn't around anymore. Yours is. Along with Danielle and Michael. Children that she did raise."

"I get that," Flynn said, ignoring some of the tightness in his chest. "But time has definitely revealed to me that I was better off. I don't respect the people that Michael and Danielle turned into. I'm glad I wasn't raised in that house. With those people. I would rather be on this side of town. I guess it's the same side that Jessie is on. I know we have a tendency to make it the Wilders versus the Hancocks, and who can blame us? But the truth of the situation is that we are the outsiders. Why? Because the insiders insist on making us that. Jessie wants to change it."

"I guess."

He looked at his older brother, at the lines that bracketed his mouth. The lines around his eyes. He wondered if he was the reason for some of those lines. Austin had had a bigger part in raising the younger siblings then he should've had to. "I know that you're the reason I turned out as well as I did."

"There's a weird compliment," Austin said.

"Come on. We're all good people. Learn how to accept praise. You're the father figure. That's why it's so easy for you to be a good dad to Emma. You were already that guy."

Austin shrugged his shoulders up, and Flynn slapped his older brother in the center of his back. "You're ridiculous, dude. You're a good guy. But you don't need to worry about me. I'm going to do what I feel like I need to do."

"Revenge is what you feel like you need?"

"Yep. I don't know if it's even really revenge. I just want to see the score settled a little bit. Like you said, it's strange to have to sit back and watch your other family be a whole thing without you. I don't want in. I never really did. But that doesn't mean I feel neutral about them either."

"Fair enough. So what are we supposed to do when people ask about you and Jessie Jane?"

That did worry him a little bit, especially considering the two people most likely to be asked were his sisters-in-law since they worked in town. Perry would smile vaguely and say something benign and dreamy. But Millie was not a liar. Not even when it came down to telling little white lies, and he also knew that Austin wouldn't lie to his wife about what was happening between him and Jessie.

"If Millie could just play coy about it, that would be great. Just say that I don't kiss and tell," he said.

"I mean, I suppose that is true. Primarily because you don't actually have relationships."

"You're not wrong."

"You know this is going to create a lot of buzz. Neither of you is really the relationship type."

"Indeed." He shook his head. "And she's not the run-for-mayor type. This whole thing is going to be a spectacle. Maybe a shit show, but a show nonetheless."

Austin laughed. "I mean, whether you win or lose, it's going to give Danielle hell."

"That's good enough for me."

It was. For once, everybody in his mother's family was going to have to pay attention to him.

He really liked to think that he didn't much care about the way he had been excluded from his family. But the truth was a little bit more complicated, he reckoned. Because these weren't the actions of a man who didn't care. No, he wouldn't want to be part of that family as they were. But if they'd been different . . .

Well, they weren't. That was all that mattered.

"You can talk to everybody else, but they're going to have to be circumspect."

"I can't control your sister."

"No. I guess not. But I really need her to get on board."

"We'll see, I guess."

"That we will. That we will."

By the time Jessie finished filing her paperwork at the court-house and placed an order for campaign signs and flyers at one of the local print shops, she was late for rehearsal.

She drove straight from town to the family homestead, which was a few miles east of the Wild West Show venue. Their living quarters were comprised of a circle of trailers with a gazebo and firepit in the center. Jessie's trailer was pink, with string lights that extended out along the walkway to the front door—which had a wreath of fake sunflowers on it. She had a little white bistro table and chairs positioned out front, and a porch goose who had seasonal costumes, along with a bright green alligator who was holding a fishing pole and wearing waders.

It was whimsical, and she liked it.

She changed into her rehearsal clothes at record speed and hopped back into her truck, driving back toward the show venue.

The food trucks were shuttered, as were the game booths, but when the show was open, food and drink flowed freely, and there were carnival games that included a pop-gun range and Whac-a-Mole.

There was a large fence painted with stars, stripes, and cartoon interpretations of the showdown in the street between Lee Talbot and Austin Wilder. There he was again on horseback carrying bulg-ing bags full of money, along with a Western Union coach on the run, and some cheeky drawings of cowgirls that always set Jessie's teeth on edge.

The fence served to hide all the RVs that were parked behind it; this was where the employees of the Wild West Show lived. It was a mini town in and of itself.

Their employees ran the carnival games, and some of them were also performers, playing small parts in various routines.

The more skilled performers had larger residences farther away from the show itself. A few team members were literal acrobats, and while Jessie and West were pretty close, their expertise was in rodeo and trick riding.

The rodeo events were held sporadically, and there was a rotating roster of riders who participated in them. Their mom still did barrel racing, and some minor tricks, while their dad was the MC. He was the face behind the Wild West Show, the magnetic force that drove it all.

Like his father before him.

The center of the show was the massive arena, surrounded by bleachers, which they routinely filled, particularly during the summer. But even this time of year, they were busy.

In addition to the shows, games, and food, there were blacksmithing demonstrations around a forge, which was one of Jessie's favorite jobs. It was how she'd gotten into doing farrier work on the side, another way she made sure they were able to pay the bills year round.

She was a Jill-of-all-trades, so to speak. But that was the life her family had always lived. A sort of patchwork existence requiring expertise in any number of random skill sets, most of them decidedly left of the mainstream.

All through the fall, they ran rodeo events, and then around Christmas there was always a seasonal performance. The weeks of January through February were pretty dead, but they were accustomed to that now and had figured out how to weather the low times, even if it meant some white-knuckling.

She parked right at the front gates, which she would never normally do, but this was just rehearsal, so no one else would need the space. She tumbled out and ran through the front entrance. West was already out on his horse, standing while the animal ran in a circle around the arena. He spotted her and jumped back down into a sitting position, using his upper body strength to keep himself from crashing onto the saddle and injuring both horse and man.

"Well, there you are, JJ," her dad said. William Hancock was a mythical sort of figure. His large mustache was gray now, but his figure was still wiry as ever. His brows were dark slashes in his face, his eyes deep set and weathered. The cowboy hat on his head had a beaded band and cards from what he claimed was a winning poker game stuffed into it. His jacket was buckskin, with fringe hanging off the sleeves. Just right for when he spread his arms wide and welcomed everybody to the show.

"Sorry I'm late," she said.

"As long as you were having a good time," her dad said, a merry twinkle in his eye.

"Yes," she said.

West had his arms crossed, and he was looking down at her from his position on the horse. "Were you?"

"Yep," she said. "Late night, early morning."

Her dad chuckled.

Not for the first time, she realized how weird her family was. Her parents, William and Lucinda, had always wanted to be friends with their kids. Not in the way that some parents tried to be, hoping to be cool. That wasn't what it was about. They wanted to be close. In a way that they hadn't been with their own parents. They wanted camaraderie. And they really wanted their kids to care about the same things they did. The show, the animals. And in truth, she and West both did.

But their whole existence was unorthodox.

She loved her parents, but in some ways, they were children. Which meant that she and West had to be adults. Her parents just wanted to have fun, but somebody had to keep things going. Another reason she was so good at wearing the particular mask she wore.

She also thought it was the reason she had some gaps in her résumé. The reason she was so good at so many things, and a whole lot less experienced in other areas.

"You need to rehearse the runaway horse routine," her dad said, gesturing back toward the holding stalls.

"Yeah, I know."

They were putting together a routine that made it look as if her horse went rogue, and while it was running laps in the arena, she did a complex series of acrobatics, as if she was trying to stay on the horse, though of course all of it would be meticulously scripted and rehearsed.

West would, of course, do a savior routine, which Jessie had initially balked at. She objected that it was sexist, but her dad had pointed out that West wasn't as agile on a horse, so he couldn't do the acrobatics that she could.

In fairness to West, it was because he was six foot four. And while he was strong and could definitely hold his own in rodeo events and balancing acts, he wasn't going to be hanging sideways off the horse or flipping himself upside down. Jessie wasn't short, but at five foot seven, she was a lot more able to do flips and other impressive saddle tricks.

Privately, she thought part of the reason West didn't want to do the routine was that it was too showy. Though he was happy to participate in certain aspects of the show, he was not in his soul a performer.

Bull riding and bucking broncos were another thing. He loved that. And he was always the house favorite during rodeo events, in which he often held his own against professional competitors.

Some of their most popular stunts were the bullfighting events, which was what West insisted they call them instead of *rodeo clown antics*. West and a few other daring performers sat at a table and played poker, waiting to see who could flirt with the bull that was loose in the arena the longest before they got nervous and abandoned the game.

West always won.

Of course, West did not wear clown makeup.

He wore a black cowboy hat and tight jeans and as a result got exponentially laid for his feats of bravery. Whatever.

"Starlight is just over there waiting for you," her dad said, gesturing to one of the holding stalls.

She crossed the distance to him and kissed him on the cheek. "Thanks, Dad."

His whole face crinkled up with his smile. He smelled like to-bacco and arena dirt. Her heart clenched. She had been feeling bitter lately. She loved her dad. She didn't need to focus on the ways in which her childhood had been difficult. And anything that held her back now . . . that was her own problem.

Yes, there were things about her childhood that were tough, but there were also things that were great.

Hell, hanging out with Flynn should be a reminder of that. His dad was gone, and his mother was in town but didn't even want to see him. Childhood trauma was a many splendored thing.

At least her parents loved her.

She walked back to the stall and started to open the gate. She didn't hear her brother approaching and jumped half a foot when he leaned in and spoke.

"What are you up to?"

"What the hell?"

"That's what I'm asking you. Where were you?"

"None of your business."

"It is my business. Because you're scheming."

"I know, I know, you're very concerned about my scheming."

"You're hiding something, and I don't like it. Because we never even had to hide weed from Mom and Dad, because they were also smoking it."

"I never smoked it, West."

He breezed right past that. "So the fact that you're stooping to subterfuge of any kind makes me concerned that it might end in a federal investigation."

"You have so little faith in me."

"No, Jessie, I have too much faith in you. Which means I don't put anything past you."

"We have a routine to rehearse, bro."

"You're really annoying, do you know that?"

"I've heard. Where's Mom?"

He shrugged. "At home. She was doing something with her crystals?"

Jessie rolled her eyes, but affectionately. Then she went into the stall and patted Starlight on the neck. She was such a beautiful horse. White with gray speckles. Jessie got on her back and leaned in. "Ready?"

West gave her a look, but opened the gate, and then she and Starlight were off.

For a little while, she forgot about everything. Any resentment over the past, all the tension of being around Flynn. The paperwork she had just filed, and the signs she had ordered. For a little bit, she was just Jessie Jane Hancock, in her element. Where none of the deficiencies of her growing-up years mattered at all, because they had made her the best at what she did here.

There were worse things.

Chapter 5

Ma thought life would be better out West. I never understood why.
Or maybe she just thought the man who promised to protect us on
the wagon train would be more trustworthy than the men she met
in alleyways in Boston. I already knew we couldn't trust anyone.
She believed in a better world than I ever could. Her hope made a
fool out of her.

—Belle Martin's Diary, November 1865

After rehearsal, when everyone else had gone home, Jessie got her
social media announcement space all set up. She had one American
flag and one Oregon State flag flying behind her, and was standing
atop a podium in the arena, with her phone mounted up. Her paperwork had been done and handed in, and her candidacy was now
legal. All that was left to do was announce.

She hopped down from the pedestal, hit the live button on her
phone, and then marched back to the podium. "Hi there. I'm Jessie
Jane Hancock, one of the founding members of Butch Hancock's
Wild West Show. My family has always been deeply invested in the
future of Rustler Mountain. Our show is a celebration not just of the
history, but of the over-the-top legends of the Old West. We believe
that the spirit of this place is what makes it so unique, and I believe
that this spirit has been suppressed for far too long. Mayor Danielle
LeFevre thinks that Rustler Mountain should shy away from its
Wild West history, she thinks we should blend in with the trendy
wine-country towns, cater to people with more money. 'The right
kind of people,' she said. Well, if they're the right kind of people that
means we're the wrong kind of people to her."

She paused for effect after she said that, and she couldn't hold back
the small smile that tugged at her lips. She was grateful Flynn had told
her that, because it was just the kind of thing to set folks' teeth on edge.

"I think that Rustler Mountain is special. It has its own unique history, its own unique identity. We already know that the truth of this place was erased from the historical record until Austin Wilder corrected the facts and shed light on the true nature of our town division into outlaws and lawmen and the story behind this town's foundation—good, bad, and ugly. I personally think we're strong enough to face the truth of the past, not sand the edges off to make a fairy tale. This is the Wild West, not the Mild West. We have the guts to contend with that. It's not a cookie-cutter tourist attraction, it's not a place where we only welcome the *right people.* Danielle LeFevre is paying lip service to a fantasy version of the past while working to destroy what we love about this town. I won't do that. I understand Rustler Mountain and all its unique glory. That's why I'm declaring my candidacy for mayor." There was suddenly a single person clapping, and she looked up and saw her brother walking toward her phone. He reached in and ended the live stream.

"Thank you, West," she said. "For your very deserved applause, and for being tech support."

"You've *got* to be kidding me," he said.

"Really? Even you're going to question me?"

"Even me? Is the other person who questioned you Flynn Wilder? Because that was actually why I was looking for you, and then I got a notification that you were live on the page. You're not keeping me informed about your schemes."

"Oh, dear brother, we are far, far past the scheming phase. This surpassed plot and has become a full-on quest."

"I hate it, thank you."

"This is why I didn't tell you. You're a skeptic, and I don't need your skepticism. You're raining on my parade, West."

"Sometimes your parade needs to be rained on, Jessie. Because you're irrepressible, and sometimes a little bit of repressing would be good for you."

"Pick a lane to yell at me from." She bunched her fingers together and waved her arm back and forth. "You're swerving all over the place."

"Flynn Wilder," he said. "You really think it's a good idea to hook up with a Wilder?"

"*You* did it."

"What?" He looked scandalized. "I did no such thing."

"You kissed Perry," she pointed out, referring to Carson Wilder's now wife.

"She wasn't a Wilder then."

"She's always been a Wilder, come on. She and Carson have been attached at the hip since they were little children."

"She wasn't married to Carson at the time, and she wanted to go out with me. So we did. Very briefly. That isn't the same. I heard that you were at breakfast with Flynn."

She looked at her fingernails and considered just telling her brother outright that she wasn't really sleeping with Flynn. But then, she found she didn't want to. Because she was tired of his superior attitude. He was no saint, and he did plenty of things that were questionable at best, so interrogating her was completely unfair. "Well, then you should be satisfied that he's somewhat of a gentleman. He paid and everything."

"Why do I get the feeling that this is all related?"

"Maybe it is. Maybe it isn't."

"Why didn't you tell me that you wanted to run for mayor?"

"Swerve," she said, waving her hand again.

"Valid swerve. What's going on with you?"

"I didn't tell you because I knew that you would try to stop me. Because I knew that you would be skeptical about my ability to do this."

West shook his head. "That's not fair, Jessie. You're brilliant. And I've always thought so. The way you transformed the finances of this place is amazing. I don't have the patience for it."

She already knew that. But then, it was nice to have West acknowledge her contribution. Nobody else ever did. Their parents were . . . They just always kind of believed that things would work out, whether by accident or on purpose. And so when Jessie had overhauled the financial structure of the Wild West Show, using a lot of West's ideas for new acts and new attractions, their parents had sort of taken it all in stride, as they always did.

She would be lying if she said it didn't matter to her that West recognized the change was because she had put effort into it, and not just because fate had swooped down and smiled merrily at the Hancocks yet again.

"Listen, Jess, I think you would be a great mayor. But I'm not sure people in town are going to agree. I don't want you to get hurt." Oh, when her big brute of a brother saved up every ounce of emotion in his body for her, it got her every time. But she wasn't going to show him that.

"I can't get hurt," she said, grinning widely and ignoring the tender feeling at the center of her chest. "I'm too feral for that."

"You want to be."

Ouch.

She made a hissing sound. "Good God, West. I ride on the back of a galloping horse standing up; I can do a somersault off and back on. I'm not scared of being rejected by a bunch of idiots in town. I just think if we never challenge the status quo, then we can't complain about it."

"That's not true. The majority of people complain. The minority challenge. You can absolutely complain while doing nothing."

"Maybe *you* can. I can't respect it, and I can't do it. I need to be active if I want things to change. And you know the taxes that she's proposing on entertainment are going to severely hurt tourism businesses. I feel like it has to do with her wanting certain kinds of people here. It's taking away all the fun. I meant what I said about the wine-country thing."

"Did she really say she wanted Rustler Mountain to be like a bougie wine town?"

"According to Flynn."

"Right," West said, understanding suddenly dawning on his face. "Because that's his half sister."

"Indeed she is."

"Well. I guess that's one reason to get in bed with the Wilders."

Her face went hot. Again, she opted not to correct him about the fact that she wasn't technically in bed with Flynn. But whatever.

"You file paperwork for this and everything?" he asked.

"Yes. I am absolutely informed on the correct processes here."

"Well, damn. Mom and Dad are going to . . . They're not going to know what to do with the fact that you're trying to become one of *the powers that be*."

"I'm doing it for good. Not for evil."

"Of course you are. But that doesn't change the fact that you're perilously close to becoming The Man."

She bit the inside of her cheek. "Shocking, isn't it?"

She held back a litany of things that she might say. About how their parents had definitely worked hard at making sure they didn't even have the opportunity to consider becoming The Man. About how their parents had done their level best to make sure that the two of them wouldn't have the skills, the experience, or education to get into such a position. Truthfully, if Jessie pulled it off, it was going to be because she had taught herself what she needed to know. And not thanks to their parents.

She really did love their parents.

But there were just . . . some wounds. But wounds didn't get better if you licked them. So you might as well slap on a big old bandage and ignore them.

"You're going to be the talk of the town," he said. "Running for mayor, and the rumors about you and Flynn and . . ." He paused again, and she knew he was getting closer to asking outright if the relationship was fake. But she wasn't going to let him.

"Worry about *you*, West. I don't need any help with this. I've got a plan."

He rolled his eyes. "Lord, girl. You are a whole lot."

"Part of my charm."

"Charm. Sure."

"That's what they tell me. Now are we going to rehearse today, or what?"

"Yeah. Get your horse, cowgirl."

"Will do."

Flynn got a late-night text from Jessie saying that she wanted to canvass in four days, which was when her campaign signs were going to be ready. He didn't care for texting. It seemed a lot of fuss when they could just talk. So he pushed the call button on the phone. When she picked up, she sounded crabby.

"I could've called you if I wanted to talk," she said, and it was way too easy for him to imagine her dressed in one of her low-cut tank tops, leaning indolently against the nearest wall or countertop as she looked at him through hooded eyes.

"I didn't want to text," he said. "I think it's annoying. You want to put signs all around town, huh?"

"I need to. I'm coming into this race behind. And I have ninety days to really get some traction."

"Yeah. And I assume you want me with you because . . ."

"Exactly. Optics."

"What do you know about optics?"

She was the most uncivilized, feral person he had ever known, and she was talking about appearances? It was very nearly hilarious. He paced the length of his bedroom, looked down at the floor. Then into the mirror above his dresser.

It surprised him sometimes that he wasn't a gangly teenage boy. He still felt like one half the time. Maybe playing games of revenge wasn't exactly helping him feel like an adult.

Or maybe it's that she makes you feel like a teenage boy on the edge of control . . .

"A surprising amount," she said. "I know you Wilders have strong opinions about our business, but you realize we have to be pretty damned good to keep a niche place like that going."

"Maybe I am not seeing it clearly," he said, and he was a little bit chagrined to admit that, because he wasn't being facetious. It was true that he probably didn't fully see the Hancock family the way other people did. It galled him to know that in this respect, he and his family weren't so different from the people who had given him guff his entire life.

The Wilders judged the Hancocks based on their ancestry. Well, and the way that the Hancocks exploited that ancestry. But Flynn himself had always enjoyed trading on the idea that he was a bit of a bad boy. How was it different really, for the Hancock family to trade on the sensational notion of outlaws, shoot-outs in the street, and other feats of the Wild West?

Maybe not so different.

"All right. So you're saying that other people like you."

"Yes," she said slowly. "You're the only one who gets scratchy whenever I ask you about taking bets. Honestly, how do you think I do things in this town?"

He felt his perspective had been turned on its head. Couldn't say that he cared for it, in all honesty.

"Okay," he said. "So . . . you're not worried about all that."

"It's going to be interesting."

"I guess so." He paused for a moment. "Do people like your family better than they like mine?"

Her laugh was a loud crack of sound against his ear.

"Are you serious right now?"

"Yes," he said. "I'm serious. I would like to know what people think of us."

"People who like coming down to The Watering Hole sure enjoy bad boys. But then I think Austin actually has stepped into the realm of respectability. Plus, Carson married Perry, and she has a business on Main Street. So . . . really, are you even outlaws anymore?"

"What about me? What's my reputation?"

"You probably don't want to go there."

"I do."

"Okay," she said. "You have a reputation as a charmer. A ladies' man."

"So, similar to yours."

"I don't think people see me as a ladies' man," she said.

"You know what I mean."

"All right. I guess so. So we're the same, basically, and us getting together is going to seem almost logical, which I find funny."

"I'm sure you do." It hit him then that he and Jessie had never really talked. Yes, they exchanged a little banter when they saw each other out at The Watering Hole, but otherwise they didn't have conversations. They had been forced to start talking over the past couple of days. It was a weird thing to realize that he knew her, but didn't especially *know* her. Because yes, he knew her reputation. He knew what people assumed about her. He knew the Jessie Jane of lore and legend, just as she knew that version of him. And now they had talked about family and fairness and Rustler Mountain, and he'd said things to her he otherwise would have only said to Austin or Carson or Cassidy.

"You're awfully quiet," she said.

"Just thinking. But yeah, I can help you canvass in four days. It's just . . . It feels an awful lot like one of those cheesy made-for-TV movies, doesn't it?"

"Maybe not enough," she said. "Maybe we should have cider and cookies. Flynn, we have to have a booth."

"With . . . what?"

"I know how to bake," she said.

"You . . . you bake?"

"Yeah," she said. "I like it."

"I don't know what to do with that information."

"Be excited. Because we are going to post signs, and then we're going to set up at the library."

"I'm not sure we're allowed to do that."

"I'll talk to Millie."

That made him feel unaccountably nervous. "You're going to talk to my sister-in-law."

"Yes. I am. Don't even worry about it. I'll follow up on the details."

"I'm sure you will."

When they got off the phone, he wasn't even entirely sure what had happened to him. Because she was like a whole herd of wild horses that couldn't be contained or denied. He was beginning to think that maybe Austin's concerns were valid. Because he had been so certain that he knew exactly what he was getting himself into. But did he?

He sat down on the edge of his bed and rubbed his hand over his chin, his whiskers scraping his palm. Well, he had made a deal with the devil. Now he was going to have to see it through.

Chapter 6

I had my sixteenth birthday on the trail and by the time I arrived in the Willamette Valley, Ma was dead and my future was decided. The men are not different out West. Men are all the same.

—Belle Martin's Diary, November 1865

Dalton was leaving the valley for a few weeks for rodeo events, and Cassidy had wheedled him into going out with her and his best friend for drinks tonight—clearly the only way Cassidy was going to get to spend time with Dalton.

Not that he really needed to be coerced into spending time with his best friend, but he was in his head a little bit about everything with Jessie.

"Nice of you to buy me a drink," Dalton said, clicking his glass against Flynn's.

"I didn't say that I was buying."

"I can pay," Cassidy said.

They both looked at her. "No," they said in unison.

"It was my idea," she said, looking at Dalton from beneath her lashes.

"Thank you," he said. "But I'm not going to have you buying me a drink. Your brother can do it. Especially since he's involved in politics now."

"Only by extension," he said.

Jessie's online announcement had gone viral locally, and it was the talk of his family all day, along with Flynn's involvement. He'd been transparent about the fact that he was going to be seen with

Jessie as a show of solidarity, demonstrating that even someone who shared DNA with Danielle had more faith in her opponent.

And also to create more buzz around the whole thing.

They were still . . . getting used to the idea.

"If you can't make campaign promises directly to me, why should I vote for Jessie Jane Hancock?" Dalton asked.

"Would you vote for Danielle?" Cassidy asked seriously.

"Well, no. And I didn't the first time she ran either. Because I have loyalty."

"I appreciate your loyalty," Flynn said. "I didn't vote for her either."

"Neither did I," Cassidy said. "And I never would."

"Well, thank you. I do appreciate the loyalty."

"I do think it's insane that your . . ."

Cassidy trailed off and looked behind Flynn.

Flynn turned and saw Jessie walk through the bar in her characteristic tight tank top, though she had a flannel shirt thrown over it. Her jeans looked like they had been painted onto her curves, and she had the ready smile on her face that she often wore when she was about to run a bit of gambling on one of the fights.

But notably, West walked in behind her.

He also frequented The Watering Hole, though not as often as his sister. But when he did, all eyes turned to look at him. Flynn watched as his sister's eyes moved up and down over the imposing figure that was West. A strange, sort of hollow look appeared in her eyes. He really had no idea what he was looking at, but it was definitely something. Cassidy's response to West was not neutral, not in any way.

"You good?" he asked.

"Fine," she said, her voice sounding scratchy. "But your girl-friend is here."

"Yeah. I see that. Thank you."

"Your girlfriend," Dalton repeated, shaking his head. "Ludicrous."

Flynn didn't mention that Jessie was aiming for fake fiancée in the coming weeks.

"Is it?" he asked.

"Yes. You've never had a real girlfriend to speak of."

"Neither have you," said Cassidy. "You are two of the most commitment-phobic men around these parts. Especially now that Austin is married."

"What about West?" Dalton said. "I've never heard of him having a relationship."

"I wouldn't know anything about West," Cassidy said.

"Ah, right, he's from the *other* side of the other side of the tracks," Flynn said. "The Wilders don't have anything to do with the Hancocks."

"You do always act like that," Cassidy said. "Which is the real reason this is weird. But hey, I totally get doing it to spite the LeFevres. I hate them."

"Yeah. Well, it would be simpler if I did."

"Don't you?"

"Sadly, kid, I don't. They're my family. I mean, I don't think Danielle is good at her job, and I don't *like* her."

He hated his stepfather. He disliked Michael and Danielle. His mother . . . That was different.

"I dunno. Seems silly," Cassidy said. "I think you should just write them all off."

"If your mom came back," he said, looking directly at Cassidy now, "and she said that she loved you, it was just that things were complicated for a while, but she wants to have a relationship with you, what would you think?"

Cassidy blinked, and he regretted the question when he saw his sister's eyes go glossy. But just as soon as the sheen of tears appeared, it was gone. "Well, it's irrelevant. Because that's never going to happen. She's never contacted me, not once since bringing me here. So I doubt that she would suddenly get a hankering to hang out with me after all this time."

"Right. Well. That's terrible. But my mom is here. And she hasn't just cut me off. That makes it . . ."

"Oh, is it harder?" she asked. There was a hard edge to her voice that Cassidy never used with him. "Must be nice, actually."

He felt like an asshole then, because maybe it was. Maybe he was the lucky one. It didn't feel lucky. It felt like having two junkyard dogs fighting over you. Neither of them worked as pets, neither of them had any idea how to be what you needed them to be, and yet they tore violently, one at each arm. That was his childhood. His whole experience with his mother and his father, or rather his feelings for them.

He looked back at Jessie, who was ordering a beer. And he realized he couldn't stay seated any longer. "I'll be right back."

He stood up and walked over to her. He stopped just short of invading her personal space, but he could feel that people in the bar were watching them.

As was West. Flynn looked up and met his gaze. "Howdy, West," he said. "Haven't seen you in a while."

"No," West said. "It has been a time. Good to see you. Tell your brother I said hi."

He knew exactly which brother West meant.

"Sure."

"And his wife."

"Now, now," said Flynn. "Why don't we avoid having a bar fight."

"Why? Bar fights with the Wilders used to be my favorite part of high school."

"Yes. I know you all used to punch each other up when you were in here with fake IDs. But I was too young."

"Just a spring chicken. And apparently seeing my sister."

Jessie turned sideways and shot West a deadly glare. "Is that what we do now, West? We comment on each other's sex lives? Because if so, I do have some opinions."

"No thanks," he said. "Not at home to opinions. Which means I'll be keeping mine to myself."

"A blessed day indeed," said Jessie. "Should we join you at your table?"

"You have some nerve, Jessie Jane, you really do," Flynn responded.

"You already knew that. I'm here because I just announced my candidacy, and what better place to be than The Watering Hole. These are my people. My constituents."

"Well, I can't argue with that."

The eclectic crowd tonight was definitely *her* crowd, and it didn't surprise Flynn totally that this was her first stop after her online announcement. What did surprise him was that she hadn't told him.

He hadn't anticipated having to wrangle Jessie Jane today, but the truth was, he had been foolish for thinking he might be able to get around it. She *had* announced her candidacy today. And he was now roped into all this.

"Yes," he said, a little bit more decisively, now that he was getting his bearings. "Come on back to the table. We have so much to celebrate."

West looked from one to the other. Well, if Jessie hadn't told her brother that her interest in Flynn was all for show, it wasn't really his place to disabuse him. The Wilders knew the truth, but it seemed Jessie and West weren't in each other's business quite as much.

When they sat down at the table, Jessie looked decidedly nervous. Which was a funny thing to see, because generally speaking, she didn't get rattled. Ever.

"You good?" he asked.

"Just great," she said, smiling.

He lifted his glass and clinked it against hers. "To Jessie Jane. Who has announced a historic candidacy today. And who will no doubt wipe the floor with her competitor."

"Amen to that," said West.

"I'll toast to that," Cassidy said, and Dalton raised his glass too.

"Right on," said Dalton.

"Well," said West. "Now that we have toasted my sister, I'll leave you to it. I'm meeting somebody."

West stood, squared his shoulders, and began to walk to the back of the bar, where a pretty redhead saw him and smiled wide.

Cassidy turned her head and stared at him for a while, and Dalton looked at Cassidy.

Flynn turned his focus back to Jessie Jane. "You aren't actually taking bets tonight, are you?"

"No," she said. "I am doing the gambling myself."

She took a drink of beer and then took a deep breath. She stood up, then walked over to the bar, where she got up onto a bar stool, and stepped onto the counter. "Hey now!" She stomped twice on the bar top.

Gus was howling with laughter from his position behind the bar, doing nothing to stop the spectacle. It was like the days of yore come into the present. Jessie Jane acting like this place was an outlaw bar, with no rules.

But then, maybe that was good. Maybe it fit. "I want everyone's attention. Just this afternoon I declared my candidacy for mayor. You heard it here first. I'm going to be campaigning around this place, and I trust you lowlifes to do some canvassing for me."

There was a lot of indistinct hollering. "I know we don't normally bother ourselves with this kind of business, but I think it's high time that we did. This town is ours. Just as much as it belongs to anyone else. For too long it's been outlaws versus lawmen. Danielle LeFevre thinks she knows what sort of person ought to be here in Rustler Mountain, and hint: it's not us." That brought a round of jeers from the crowd. "But I like us. I like this town. So tonight I'm buying everybody a beer. All of you. You heard me, Gus. It's going on my tab."

Gus hollered, "If you say so, Jessie."

"I say so," she said. "And I want you to remember me whenever you take a drink of your favorite brew. And then I want you to make sure to fill out your ballot on election day. We have mail-in ballots, so you have no excuse. Even the laziest of you ought to be able to do something."

"Not the felons," said one of the men in the back.

"True enough," Jessie said. "So those of you who can't cast your own vote need to encourage other people to do it."

"Are you going to make gambling legal?"

"Well, I don't have the power to change laws. But I'll have the power to oversee local ordinances."

"And what good does that do most of us?"

"Maybe nothing," Jessie said. "Maybe there won't be a damned lick of good that I can do directly for some of you. But if there is, I'll listen to you. And that's more than you're going to get from the likes of Danielle LeFevre. Also, I'm cooler than she is." To punctuate the point, Gus handed her a glass of beer, and Jessie started to drink it down, to the cheers and encouragement of the people in the room. And in just a few seconds, she had drained it. She set it down hard on the bar top. "Vote for Jessie Jane Hancock!"

Then she hopped down off the bar, bypassing the stool completely, to a round of thunderous applause.

"She is a lot," Cassidy said.

"Yeah. God damn."

At that point, Jessie was swarmed by bar patrons who all had some story to tell her about Danielle, or a comment to make about what her platform should be. "What about you, Wilder?" One of the older men, Nate Schloot, looked down his long nose at Flynn.

"I don't just endorse her," Flynn said. "I'm dating her."

The sound that arose from the bar was riotous. "You heard it here first," Jessie said. "He'll be the first man."

"That I'd pay to see," Nate said, laughing until tears ran down his cheeks.

Well, they were certainly making the splash she had hoped they would make, though it was with the crowd most likely to be friendly to them.

"You don't have to pay," Jessie said. "You just have to vote. Now, I am buying you all a drink, but if you want to contribute to my campaign, you can play darts against my brother, or pool against me." She spread her hands wide. "Loser gets to help support my domination of Rustler Mountain."

And that really kicked things off. He would say this for Jessie, she was definitely one who knew how to cause a scene. Although West didn't seem to be picking up his darts too quickly. He did eventually, though. Flynn knew what it was like to have a younger sister who could talk you into almost anything.

The alcohol was flowing, and Jessie was handily beating people at pool. "Challenge your lady," Dalton said. He was getting a little deep in his cups and apparently wanted to be punched in the face.

"Oh, I am already giving to her campaign."

"Come on," Cassidy said. "Play."

"You better watch it."

"Flynn?"

He turned and looked across the bar to see Jessie standing there looking at him.

"I'm going to win," he said, standing up and making his way toward her.

"Are you?"

"Yes, Jessie, I am. But either way, I support your campaign."

Everyone was watching them, and his heart was beating just a little bit too hard. Because there was something about her. There was just something about her.

She held a pool cue out to him, and he grabbed it, but she didn't let go, so he ended up pulling her bodily toward him. She looked up at him, a small smile on her lips. "I'm very good at this." She moved her hand up the pool cue just slightly, and he felt the motion resonate in his dick.

They were performing, and he knew that. Except, had they ever really been performing?

In spite of himself, he was taken in by her performance. He knew that it was for the people around them and had nothing to do with the thing between the two of them, but still . . . He just couldn't be immune to her. And it was damned ridiculous, because he had known this woman for years. And all that time, he had managed to keep his distance. Here he was. It was like a study in self-sabotage.

But why not? Why not give in? You're already working with her. You're already helping her with her election. What difference does it make if the two of you blow off a little steam?

Except there was something inside him, the thing that had always resisted getting involved, that pulled him back even now. A part of him had known all this time that he needed to stay away from Jessie, whether it was because she was a Hancock, or because of the intensity of the attraction between them, he couldn't say. But there had always been something. Just as the attraction had always been there, so had the aversion to giving in to it.

And yet he found himself grasping hold of the pool cue, right over the top of her hand, and rubbing his thumb across the back of her knuckles. "I'll play, if you let go of the stick."

Her face went bright red, and she released her hold on the pool cue. That made him feel that he had a little bit more power here. That he wasn't being completely dog-walked by her.

He had so much experience with sex. He knew what he wanted, and he got it whenever he needed it. It had never made any sense that she felt like this mythical creature. This person right in front of him that he couldn't reach out and touch no matter how badly he wanted to.

No. It had never made sense.

And yet, she did the same thing with him. Rumor had it she went after whatever she wanted. She was happy to flirt, happy to tease. By all accounts, she was a great time. Yet she stayed away from him. Acted as if he was as ridiculous an option as she was to him.

Maybe that was why the attraction was so hot after all this time. Maybe that was why it didn't go away. They were the fantasy each had never indulged.

He shouldn't be thinking about this while he was about to play pool. Because he was going to beat her. Goddammit.

She wrinkled her nose and stepped away from him, taking hold of her own pool cue and setting the balls on the table with a flourish.

"Ladies first," he said. He felt magnanimous, actually. And of course he would never get any credit for the gesture, not from her.

Not that he needed it. He would beat her no matter who went first.

She leaned over the table, and he couldn't help but look at the way her breasts spilled over the top of that tank top, drawing all his attention away from the game and right to her body.

He tried to focus on what she was doing, but it was difficult. She didn't even look at the balls but made eye contact with him as the pool cue slid smoothly through her fingers and the white ball cracked against the colored ones with a loud sound that should've jarred him out of his haze, but didn't.

Because he was a disaster.

This girl.

"I'm solids," she said.

"Stripes it is." He was in a pretty advantageous position, so when he set up, he easily sent the white ball into a stripe, knocking it into the pocket. The cue ball rolled just to the edge of the velvet, but didn't tumble in and cause a scratch.

He grinned.

"Impressive," she said, but in a way that was a little bit too smooth. A way that felt like she was stroking him.

"It's really too bad you don't need any instruction," she said. "I would've loved to give you some guidance." She knew exactly what she was doing to him.

"Well, if you need me to show you how it's done, I'm happy to."

She set up next to the shot he had left her, which was difficult no matter how good you were. "Oh, Flynn, I know my way around balls. I definitely don't need you to teach me." The cue glided through her fingers, striking the white ball, which hopped and hit the top of a solid so that it rolled straight into the opposing pocket.

"Damn," he said.

And then he ground his teeth together, because she was as hot as she was annoying.

They went back and forth like that, until there were very few balls left on the table. As he set up to take another shot, she stood there, arms crossed under her breasts, looking at him, refusing to move.

So he turned, brushing his hip against hers as he leaned in to prep for his shot. And then she leaned in, her breath hot against his ear. "Don't mess up."

He turned his head, and their mouths were only a whisper apart. It would not be out-of-pocket for him to kiss her, actually. Because they were pretending to be a couple. Because this was all part of the ruse. Certainly, the people around them were all entertained.

His pulse began to pound heavily. But he distracted himself by watching as the color mounted in her cheeks. Watching as she began to get short of breath. She was turned on. She had flown too close to the sun. She meant to mess with him, and she had messed with her damn self.

He took a shot and sent his ball in, leaving the white one in a precarious spot. She cleared her throat and rounded the table, but he went right with her.

"What are you doing?" she asked out of the corner of her mouth.

"I'm helping you. Just like you were helping me."

"You are not helping."

He leaned against the table just as she bent down, keeping their faces close. "Don't mess up, Jessie."

She arched back, scratching, sending the white ball flying off the table.

"You did that on purpose," she said.

"Not at all. I was just being affectionate."

"You are the worst," she hissed.

"Many women would agree with you."

"You shouldn't brag about that."

"Well, I'm the worst, so I'm often unclear on what exactly I should be bragging about."

She huffed.

And then it was his turn.

He only had two more balls left to sink, and with a trick shot, he could do it. So he was going to give it a shot. Because she was playing with him, and he was over it. He was going to help her out with her scheme, but she didn't get to be in charge. She didn't get to dictate how he felt or crash his get-togethers with his friends. He was a man who had control over his life. The last time he'd let anybody yank him around . . .

He just didn't do it. The end.

He took the shot, and knocked one of the balls against the other; then both rolled into the pocket, the white going just to the edge and resting there.

He slammed the end of the pool cue down the floor and blew across the top of it as if it was a smoking gun. "I win."

But there was a feral light in Jessie's eyes, and he knew that he had pushed her a step too far. That she was about to get her revenge.

She walked toward him and grabbed the front of his shirt. "I think we need to have a campaign meeting."

And then she tugged him away from the pool table, down the narrow hall, and straight into the single-occupancy bathroom. Where she slammed the door and locked it behind them. He could hear cheering and hollering from the bar.

"What the fuck?" he asked.

She stared up at him, her breathing hard.

Her cheeks were flushed, her eyes bright. She wanted him. He wanted her.

He didn't think he could fight it anymore.

He grabbed her arm and pushed her back against the wall, his own breathing unsteady. Were they doing this? With everybody outside, were they doing it as part of a performance? Finally. He reached out and moved his thumb over her lower lip, and the sound that escaped her lips was something like a wretched cry. And then she ducked under his arm, unlocked the door, and scurried out. He went out after her, and looked toward the bar, then looked out toward the back door, which was just closing.

"For God's sake."

He followed her outside, into the alley behind the bar. "What the hell are you doing?"

"We can't be taking up the bathroom. We can just cool our heels out here for a minute."

"To what end?"

"The show, Flynn."

"That wasn't a show."

"It was a show," she said. "That's all this is. Don't let it go to your head."

"My head? That's not where it went to, Jessie, and I think you know that."

"Darn. I didn't realize that you were as gullible as the rest of them."

Oh, that did it. That brat. "You are not unaffected by this, Jessie Jane Hancock."

"I am going home, Flynn Wilder."

"We have to leave together," he said.

"They'll think we did." She picked up her phone and was on a call before Flynn could say anything else. "Gus? I'll come by and square up tomorrow. No. I swear. I'm good for it. I gotta go. See you."

She hung up and started to walk quickly away from him. "Now I have to leave."

"Yeah. Guess so." He paused. "You know, you really made this a miserable evening."

"You're not the first man to say that to me."

And with that, she left him standing there in a nearly empty street staring after her hips as she walked quickly to her truck and got in.

He was not leaving. He was going back inside. He stormed back into the bar and walked up to Gus. "I'll pay Jessie's tab."

He said it loudly. Loud enough for everyone to hear.

"She said she would square up tomorrow."

"I know she did. But I've got her."

Then he went back to the table, anger he couldn't quite sort out rolling through him like a thundercloud. She wanted him; she didn't want him. It was part of the game.

It made him think too much of his childhood, and if that wasn't the most messed-up thing . . .

"You good?" Dalton asked.

"Great," Flynn growled. He did not take a drink from the beer bottle his sister slid in front of them, because he had a feeling that right now he would end up biting the end off and chewing glass.

Somehow, he and Jessie were going to get through this. Because he had thrown his hat into the ring, and he was going to see it through. It was just a real damn shame that dealing with her made him think of . . . Well, all the reasons he was involved in this to begin with.

One of the reasons he didn't do relationships was that he wanted everything to be on his terms. And that just wasn't how romance worked. It also wasn't how parent-child relationships worked. Because when you were a kid, they had all the power to make you feel wanted, unwanted . . . whatever. To be invited to Christmas one year and given extra presents to assuage someone's guilt, or maybe even because they cared, to being skipped the following year for no reason you could fucking figure out . . .

He didn't do hot and cold. He didn't do uncertainty. He sure as hell didn't want anything to do with people who didn't want him.

And that included Jessie Jane. His feeling for her wasn't that deep. He wanted her, she had teased him a bit. That was all. But there was a burning something in his gut. Something that made him want to push her too. Made him want to get her to admit that this back-and-forth wasn't part of the show.

He wrapped his hand around the beer bottle, until he was afraid he might break it.

And he realized he couldn't even dance with one of the women here. Couldn't even hook up. Couldn't do a damn thing to get rid of the tension in his gut.

Damn Jessie Jane.

"I'm about ready to go," he said.

Cassidy's eyes widened. "Already?"

"I'll take her home," Dalton said.

He looked from his sister to his friend and back again. Cassidy had such a crush on Dalton. And honestly, Flynn wouldn't mind if the two of them hooked up. In fact, he thought it was about time Cassidy hooked up with *someone*. Dalton was a better option than . . .

His gaze drifted across the bar to West, who was practically being climbed by that redhead, and at the same time, Cassidy seemed to notice as well.

Yeah. It was good to have Dalton take her home.

"Great. I gotta call it. See you both tomorrow, I guess."

He would also see Jessie in the next couple days, whether he wanted to or not.

You couldn't choose your family, but he had chosen a pretty miserable partner in poking at his family. One difference between the emotional torture he'd experienced at the hands of his mother and the physical torture he was currently experiencing at the hands of Jessie was that this was his own damned fault.

Flynn Wilder, king of bad decisions.

For the first time, his outlaw status annoyed him. Because it had damn well gotten him into this situation. And the problem with being great at causing trouble was that it was kind of hard to know how to get out of it.

Chapter 7

I don't know why I keep on moving. Except men are the same everywhere. The only thing I can change is the scenery.

—Belle Martin's Diary, February 1866

Jessie hadn't slept well at all the previous night. The evening's interactions with Flynn played through her mind on a loop.

It had almost happened. The thing she'd felt—feared—could happen if she ever got too close to him. But this was not the time.

Will it ever be the time?

No. Not with him. Not with him.

She was playing with fire, but she was Jessie Jane Hancock, so she ought to be able to handle that.

He'd been pissed off, though, when she left. Probably because he was a man and he'd had a moment there when he'd thought he might get laid, and then he didn't.

She needed to focus on what was in front of her, which was not Flynn Wilder, but her campaign.

That's why she was headed to the library to talk to Millie about setting up a little campaign booth in the parking lot. Just as she walked into the library, Danielle Lefevre was walking out.

"Jessie Jane," Danielle said, managing to orient her body so that she barely missed running into Jessie, all while smiling in such a toothy manner, Jessie thought she might have been dropped into a toothpaste commercial.

"Danielle."

"Declaring for mayor. Really?"

"Yes. Really. As anyone can."

"You're not . . . It's not . . . It isn't serious, is it?"

"I filed paperwork, Danielle, and I'm not about to engage with bureaucracy for the sake of empty entertainment."

"It isn't going to bring me any joy to beat you as soundly as I'm going to."

The door opened behind Danielle. "Jessie," Millie said, smiling wide.

The small, brown-haired woman was wearing a floral dress. She had very large glasses perched on the end of her nose, and a person who wasn't observant could be forgiven for labeling her as mousy or retiring. But Jessie paid attention to people. It was one of her strengths. Part of what made her charismatic, if she was going to call herself that, and she just might.

"I thought you were on your way to an appointment?" Millie asked Danielle, pointedly.

Jessie knew that there was bad blood between the two of them. It was why she thought Millie might make a good ally. And why she was totally surprised to see Danielle at the library.

"Yes. But of course I had to stop and talk to Jessie. We might be rivals, but I have compassion for the fact that she's about to go through a difficult time." Then she turned her glittering blue eyes to Jessie. "I guess I'll be seeing you soon. For a debate at town hall?"

A debate. Fantastic. Jessie could think of nothing better, especially when she got all her favorite cowboys, barflies, and buckle bunnies to attend. "I would love to."

Danielle walked quickly to the parking lot and got into her big white SUV.

Jessie turned toward Millie. "I assume there's a story here."

"A little bit of one," Millie said. "You know how she is."

"I do know how she is, but I'm shocked she'd come into the library after what she did to you."

Millie wrinkled her nose. "Shocked? Really? She is . . ."

"Fair enough. People think I'm shameless, but I got nothing on her."

"No indeed." Millie cleared her throat. "She was wanting to put election materials up on the library bulletin board. I told her I would have to consider it. The library can't be partisan. It's funded by taxpayer dollars."

"Danielle wants to take library funding."

Millie grimaced.

Jessie tapped her chin. "What if you let her put her flyers up on the board, and then I can do a booth in the parking lot."

Millie blinked. "Come in."

Jessie stepped past the threshold and into the library. She'd never been inside the library before. It was a lovely facility, all new and nice—which meant it had been built in the last twenty years. There were lots of cushy chairs, desks and tables, nice nooks to read in. It was a bit more industrial and less cozy than Jessie would personally prefer, but it made her feel a little sad that this was the first time she had been in the building. Another way that she was just . . . odd, an outsider.

"What is it you'd like to do?"

"Flynn is helping me out with my canvassing, and he mentioned that it might be a good idea to have a booth with drinks and baked goods. I thought it was a great idea, and I thought the library would be a good location, seeing as you're his sister-in-law . . ."

"And Danielle stole my fiancé?"

Jessie choked on a laugh. "Well. I thought that might not hurt."

"I don't care that she took him. In fact, it's the nicest thing anyone ever did for me."

"Well. You're not wrong. That guy is a weasel. And so is she. That's why I'm running against her."

"I can list a hundred reasons why it's good you're running against her. And Austin . . . He explained to me that Flynn is involved because . . . you know how it is."

"I'm getting the picture, yes. As far as the town is concerned, we're dating."

Millie looked at her, her eyes bright. "You aren't, though?"

"No. I think Flynn would rather take some of my hairspray, douse himself with it, and set himself on fire than actually date me."

"That wasn't the impression I got," Millie said softly.

"Oh, he thinks I'm hot," Jessie said. "I know that. But he doesn't like me. I think he might sleep with every woman in this town before even considering me. In fact, he seems to be attempting to prove that theory right."

She felt overly hot and sweaty just saying that, but knew her agitation wasn't showing. She was being exactly what someone like Millie expected her to be. She was being a straight talker. She was being that honest, slightly risqué version of herself people responded to so well.

"I have no issue with you and Flynn using the parking lot to distribute materials, and I'll let Danielle hang up her campaign poster."

"Perfect. And honestly, if she complains, it's going to look like she feels threatened by me."

Millie regarded her for a moment. "She should be. I think she's overestimating her popularity. When I went up against her on the issue of funding Gold Rush Days, her stance wasn't popular enough to win the vote. She was close, but the loyalty people have to her is directly related to what they think she could do for them. Yes, there are some people who aren't going to want to give up that connection, but there are plenty of people that will jump ship. The thing is, Danielle isn't loyal. Because of that, she doesn't engender a lot of loyalty."

"That's what I'm counting on. And the truth is, a lot of people don't get involved in this community because they don't think there's any point. I'm hoping to bring them out of the woodwork."

"Smart plan."

"I'm smarter than people think."

"Do you want to come have dinner at our place tomorrow night? I'm going out with my friend Heather tonight, but tomorrow . . . You and Flynn could discuss your plans, and the whole family can get their story straight. And we could discuss them canvassing when and where you'd like them to."

"Great. I've also got my horse-shoeing clients. I'll be talking to all of them. What I'd really like is to hear the concerns that Austin and Carson have as ranchers. Flynn obviously has had a chance to weigh in already."

"And that is very smart. Because this town isn't just about tourism."

"I feel like I occupy a middle position, between businesses that cater to tourists and ranchers. I think we can serve both parts of the community."

"If anyone can, I think it might be you. I've always admired you, Jessie. People have always thought that I was nothing more than the quiet librarian. And for a good portion of my life, I suppose that's been true. But I've always thought you were a badass."

Millie looked slightly thrilled that the word "badass" had come out of her mouth, even if at a low volume. Jessie could only smile. "And I've always known that you were actually a force to be reckoned with, Millie Wilder. Your marrying Austin made it clear that I was right all along."

"I suppose it did," she said.

"Well. I'll see you for dinner. And then for the booth. What's your favorite baked good?"

Millie frowned. "My favorite baked good?"

"I love to bake."

"Lemon bars?"

"Then there will be lemon bars. And thanks for the dinner invitation."

Jessie was halfway back to her truck when she realized that she had just been invited to Austin Wilder's house for dinner.

Likely, Millie was going rogue with the invitation. Because she could not imagine that Austin would be any too pleased about it. Hell, come to that, Flynn probably wouldn't be too pleased either.

Jessie felt amused down to her socks.

When Flynn showed up at his brother's house for dinner with a cooler full of elk steak, he was greeted with a phrase so insane, he was convinced that he had misheard it: *Jessie ought to be here in about a half hour.*

"Excuse me?"

His sister-in-law grinned at him. "She didn't tell you? She stopped by the library and talked to me about the two of you doing a booth there tomorrow."

"I hadn't received those details."

"I invited her to come to dinner, because honestly, I thought we should all have a unified story. Also, I want to make sure that I support her mission in any way I can."

"Still feeling frosty toward Danielle?" Austin asked, from his seat on the couch where he was holding Emma.

"Yeah. I do. I don't mourn the loss of Michael, don't get me wrong, but I still think she's an awful person. And I'm not over the things she said about you when we started dating."

"Dating," Austin said. "Is that how we are reframing that?"

Millie went scarlet. "Eventually we dated. Well, eventually we got married."

"We never did anything half so civilized as date, Millie Mouse."

Millie made a *tsk*ing sound and moved to the couch to steal the baby.

"I'll tell you what, Jessie Jane is smart," Flynn said. "She managed to find a family with two built-in allies."

"She did," Millie said, holding Emma on her hip. "I'm more than willing to support a change in regime."

"But Jessie Hancock?" Austin said. "I'm really not sure how I feel about this."

"Why?" Cassidy asked, leaning in the doorway, holding a bag of chips. "I mean, if you don't like Danielle anyway . . ."

"Better the devil you know?"

"I'd rather have the devil I don't know," Cassidy said. "It's more interesting."

"There you go. From the mouths of babes," said Flynn. "Also, it makes a fucking difference to me, Austin."

Austin looked sheepish. "Sorry. The thing is, I don't think of them as your family. We're your family."

"Damn straight," Cassidy said, talking around a mouthful of

crumbs while she wiped her hand on her jeans. "And they don't deserve any of the wealth they have. I'm all for this targeted takedown, even if it does involve the Hancocks. But none of us have ever had quite the beef against them that you have, Austin. You're the one who needs to relax."

The front door opened, and Flynn's stomach clenched, until his brother Carson and his wife Perry walked in. Of course it was Carson and Perry. Not even Jessie was feral enough to walk in without knocking.

"Oh, am I missing the Flynn/Jessie Jane gossip?" Perry asked, looking genuinely upset that she might have.

"There's no gossip. Anyway, Jessie is coming soon."

"Really," Perry said. "I am living for this."

"There's nothing to live for, Perry," he said to his sister-in-law. "This is just two people engaging in small-town talk. That's it."

"Well, that's interesting enough in and of itself."

"Get the grill going," Austin said. And then Flynn found himself out on the porch, grousing as he ignited the grill and put the steaks on. That's where he was standing when Jessie Jane pulled up in her old blue truck.

His body reacted. Which just made him madder. Madder at himself, madder at her for what had happened at The Watering Hole. Just mad.

She grinned at him from the driver's side window as if they hadn't left each other hot, panting, and furious last time they'd talked, and then parked next to Carson's truck. She got out of the oversize vehicle, jumping down to the gravel and making her way over to him. "What are you grilling?"

"Elk," he said, his voice clipped.

"Cool. Thanks for having me up for dinner."

"This isn't my house, and I'm not the one who invited you."

"You're such a romantic, Flynn. How is it that a girl hasn't snapped you up yet?"

"I don't know, Jess," he bit out. "Maybe the same reason a man hasn't made an honest woman of you."

"You got me there," she said, pointing finger guns at him.

Finger guns.

Like she hadn't locked them in a bathroom and then run when it got too intense.

His blood felt hot. Felt like it was running just a little bit fast. He didn't like it. He was used to being in total control of his attraction to women, and maybe that was the real thing that bugged him so much about Jessie. The control seemed to rest entirely with her.

"Be forewarned that my family is about to descend upon you like a pack of ravenous wolves," he said.

Jessie did not look concerned about this at all. In fact, she looked as irrepressible as ever. "Excellent. Being invited to a Wilder family gathering. It feels like a Discovery Channel special. I'm about to see a rare creature in its natural habitat."

"We aren't all that rare."

In truth, though, he supposed that he was. The only one of his kind. Part Wilder, part Respectable Family About Town. But that wasn't what she was talking about.

"You get to give your little speech again."

"I love a speech."

She walked up the steps, but she didn't knock on the front door; instead she came to stand beside him, craning her neck to look at what he had on the grill.

"Jessie," he said, his tone warning. "Don't make a nuisance of yourself."

"But that's what I do."

He turned his head to look at her, and she was far too close. He wouldn't take money for helping her, but he knew exactly how he would like to extract payment from her.

That was . . . not a thought he needed to be having right now standing on his brother's front porch while grilling steak. No, it wasn't.

But he felt compelled to make her pay for last night, or at least make it clear he hadn't forgotten.

"Don't push," he said.

"Or . . . ?" she asked.

"Don't ask questions you don't want to know the answer to."

"Maybe I do want to know. I heard curiosity killed the cat."

"Curiosity might result in something else for your kitty."

She stood there for a moment, not getting the double meaning, and then her eyebrows lifted just slightly.

"Oh."

Right then the front door opened, and Millie rescued them both. "Jessie Jane!" She rushed forward as if Jessie was an old friend. "Come in!"

"Thank you," Jessie said. "Sorry I didn't bring any lemon bars tonight, but I will have plenty for tomorrow."

Lemon bars. What?

"I'm excited. I have to warn you, though, that I put up a little informational thing about the booth tomorrow, and now Danielle is coming."

"What?" they both asked.

"Well . . . basically I was hoisted by my own petard. Because I initially declined to let Danielle hang her posters up based on non-partisanship, now I have to allow her to have a booth in the parking lot."

"Great," Flynn said.

"Great indeed," said Jessie, unflappable as ever. The woman was like Teflon. Whatever you threw at her just seemed to bounce off.

Though for a second there, when he had dropped that innuendo, she hadn't looked quite as balanced as she usually did.

He didn't know if he was proud of himself or ashamed.

"It will give us a chance to really stand in contrast to her. People don't like Danielle."

"Well, that is true. People think they have to like her. And that's not the same thing."

Jessie laughed. "You're telling me."

Jessie and Millie disappeared into the house, leaving him alone on the deck with his ruminations. That was when the door opened again, and Carson came out with a beer in hand, which he thrust toward Flynn. "I thought you might need this."

"Thanks. Are you not thrilled to have Jessie in-house?"

"Oh, I have no issue with her," Carson said. "You were all wound up about me and her. There was never anything to it. All she ever did was ask me to do a little bit of work for her. There was never any . . . There was nothing on my end." He paused for a moment. "Now, West on the other hand, I might have issue with. Considering he did kiss my wife."

"She wasn't your wife then," Flynn pointed out.

"I guess not. But I still don't have to like the guy."

"I guess not, Carson, but it seems a little bit disingenuous considering you were married to somebody else before you married Perry."

Carson cleared his throat. "Listen. We all have a past. It's fine. It just so happens that West kissed Perry when I wanted to kiss Perry and—"

As if she had been summoned, Perry appeared, looking sunny and beautiful as ever, her long blond hair a beautiful tangle around her shoulders. "I'm sorry, what?"

"Nothing," Carson said.

"Carson still has sour grapes about you making out with West."

Perry smiled. "Really? Maybe you should talk to someone about that, Carson," she said.

"I'm good," he said.

"You know what else was good? West. He's a good kisser."

"No," Flynn and Carson said at the same time.

Carson and Perry had been best friends their entire lives, and in reality, in love for most of their lives, but running from it as if it was the most terrifying thing either of them could imagine. Carson had gone away to the military, had gotten married, and had been widowed only a few years later. In the aftermath, he and Perry had finally worked out their feelings for each, but Lord, it had been messy. Their foundation was strong, and their feelings were intense.

That kind of commitment made Flynn want to turn and run in the other direction.

In his estimation, love was . . . labor. Austin and Millie, for what it was worth, had a much less tempestuous relationship, but Perry and Carson had fallen in love kicking and screaming, wounding each other the whole way.

He was glad they were together now, but good God, you couldn't pay him.

He'd been through enough when it came to love, even if it was of a different variety.

"What?" said Perry. "I wouldn't have been thinking about West except you brought him up."

"Well, his sister is here."

"Thank you for that," she said. "I did notice. But I also acknowledge Jessie's identity apart from her family. Anyway, I'm primarily curious about your-all's scheme."

"You can't tell anybody," he warned.

"Yes, that has been said to me about fifty times. I know I can't tell anybody. We are united in this whole beat-Danielle thing. The restaurant tax would have such a detrimental impact on tourism in town. And anything that impacts tourism negatively is a hundred percent not for me. Plus, I don't like her."

"Nobody does," Flynn said. "Well. That's not true. Plenty of people do, or she wouldn't be the mayor. But it's a particular sort of thing. The kind of liking that has a clause. They'll all turn on her if the tide shifts."

"True that," said Carson.

A minute later, the steaks were done. He carried the meat in and was unsurprised to see that Jessie Jane was holding court in the living room. He had just come in at the end of a full-on campaign speech.

Millie looked delighted, Austin looked dubious. Cassidy gave a fist pump of admiration.

He wished that Dalton were here, but he had gone down south to compete in a rodeo event and would not be present for the next couple of weeks to pass judgment on the situation. Very irritating.

It would've been nice to have his input.

"I think it sounds great," said Cassidy. "Anyone who's going after Flynn's useless-ass family is good in my book."

Oh, Cassidy. She drove him nuts, but she was so resolutely on his side. The truth was, he was the only one, and so was she. Carson and Austin were full brothers. Danielle and Mike were full siblings; Flynn was the half. And Cassidy was in much the same boat. She was one of the halves. Cut from a slightly different cloth, and never really quite sure what to do about it.

He had really needed her when she had come to the house, and he wasn't entirely sure if he had ever communicated that to her. But her arrival had upended things in the best way. Having a nine-year-old girl to look after had taken the focus off his own pain. And it had made him feel a little bit less alone. And hell, her loss had been a lot more important. A lot fresher, and it had given him a purpose.

"Thank you," he said. "You know I don't hate them."

Did he? It was complicated. Sometimes the LeFevres felt like strangers. But strangers didn't have their hooks in you, he supposed. Strangers didn't have complex scaffolding that they had built inside you, residences that made you feel a certain way about yourself and everything else.

"Well, I don't like them," he said.

Danielle and Mike, anyway. His feelings for his mom were more complicated and always had been.

His stepdad could die in a fire. He didn't even think of him as his stepfather but as his mom's husband.

"What I really want to know," Jessie said as they all moved into the kitchen to eat, "are your primary concerns as ranchers."

That question opened the gate, and Carson and Austin were off to the races. They had plenty to say about the nuances of water rights and other issues affecting ranchers.

"I fear there's probably not much I can do on a local level about some of that stuff. But what I would be committed to doing is having a quarterly meeting with the ranchers to find out how we can better serve different agribusinesses in the community. It's important. Tourism isn't all Rustler Mountain is, even if it has historically been my family's concern."

He watched her closely, trying to tell if she was being genuine, or just a genuinely good politician. It was hard to say with her.

There was always a cheeky grin on her face, and that swagger in her step. He had no idea if that was who she was, or if it was a bit she was doing.

But when she was talking about ranching, there was a light of real concern in her eyes.

He watched as she charmed everybody, complimenting each and every dish, and even managing to make Austin smile.

She was a force of nature. She didn't charm people by being bland or saying things that were easy to digest the way Danielle did. Danielle was expected. Exactly the kind of person that you would think would be mayor of a small town. Well, until the sex scandal. But even then . . . Even that scandal seemed pretty on brand for a politician. He was only surprised that as a woman, she had managed to slide around most of the judgment. Jessie was a maverick. She was unlike . . . well, anyone.

"I'm shocked that you're trusting us with the fake-dating story," Cassidy said, breaking open a dinner roll and slathering it with butter. "I mean, there are a lot of loose lips over here that could sink your ship."

Jessie laughed. "It's better than trying to maintain a lie with the people who know us best. Better to have you all on our side. And in the know. I don't know if Flynn wants me bunking at his place every night."

He cleared his throat. "No," he said shortly.

"What's the story?" Perry asked. "I mean, the official story of how the two of you got together."

"We hooked up," he said. "That night at the bar."

"Really?" Perry asked, squinting at him. "That's the best you can manage, Flynn? Making the woman you're dating no more special than anyone else you've ever been with?"

"That's what everybody saw," he said. "I'm just keeping it simple."

"Nobody wants simple," Perry said.

"Oh, but if the story's too elaborate, I might mess it up," Millie said.

"No, you won't. Because you know what makes a good story, Millie," said Perry. "You love books. Is this a satisfying romance?"

Millie wrinkled her nose. "I guess not."

"So what should the story be?"

"Maybe the story should be that they were friends, and then she almost hooked up with someone else, and he got mad and took her out back behind the bar and kissed her." Cassidy said this deadpan, staring at Perry, and Flynn wanted to give his sister a high five.

Perry bared her teeth at Cassidy. "You know, I think that story might be taken."

"Sorry for plagiarizing your life," she said, stuffing the roll into her mouth.

"Yeah, I'm good. I think if this is going to be a really satisfying enemies-to-lovers type story, then there needs to be a dramatic culmination," Perry said.

"Oh indeed," said Millie. "A lot of will they, won't they?"

"You're describing the last three years of all of their interactions," Austin said.

Flynn felt like his brother had hauled off and punched him. And Jessie Jane, being Jessie Jane, just laughed.

"Well there," she said. "There's the story. We did hook up that night at the bar, but there were years of denying it. Years and years." She laughed as though it was the most ridiculous thing she had ever heard, as if she wasn't resisting a damn thing. As if the heat between them was entirely a by-product of his siblings' imaginations. And his.

He didn't like that. He didn't like it at all.

"Fine," he said. "Great story."

"I think so," said Jessie.

"And," he added, "I encouraged you to run for mayor. Because I knew that you had a lot of great ideas for the town."

"Excuse me, why am I giving any of my power over to a man?"

"You quite literally asked me to pretend to date you in order to help validate your candidacy?"

"Still. It was my idea to run for mayor."

"I get that. But you've involved me, and the current mayor is my half sister, so don't you think I ought to be involved?"

"He has a point," said Carson.

He had the feeling that his family was enjoying this way too much.

"I do have a point," he said.

"I'll think about it," said Jessie. "We'll see how it goes. What I really want is for you to wear a flannel shirt and carry an ax, like you're about to chop down some firewood. It would be the perfect vibe."

"It isn't Christmas."

"No, but it would give you that wholesome vibe."

"I am not wholesome," he said.

She shrugged.

He had lost control of the conversation. His family was bantering back and forth about all the ways in which he and Jessie could be the most convincing Hallmark movie the town had ever seen. And he was not into it.

Finally, when dinner was over, Jessie excused herself because she had to go home to make her cinnamon-roll dough.

"What time are we meeting tomorrow?" he asked, standing and preparing to walk her out, because, goddammit, he actually was kind of a gentleman.

"Ten. I want to get there before Danielle shows up. Since apparently we are sharing the parking lot." He opened the front door for her and held it. "You don't have to walk me out. My car is right there."

"Consider it practice. You know, you're telling this whole story like it's kind of funny, but the reality is, we have to have one, because people are going to ask. And frankly, I think Danielle is going to be suspicious."

Because their getting together was a little bit too neat, and he could see that. Looking at it from above, explaining all of it to his family, and constructing the story of how the two of them had gotten together, he could see it clearly.

"It's just . . . people will believe it," she said. "Your brother even made that comment about us. About . . . I don't know, whatever nonsense he was on about."

"Nonsense?"

"Yes. I know people think that just because we . . . banter on occasion, there's something between us."

"And there's not?"

"No," she said, tilting her chin up toward him. "Not on my end, anyway."

"Really?"

He shouldn't let her push him. Hell, it shouldn't matter. Because he had done his level best to ignore the attraction between the two of them for years. Why it should make him mad that she was denying it, he couldn't say. Except that she tormented him. But then, she had waltzed up to this ranch and asked Carson to fix that historic Conestoga wagon for her family, and had practically acted like he wasn't here. And it had made him feel . . . decidedly bent out of shape. Because hell, he had always kind of thought that if one day they crossed that line, that threshold between his family and hers, it would be the two of them. And for a moment it had seemed as if it was maybe going to be her and Carson, and he hadn't particularly appreciated it. It had felt like years of foreplay between them.

Years. Starting somewhere around high school, in fact, and now she was just acting as if it was all in his head.

"Yes," she said. "Really."

He took a step toward her, irritation fueling him, and grabbed her arm and pulled her toward him. "Let me tell you something, Jessie Jane. My family—hell, everybody—seems to be pretty damn charmed by your carnival barker schtick. It's bullshit. I don't buy it. Everything about you reads like an elaborate bit to me, and I don't believe for one second that half of what comes out of your mouth is genuine. Yes, I want you to beat my half sister in this election. But that's because of my own feelings about them, and nothing to do with you. I'm suspicious of you."

"Why? Because you're suspicious that a woman isn't gagging to get into your pants?"

He moved nearer to her, and he could smell her. Vanilla and lemons. Probably just because she'd been making lemon bars. That made it even worse. "No, because a woman wants to, but is lying about it."

"Well, maybe think about this," she said, pulling away from him. "Maybe consider that to some women it's worth resisting you either way. I've got pride. And standards."

"Apparently not. Because you're more than happy to use me when you need me."

"Well, maybe I am. And maybe I thought we were even close to getting along, but your ego is getting in the way."

"Your lying is getting in the way."

"What difference does it make? Nothing is going to happen between the two of us."

"I don't want you to pretend."

"The whole thing is pretend, Flynn. Deal with it."

"You're a coward, Jessie."

She didn't look back at him.

She headed toward her truck and got inside, closing the door with an exaggerated slam.

That was stupid. There was no point in starting a fight with her, and the two of them had to meet tomorrow morning to do this whole political thing. Maybe he had been stupid to think that it could work between them. That they could get along even for a limited chunk of time. Now, they were going to have to pretend to be a couple. And that meant . . .

That meant touching her. Maybe even kissing her.

Well. He supposed there were only two potential outcomes to that. Either she would prove her point, which might be better for both of them, or they would spontaneously combust. And set this whole fucking place on fire.

And hell, given the way wildfires spread in the West these days, he had legitimate fear about what that could mean.

He just needed to get a grip on himself. Get control. But the other issue with pretending to be Jessie's boyfriend right now was that he wasn't going to be doing any hooking up.

Nothing to relieve the growing tension inside him, the disastrous consequence of being around Jessie more than he ever had been.

If there was one thing Flynn was good at, it was not letting people get the better of him.

He had let her do that tonight.

It wasn't going to happen again.

Chapter 8

Jacksonville, Oregon, is filled with men who have gold fever. A fine place for me to settle for a while. The El Dorado Saloon is comfortable, and the owner makes sure no one harms his girls. I know I could do worse. I only wish sometimes I could do better.

—*Belle Martin's Diary, April 1867*

The cinnamon rolls had turned out perfectly, so there was that. But she had spent way too much time wondering about what she should wear, which was very stupid, because she knew she had to look like herself. Well, a more put-together version of herself. She had momentarily toyed with the idea that she was going to need to buy new clothes, but no. She was going to stick with the bedazzled, rhinestone look that she always favored. Because that was who she was, and that was the woman who was running for mayor.

Outlaw ticket.

She didn't know why she had been so confrontational with Flynn last night.

Maybe the same reason you ran from him in the bar . . .

It was all building. She'd felt embarrassed. Embarrassed when Austin had brought up the notion that there was something between her and Flynn, because she didn't like to acknowledge it.

Because it made her feel small and afraid, and she wanted to run from it. But of course, that didn't make any sense to Flynn.

Because when he looked at her, he saw the same woman everybody else saw.

The one she was pretending to be today.

She had on a white cowgirl hat, a fringed jacket, a white tank top, and white bedazzled jeans. Her boots were bright pink.

She had chosen lipstick to match, not even bothering with subtlety. Subtle had never been her grift.

Flynn had texted her that he would come pick her up in the morning, and she had decided not to argue with him. It really made more sense for the two of them to meet in town, but she supposed the optics of their rolling in together were better.

She had West drive her to the end of the long driveway with all of her signs, baked goods, and flyers. Along with a spangled tablecloth for the folding table that Millie was providing for them.

West gave her a sidelong look from the driver's seat.

"You look good."

"Thank you."

"Am I going to have to vote?"

"Do you normally not?"

He shrugged. "I don't give a shit what happens in this place. Not on that level."

"You . . . you have to . . . West."

Her brother was the definition of unbothered. Unless he chose to be. He was always one badly placed insult away from a bar fight. Or one disastrous affair away from one.

West really didn't have a single fuck to give, and sometimes she found him to be a charming renegade, but currently, she found him annoying.

"Sorry, I've inherited Mom and Dad's apathy for civic duty of any kind."

"Well. Well."

She really was going to have to talk to them about this. But every time she had seen her dad this week it had been for show rehearsals, and her run for mayor hadn't come up.

"Oh, it's come up," West said, as if he was reading her mind.

"It has?"

"Several times."

"Well, why didn't they say anything to me?"

"Because you haven't been around. You've been with Flynn."

"Well, that's my business, isn't it?"

"For sure. You know we all live and let live."

"Yeah. Sometimes too much. It might be nice to know my parents' opinions on this major decision I've made."

"You mean Flynn or do you mean running for mayor?"

Right. Because her family didn't know that Flynn was a ruse.

"Both. Maybe it's getting serious with him."

West lifted a brow. "Is it?"

"No."

Right then Flynn rolled up, and she could feel West's tension increase.

"Oh, stop it," she said. "It's a bit rich coming from you. Also, it's a bit rich that you care now."

"It's because he's actually involved in your life. And you seem to be . . . hanging out with his family. Sex is one thing, Jessie, but relationships are another."

"What would you know about relationships?"

He grinned. "Nothing. But I definitely worry about you being in one with the wrong idiot."

"Let me worry about the idiot."

"Sure."

Poor West, he knew less about her than he thought. But then, he was in good company.

What really galled her about her discussion with Flynn last night was that he was closer to the truth than just about anybody. He had called her out. On the bit.

The persona that she was so dedicated to. He was the only person who seemed to realize that's what it was, and he was the last person she wanted realizing that.

But the trouble with playing a game like this was there was no easy exit ramp. At a certain point, you were completely committed to playing a role, and what else could you do?

What else could you do?

She got out of the truck with as many things in her arms as possible. West grabbed a stack of signs and a tray of baked goods and followed her out, even though she was grumbling.

Flynn got out of the truck, went around to the passenger side, and opened the door. She stood there, clutching all her things, gazing up at him, willing him not to say anything about their fake dating. Willing him to . . . something.

"Looks like you're all ready," he said.

He looked up, and West was staring at him. She had never experienced her older brother being overprotective in this way.

He had always been pretty relaxed with the guys he thought she was seeing. But he definitely had his hackles up right now.

"I'm good," she said, shoving her brother's shoulder.

"Good to see you," said Flynn.

"Yeah," West returned. "Give your sister-in-law my regards."

Flynn chuckled. "She can get them from you herself if she wants."

"Take care of my sister."

"Oh, West, your sister can take care of herself."

Jessie climbed into the truck, and Flynn firmly closed the door behind her.

They exchanged a few more words that she couldn't hear, and then Flynn opened the driver's side and got into the truck. "I take it your brother doesn't know that we're not really sleeping together?"

"No," she said.

"Why didn't you tell them?"

"Because he was being a dick about it, so I didn't want to give him the satisfaction of knowing that it wasn't real."

"Great. So if I end up getting my spine pulled straight out of my back, that would be why. Because of your pride."

She also had a feeling that he might be referring to their interaction last night. And her pride.

"Yes," she said, doing her best to sound cheery and not sincere at all, because he wasn't going to make her break, not right before they met the public.

"I would've driven up to get you. West didn't have to bring you down."

"It's fine."

She felt allergic to the idea of his seeing her trailer. She could live in a house somewhere else if she wanted to, but it didn't make any sense. It was a lot more logical for her to continue to stay on the family property and save money, but old habits and baggage clung tightly to her, and she didn't want . . . She didn't want him finding out that she lived in a camper. That she was weird. She didn't want him to see her personal things. She didn't want him to see her.

Because as long as people didn't see you, they couldn't really hurt you. If they didn't know you, what could they say? What could they do?

"I'm sorry," she said, feeling that they really had to clear the air or the day was going to be a disaster. "About last night. The thing is, we have to work together, and I don't know how to do that if we're . . ."

"What?"

"I can't do physical stuff with you."

"A level of connection will be inevitable—we're pretending to be in a relationship. Which was your idea, I might add. You came to me. You wanted to do this and now you're acting all put upon about it."

"Well, I . . . underestimated some things," she muttered.

"I can accept a truce," he said.

"Great," she said. "Truce."

"All right, so now we have to focus on the fact that we are about to stare Danielle down for two hours."

"How often do you see her?" she asked.

"In what capacity?"

"As . . . *family.* I mean, I got the impression from last night that it's definitely complicated."

"Yeah. It's complicated. It might be easier if we were totally estranged, but we aren't. It's more a weird, uncomfortable kind of competitiveness. I think she doesn't love the notion that her mom had sex with my dad. Because honestly, if you know my mom, that's kind of an insane thing. She is the most buttoned-up . . . I dunno, she fits with them, you know? She doesn't make any sense with my dad. She doesn't make any sense with me. I'm completely and totally the odd one out."

"But you do see them."

"Sometimes I go over for Thanksgiving. Christmas. Other holidays. I never lived there."

"Oh. So you never really see her and this is the first time, and I'm traumatizing you."

He laughed. "No. I went over on Memorial Day for barbecue. Didn't do Fourth of July this year. So I guess it's been about four months since I've done anything with the family? But we all stood around and made polite conversation. Things are a little weird now that Danielle and Michael are together. You know, the Michael who isn't our brother."

"That was truly a bonkers decision on her part," she said.

"It was. And now that I am related to Millie, the whole thing is even weirder, names aside."

"Right."

"I never wanted to be part of that family," he said.

"And you don't like them."

"No. Especially not Danielle and Mike. My half brother, I mean. Though I don't like him either."

"So you're not in contact with them but . . ."

"It's just very complicated."

She left it at that, because she didn't know what else to say.

"Can you swing by Scallywag's? I put in an order for a dispenser full of coffee, and one with hot water."

"Sure."

She felt she was pushing the limits of his goodwill. Last night's confrontation had been intense and unpleasant. She wanted to put it behind them, but even when they had nice moments of conversation, they hit speed bumps where they just clunked and quit moving forward.

They got the beverages and cups, then made their way to the library, where they began to set up the station. Millie came out with the table and chairs, a pop-up tent and also some balloons, which Jessie thought was a nice gesture. They were getting all the food set out when Danielle pulled up in her white SUV. Michael was with her.

She looked at Millie to see if she was upset by his presence, but she didn't seem perturbed in the least.

Then she looked at Flynn. His face was as smooth and implacable as ever. But there was a level of intensity in those green eyes. Intensity that made her stomach tight.

He wasn't happy with her; that much was obvious. He was here to play the game, and obviously Danielle's presence ignited something competitive in him. However, last night, she had made a misstep with him. But what was the alternative?

Admit that she was attracted to him? Absolutely not. The very idea made her want to run and hide.

She needed to focus on the here and now.

Danielle was dressed all in black, and Jessie thought that was an interesting contrast, considering *she* was the outlaw. Yeah. That was a pretty fun contrast, honestly. But instead of looking at her opponent, she looked at her own setup. Thought about the things she wanted to say. Because if there was one thing she had learned in life, it was that focusing on other people didn't help. It only gave you a lean, hungry look that vultures recognized.

It made you look wilting and weak, as if you might die. That was when they started circling. It was why Jessie led with confidence. It was why she looked content with her own company at all times.

Flynn looked down at the table, then back up at her. "You really bake these?"

"I did."

For some reason she felt she had just opened her chest up and showed him her heart. Squishy and tender. She hated that feeling.

But she had figured she might as well bake the things she was bringing, since she enjoyed doing it. But maybe she shouldn't have. Maybe it had been a bad choice.

Maybe she should've just bought some cupcakes.

And then nobody could criticize her baking, and no one could criticize her. And Flynn couldn't say it was weird or silly or girly that she liked to bake.

"Looks good," he said.

And she realized that being exposed and wounded were perhaps not the two worst things that could've happened. Because his praise made warmth spread through her like melting butter. It made her heart trip over itself. Made her feel like she was floating.

"They are," she said, because a comeback was always a great defense. Always.

"I trust you."

"You should try one. Have a cinnamon roll and some coffee. That way people will know that they can just grab stuff."

"You think that will make them grab baked goods?"

"Yeah. People always need someone to be modeling the behavior."

"Is that so?"

"Well, I'm going to have a lemon bar," Millie said, reaching out and taking one, and then pouring herself some coffee. "Austin is going to come down with Emma a little bit later."

"Great. Give Jessie a chance to kiss a baby."

Jessie wrinkled her nose. "I generally don't kiss babies. I'm not . . . used to small humans."

"Really?" He shrugged. "I like them. Especially when I can hand them back to their parents. Being an uncle has been a lot of fun."

His observation made her feel twitchy. She didn't want to think of him as being good with children. She liked him in his box. But unfortunately, she was seeing him out of it more and more lately.

"Storytime starts soon," Millie said. "Which means that the crowd will pick up a little bit. And then there's a book club that meets here in a couple of hours. Older ladies who are retired and like to talk about romance in the middle of the day. I always join them."

"You read romance?" Jessie asked.

"I didn't use to," said Millie. "But . . . I started about a year and a half ago. One of my regular customers talked me into it. She thought I might learn a few things."

Jessie considered her confession. Millie had gone on to hook up with Austin, who was a far better man than Michael could ever be. She looked across the space at Danielle. She couldn't imagine Millie with the more diminutive man in slacks who was helping arrange Danielle's balloons.

Millie and Austin might appear to be an unlikely couple, they might appear to be opposites, but they fit. Complemented each other.

Jessie knew that love was real; she just couldn't claim to be an expert on what produced real, healthy love and also created a healthy family. Her parents had always been obsessed with each other. But they were the same kind of strange. And that meant they had raised their kids to be the exact same kind of strange. She supposed most people were like that; they just weren't completely unorthodox. Danielle and her fiancé Michael Hall certainly had the same energy. Correct and officious; likely they fancied themselves subtle, when they really weren't. They were clearly upset about this whole turn of events, and that delighted Jessie.

She supposed she and Flynn also looked like two sides of a coin. Which meant their relationship would make sense to everyone in town.

A few cars began to pull into the parking lot, and Danielle took her place at her table, while Jessie took her place at her own.

"Eat a cinnamon roll," she said to Flynn.

"Jessie Jane, have you noticed that I don't take orders well?"

"Well, you're supposed to, because you're supposed to be my boyfriend."

"What leads you to believe that even as a boyfriend I would take orders?"

He was not wearing a flannel shirt. In fact, in spite of the relatively cold weather, he was wearing a tight black T-shirt that outlined his muscles, and a pair of blue jeans. He really did choose violence today.

"Probably the reason you aren't actually anyone's boyfriend," she huffed.

"Probably."

But he did put a cinnamon roll onto a paper plate and pour a cup of coffee.

Right as the first person was about to walk by, he took a bite of the cinnamon roll and made a noise that verged on obscene. She felt it, in her stomach, between her legs.

"Good," he said.

The word skated down her spine, made her fingers feel loose and languid.

She looked over at him, and their eyes met. She couldn't breathe. "I'm glad you like it," she said, knowing she sounded wooden and strange. Knowing she sounded like someone who cared an awful lot that someone liked their cinnamon roll, and maybe even got turned on because his response to the cinnamon roll was hot, and she was only a girl.

But then she had to focus, because a woman was standing there holding a toddler, looking between Danielle and Jessie.

"Hi," both Jessie and Danielle said at the same time.

"I'm running for mayor this year." Jessie rushed to get that last part out before Danielle could say anything.

"You're running?" the woman asked, stepping toward Jessie Jane's table.

"Yes, I am," said Jessie. "I truly believe that I can effect some good change in this town. If you don't feel like your needs have been represented, consider the alternative. A more unorthodox choice."

"Your family does the Wild West Show, right?"

"Yes. We do."

"I've never been to it."

"Come out sometime. Kids love it. There are lots of games. And we have food trucks and all kinds of fun things. You can get a sense of who my family is."

"You're the outlaws," she said.

"That's right," said Flynn. "They are."

"Oh. Flynn."

Flynn looked momentarily confused. "Yes," he said. "Flynn Wilder."

"I know," the woman said with a bit of reserve.

She gave Jessie Jane a warm smile as she began to leave the table.

"You can have coffee. And a cinnamon roll and a lemon bar," Jessie offered.

"Oh. Thank you."

She took a plate, and Jessie served her a cinnamon roll and a cup of coffee. "Good luck balancing everything," she said.

The woman went into the library, and Jessie looked at Flynn. "What was that?"

"I don't know—oh."

"What?"

"I think I slept with her."

"For God's sake," said Jessie. "I did not consider that."

"You wanted the outlaw ticket."

"She's *married*."

"She wasn't. It was like five years ago, I think."

"Oh, Flynn." Jessie tried to project disgust and disappointment, but in truth, she felt a raging, twisting jealousy.

A feeling that she ignored often when she saw Flynn doing his thing at The Watering Hole. Because the reality was, he was everything she pretended to be. Not that she had consciously pretended to be the kind of person who engaged in casual hookups. It was just that people looked at her and made assumptions. Based on her parents, based on her manner. And people had spread rumors, which had done a whole lot of work she had never done. Even her brother thought it was true. Her reputation didn't bother her. She would have to think there was something wrong with hooking up in order for it to bother her, and anyway it made her seem more interesting than she was. It gave her a mystique.

It covered her vulnerability. The vulnerability that she for some reason felt keenly right now with Flynn standing there eating her cinnamon roll, being Flynn.

"Well, we can't exactly claim to be running as the paragons of Rustler Mountain society."

"That's true. We are the dregs," she said.

He huffed a laugh and took another bite. "This really is good."

Half a dozen more people came through in the next few minutes, and thankfully, Flynn hadn't hooked up with any of them. They took cinnamon rolls and lemon bars and cups of coffee, and chatted with Jessie. They were considerably busier than Danielle and Michael, and Jessie felt totally smug about it.

There was a slight lull in foot traffic when storytime ended, and the book club hadn't yet started, and Danielle walked across the parking lot to their table. "Flynn," she said. "I haven't seen you in a little while."

"Nope," he said.

Jessie was aware of the tension beneath their smiles.

"I didn't realize that you and Jessie were in a relationship."

"Well, that would be because you and I haven't seen each other in a while."

"I'm not convinced—"

Jessie Jane waited for Danielle to finish the sentence. As if she wasn't convinced that Flynn would have told her even if they were close. But there was no more to the sentence.

"Excuse me?" Jessie asked.

"I don't think the two of you are in a relationship," she said. "I think this is some weird thing where you're conspiring against me."

"Danielle," Flynn said. "I have no idea what you're talking about."

Oh. He was a liar. And he was a smooth one. She shouldn't find that hot, except he was doing exactly what she needed him to do, so she did find it hot.

"It's too coincidental. You're suddenly with her. She's suddenly running for mayor."

It was exactly what he'd said. That Danielle was going to be suspicious. Well, apparently he knew his half sister better than Jessie did. And maybe on some level Jessie Jane had been a bit deluded. Because generally, with sleight of hand, she could impress people enough that they didn't ask a lot of questions.

But she had gone right into Danielle's territory, so of course the other woman was going to be fixing her with the evil eye.

"I think you're trying to cause a ruckus about town, to get some eyes on her campaign. Because God knows nobody would take her seriously otherwise."

Flynn laughed. Smooth and effortless. "And you think I am going to lend anybody credibility? We both know that isn't true. Also, this isn't a Hallmark movie. This is the real world."

"But you are you," Danielle said.

And just then, Flynn wrapped his arm around her waist, as if he owned her. As if he had done it a hundred times and had the right to do it a hundred more. "Listen, you can call me any number of things, but call me a liar and we are going to have a problem. Especially when you start insulting my girl."

Jessie felt dizzy.

"Not all of us use relationships as guerrilla warfare," Flynn continued.

Danielle looked toward the library, and then back to him. "You honestly think my long-term relationship was some sort of . . . plot to hurt the librarian because I had funding disagreements with her?"

"Stranger things have happened. But I'm just saying, you're suspicious because you were doing someone dirty the last time you got into a relationship. But that doesn't make us all like you."

"I'm the mayor of this town. I'm going to continue to be the mayor of this town. Whether she runs or not."

"You have nothing to worry about if you're so confident of winning," said Jessie.

"I do think people would find it interesting to know that you're faking a relationship for attention."

"Sticking with that? I mean, go ahead and spread it around," Flynn said. "It sounds paranoid."

He wasn't wrong. It did, in spite of the fact that it was also correct.

Danielle huffed, then turned around and walked back toward her booth.

And that was when a new wave of cars began to pull into the parking lot. "I'm about to kiss you," he said.

"What?"

"Just a fair warning."

He wrapped his arm around her waist again, but this time, he turned toward her and closed the distance between them. His mouth was shocking. Hard and hot and everything she had ever imagined it might be. Everything she had ever tried not to imagine it might be. As she lay in bed at night and thought about Flynn, only Flynn, because he was the only man ever to get under her skin that way.

Her whole body was lit up like a Christmas tree. At every point where he was touching her. His hands on her hips, his hard chest crushed up against her. His mouth . . . Oh, his mouth. She was dizzy. His tongue touched hers, and she whimpered. Her knees went weak, and an insistent pounding made itself known between her legs.

It was over in about fifteen seconds. It hadn't been a meaningful space of time, and yet it had been a moment in which everything had changed.

Because before, she hadn't kissed Flynn Wilder. And now she had.

She could never go back to pretending that maybe, just maybe, all the sparks between them were just in her head.

More to the point, she had gone from not being kissed to being kissed, but she had a very stark and terrible feeling that it really only mattered that it was him. And any other time, any other way, it simply wouldn't have been the same.

It was a pretty tame kiss, as kisses went. She had to try not to look shocked, but she didn't think she was managing it.

"Okay, now you got your next wave of people."

But her knees felt like jelly. How was she supposed to go on? He seemed unaffected. And suddenly, she had an inkling of why last night had frustrated him.

Except . . . Did he really feel much of anything for her if he could kiss her like that and then go back to whatever he was doing? He must not.

And oh, it was galling.

"Hi," she said. "I'm Jessie Jane Hancock."

For a while she chatted with a woman called Alice, who was a big fan of romance novels, and who told her all about the newest vampire book she was reading.

She thought she did a pretty good job impressing the older ladies, but truth be told, it was clear that they weren't the type to be impressed by someone like Danielle. They liked a little bit of spirit, and therefore liked her.

That realization gave Jessie some of her equilibrium back.

When Millie popped out about forty-five minutes later, Jessie had been so busy, she hadn't been able to exchange even a glance with Flynn. Or maybe she hadn't exchanged a glance with him on purpose because if she made eye contact with him right now, she might die.

"Everything going okay?"

She watched as Millie flicked a glance over to where Danielle was standing at an empty table.

"She should have brought cinnamon rolls," Jessie said, not bothering to keep her voice down. "Or Flynn," she added.

Millie laughed. "Those Wilder men really are a draw."

As if on cue, Austin pulled into the driveway, parking near to their booth and getting out so he could unbuckle Emma.

Millie's entire face lit up. She took her baby into her arms, and then Austin wrapped his arms around both of them and kissed them. The obvious affection between them made Jessie's heart ache. Yeah. There were a lot of different kinds of love.

She sneaked a glance across the way at Michael and Danielle. The way they weren't watching Millie and Austin was so pronounced, it was almost comedic. She knew there had been an incident between the two men. Austin had been arrested for assaulting Michael in the street. Really, he had just punched him in the face. The sheriff hadn't held him for very long, but the entire incident had been pretty dramatic. She knew neither Danielle nor Michael would start anything with Austin here, because Austin had already proven he wasn't afraid to lay Michael flat out if he needed to.

It was obvious to her that Michael and Danielle were stuck together because they had made bad choices to start their relationship and were therefore trapped in it.

Whereas Austin and Millie had chosen each other out of love. And would do it again every time.

"You all about done here?"

They had gone through almost all their baked goods, and the coffee had long since dwindled.

"Yes. I think now we're going to go put signs up wherever we can manage."

"Sounds good."

Austin gave Millie a kiss and got into his truck, leaving Emma with Millie. "Will I see you later, Flynn?"

"Probably not. Dinner at my place, most likely."

"All right. Good luck with your canvassing." Millie grinned just slightly. "This was fun."

Jessie laughed. But then she was left alone with Flynn. And the memory of that kiss echoing between them. Or at least it was echoing within her.

"Anyway, that was an experience," she said.

"Yep."

They tore down the booth, and Flynn drummed his fingers on the side of his truck. "Do you have a list of places you want to go?"

"Well, first I want to go to The Watering Hole. Obviously, that's going to be my main base. Because that's where most of my constituents are."

"You definitely need to do a campaign event there."

"Agreed."

She smiled at him, and her heart ached.

"Hey, Jessie?" His green eyes burned into hers.

"Yes?"

"Don't pretend you don't feel anything."

With that, he got in his truck, leaving her standing there, feeling as if she had been dipped in hot oil.

Nobody got the better of Jessie Jane Hancock.

But Flynn Wilder might be coming closer than anyone else.

By the time they drove back up to the Wild West Show, Jessie felt as if she had ants crawling under her skin. She needed some distance from Flynn.

She also recognized that they had just set off a pretty intense rumor mill.

"We need to have a date night. Something that isn't part of the campaign. Because Danielle is suspicious," she said, when he drove up to the end of the driveway. "You can just leave me here."

"No, I'm going to drive you up to your house. I'm not leaving you at the end of the road."

"You . . . I can text West."

"Don't be silly."

She really hadn't thought this through. But she also had passed the point where she could try to dissuade him without making it even weirder. She just needed to keep her feelings to herself at this point or it was going to look as if she didn't want him to see the trailers, and since he was going to, she had to let it happen.

Not act embarrassed.

She would not act embarrassed.

"All right. Suit yourself. I didn't want to put you out any more than I already have."

"I think you want to get away from me."

That was almost preferable to him thinking that she was embarrassed by her home. "Why?"

"Because I proved that you're a liar."

"Oh, please. You think that I'm perturbed over a kiss?"

"Yes. I do."

"Save it. For date night. We'll probably have to do it a few more times."

"You could save us both a lot of trouble by admitting that you're attracted to me."

"Okay. I'm attracted to you." Because again, she had reached the point where protesting was going to start to seem weird. It was going to make him feel that he was significant. He was, but he didn't need to know that. "So now what?"

"Nothing. I just wanted to hear you say it."

"Oh, does that make you feel good, Flynn? You need to know that every woman within a hundred-mile radius is attracted to you?"

"Just you."

"Doesn't mean I like you."

"Great. Doesn't mean I like you either. But just so we're both clear about what's going on here."

"That we act like children on a playground who like each other, and therefore must pull each other's hair?"

He chuckled. "Yeah. That. Though if I pulled your hair, Jessie, it would not be playground stuff."

She gripped the door handle. "This is not a good idea."

"Agreed. But the problem is you and I are known for our bad ideas."

"I am not," she said.

"Says the woman who does borderline illegal gambling at the local bar?"

"Well . . ."

"The woman who is currently running for mayor?"

"It's just . . ."

"The woman who is pretending to date me to create conversation?"

"Okay. Bad ideas are kind of our thing. Because you're involved in all this too, so you can't put it off on me."

"I wasn't going to. I absolutely acknowledge my part in the bad decisions."

He was going to ask why not just have sex. She could feel the question hovering in the air between them. Because if she was who she said she was, then why wouldn't they?

But the trouble was, she wasn't. The trouble was, this made her feel like she was exposing parts of herself that she wanted to keep hidden forever. The trouble was, she was operating above her pay grade now, and everything that was coming out of her mouth was nonsense. It wasn't her. Not really.

She was grateful when they pulled up to the fork in the road that would take them to the trailers.

"Turn here."

"Okay," he said, turning away from the sign that indicated that they were near the Wild West Show.

She was committed to just getting through this. Besides, it was Flynn. She was overthinking this. She wasn't exposing herself, because he didn't care about the intricacies of her life. He wanted to sleep with her, at most. She ignored the physical attraction that swept through her, ignored the memory of the kiss they had just shared.

She had kissed Flynn Wilder.

For show. That was all it was. That made a difference. It wasn't as if they had spontaneously given in. Hell, she had resisted him in the bathroom at the bar. Then she had pretended that it was nothing, and he was upset about it. What did that mean?

It was just male ego. That was it. She didn't need to go romanticizing his response.

She didn't do romance for very specific reasons.

The road narrowed and started to wind toward the little lane where all the family trailers were parked. Hers was pink, set back in the trees. It was cute, really. If you squinted.

"This is where y'all live?" he asked.

"Yes. I'm over here," she said, gesturing toward her place. As if it didn't matter. As if it didn't feel intimate for him to see it. She had been to his house. But his house was nice, in the way that something could be nice when you had some money. The kind of nice that a million other people would like. When you lived the way she did, it was the kind of fixed up that people understood when they'd had to do things on a budget. It was the kind of nice that people would call quirky. And there were maybe a couple hundred other people who would like it. Particularly the alligator.

"Well," she said, dumping herself out of the truck when he stopped. "It's been great. See you tomorrow."

"Dinner. I'll pick you up here. Don't have your brother drop you off at the end of the road."

"And what if I disobey you?"

"Keep playing risky games if you want."

What would happen if she invited him in? Right now. What would happen between the two of them? That very thought made her feel as if she was falling off a cliff. Endlessly, endlessly. There was nothing stopping her. That was the insane part. The only thing stopping her, all this time, was her own fear. She had the courage to put herself in front of the town like this, run for mayor, but the idea of inviting Flynn Wilder into her trailer to maybe have sex terrified her.

Her family wouldn't care. Wouldn't judge her. She wouldn't lose anything.

Just her virginity. Finally.

"Bye," she said. She slammed the door resolutely, and she didn't look back at him. If she did, she might just keep falling.

Chapter 9

*I caught his eye on the street and for a moment I felt like I could
be a lady. Any lady. One walking down the street to buy a new
ribbon, clean and new and the sort he might want. I forgot myself.*

—Belle Martin's Diary, April 1868

It had been a cloudy day, which was a relief in some ways. The summer heat hung on late in this part of the state but as the year faded into September, there was more chill in the morning, more bite at night.

The silver clouds that hung over the mountains were swollen, and he was surprised that they hadn't burst yet.

He was making small talk in his mind.

Talking about the weather so he didn't think about Jessie and taking her out to dinner tonight.

He had made a reservation for the two of them at the best restaurant in town, and he was trying to decide if he should text her and tell her to dress up or see what she came up with on her own. He knew that he was playing games, but he couldn't help it. Or maybe he could, and he just didn't want to. What he didn't expect, and yet didn't find a complete surprise, was for his mom to call. But just as he was about to turn on the shower so that he could get cleaned up before getting dressed, his phone rang.

He groaned. "Hello?"

"Hi, Flynn," she said. Always hesitant, as if she had cold-called a stranger. But in some ways, he supposed that was true.

"Hi, Mom."

"How are things?"

"Good. Good. I have some new elk coming, going to go ahead and increase the herd because the initial investment has been so successful. But I don't think that's why you're calling me."

The silence on the other end was indignant. He had done it. He had called her game, and she never liked it when he did that. She always wanted to pretend that she was just a mother calling her son. She never wanted a reminder that they were the furthest thing from a conventional family.

"I talked to your sister."

She always said that. *Your sister.* As if Cassidy didn't exist, as if he didn't have a sister that he considered far more of one than Danielle. As if she could only be talking about one person.

"Danielle?" He didn't insult either of them by asking which sister, but he did decide to make it a question.

"Yes," she said. "She said that your girlfriend is challenging her in the election?"

To his mother's credit, he had a feeling that Danielle had not put it that way at all. He had a feeling that she had gone in ranting and raving about him and Jessie Jane lying. At least his mother was not coming at him with that. He almost felt bad. Because they *were* lying. Because he was doing this to mess with Danielle. It would've been nice, actually, to be on the high road, looking down on his suspicious sister from a great height of moral superiority. But he wasn't. He was as bad as she suspected. But then, that was the whole game, wasn't it?

He was born of a sinner. And therefore he could never be a saint. Not like them.

"She is," he said. "And I know that Danielle is upset about it, but first of all, I don't tell Jessie what to do, and I wouldn't think you would approve if I did. Second of all, if Danielle runs a good campaign, she shouldn't be nervous."

"It's . . . it's just upsetting, of course, to have you two in tension this way."

Again, he held back the meaner response. "Well, Jessie Jane isn't your daughter, so there doesn't need to be any tension for you."

"Is there any for you?"

"No."

Maybe that was cruel. But in this instance, he wasn't in the mood to hold back.

"I see."

"You can't magically be close to someone you've never even spent any time with. Genetics don't magically make that happen."

Maybe they did for some people. He'd seen videos of kids who were given up for adoption meeting their birth parents for the first time as adults and clearly feeling an instant bond by virtue of that connection. He didn't feel that for his family. He just didn't.

"I just would hate to think that you were doing any of this because you're angry with me."

She sounded sad. Upset that her children were at odds with each other. And he felt . . . he didn't know what he felt. But he never knew what he felt for his mother. The trouble was, he did love her. But his love had turned into a sore spot over the years. It wasn't a nice feeling; it wasn't a comfortable feeling. It was like a bruise. And when it got pressed, it hurt. He couldn't take any joy in her being upset. But it wasn't going to be enough to change his course either.

"I don't know what to tell you," he said. "I'm sorry that you're upset. But I don't think Danielle is a good mayor. And I think Jessie will do a better job." He had really done it now. The silence on the other end had barbs.

"Danielle tries to be the best at everything she does—"

"Mom, she's a self-serving brat. The reason you're calling me is that she's bent out of shape because of Jessie's event yesterday, and she wasn't nice. She's not nice. I don't know what else to say about it."

"I just wish you had a better relationship."

"How?" The words were raw, more fractured than he would like. "How am I supposed to have a good relationship with her? I don't know her. And what I do know isn't nice, isn't welcoming."

"You're all my children."

He was at a loss for words. He wanted to say that wasn't true.

Not in the way she was saying it. And she ought to know that. He wanted to say it would never be an equal playing field, but what was the point? He always had the feeling that if he called her out too directly, he was going to lose her completely, and he didn't think he could bear that. He also couldn't explain why. But his father was dead; his grandfather was dead. He had this one link to a parental figure, and he just didn't want to break it. He didn't want to hurt her. Which was insane, because the truth was, they hurt him all the time.

He wasn't them, though. He never had been.

His mother particularly seemed to walk through life with blinders on. With a very deliberately obscured idea of their relationship. Of what they could be to each other. He saw everything far too clearly. He didn't have the luxury of blinders.

"I've got to go. I have to take a shower. I have a reservation for dinner with Jessie."

"Are you serious with her?"

God, he couldn't do this.

"Pretty serious. Pretty serious. Thanks for asking. But I have to go."

He hung up the phone, and stripped his clothes off, got in the shower, and rinsed as aggressively as possible before stepping back out and putting on a pair of black pants and a black button-up shirt that he tucked in. He knew how to clean up. He put on a black cowboy hat and a pair of black boots, and got in his truck, heading down to Jessie's without replaying that conversation with his mother. He refused to do it, in fact. Instead, he thought about the glimpse of the little trailer he'd seen when he'd dropped Jessie off yesterday. She had been funny about it. Like she didn't really want him to see. Did she think he would care about something like that?

His family had land, but growing up, they hadn't had any money. He wasn't snobby about things like that. He was a little surprised, given that he assumed she made decent money, but maybe she just chose to live in a trailer. Whatever the reason, it was nothing to be ashamed about.

He pulled up to the front of her trailer and got out. He didn't text her, because he wanted to walk up to the front door. He felt compelled to look inside. The truth was, Jessie Jane was something of an enigma. A frustrating one. There were times when she was exactly what he thought she was. And times when she just . . . wasn't. Times when she seemed softer and more vulnerable than he expected. Times when she seemed younger.

The front of her trailer was clean and decorated. There was a girly little table, a goose dressed in a costume, and . . . an alligator. He shook his head. He knocked firmly on the door, and the sound was a metal rattle beneath his knuckles.

"Just a second!"

The trailer shook a little bit, and then the front door opened. Jessie popped halfway out, wearing a red dress that was formfitting and showed her figure off in a way that made his body howl. Her dark hair was wild, and she had one earring in, easily putting in the other.

"I'm almost ready."

She turned away from the door and started to put her shoes on. He got a quick peek into the trailer. Saw a turquoise curtain, little tea towels with apples on them, a bright pink refrigerator. He turned toward the area with her bed, and that was when she stepped right in front of him and out the door. "Nosy," she said, brushing past him and shutting the door.

"Yeah. I am. I have to say, I didn't imagine this was the sort of place you lived."

"I'm trailer trash," she said.

"That isn't what I meant. It's very girly."

She looked at him, and a little pleat appeared between her eyebrows. "I'm girly, Flynn."

She was so perplexed that it made him chuckle. "You are not. You're tough."

"Well, I am tough. But I am also very girly. I have rhinestone jeans."

"You do." He looked up at the sky. "Do you want to bring a jacket?"

"I'm good."

"I think it's going to rain."

She shook her head. "It won't. We need it too badly. You should come to the show tomorrow night, by the way. We've been rehearsing a new routine."

"Yeah. Well. Assuming you don't kill me during dinner. Or that Danielle doesn't hunt me down and do it. Or maybe even more likely, her father."

"Is her dad mad at you?"

"Oh, I'm sure he's about to be. My mom called. She's all wound up."

"Oh."

He opened the passenger side door of the truck. "Get on in."

He got into the driver's side and thought again how stupid it was that they were playing this game. "You look great, by the way."

He looked at her out of the corner of his eye, and her cheeks were lit up pink. "Thanks."

"You're welcome."

"I mean, you look great too. You do."

"Thanks."

"I don't really know to do this. Dates."

He laughed. "Me neither. But here we are. It's a great excuse to go to Adeline. I hear the food is amazing. Farm to table and all of that."

"Well, that sounds decidedly above my pay grade." He looked at her again, and she squared her shoulders, seeming uncomfortable. "What?" she asked.

"Nothing. You just seem a little bit more feral than normal."

"I don't ever bring anybody out to my house. I do have money, actually. It's just I'm used to the way I was raised."

He put his truck in reverse, turned around, and headed back out toward the road. "I'm the last person to judge anyone about something like that."

"Well. Good. Because I'm not home to judgment. I dealt with enough of all of that back in school."

He frowned. From his memory, Jessie was really popular in school—at least with a certain crowd. No, it was never the preppy kids, like the pack his half siblings ran with, but she had been very well liked in general.

"I remember you having a lot of friends."

"Sure. Later. But not when I was really young. I barely had any. Nobody wanted to hang out with me. I was . . . one of the weird-ass Hancocks. And I just . . . I carry that with me."

"You don't seem to care about what anybody thinks."

He could feel her staring at the side of his head. "I'm a performer. Who's also running for mayor."

They were silent for a moment, and he let her words sink in. Let them get under the top layer of his skin. Well. The things she was doing definitely indicated someone who cared what other people thought. But she just . . . She was such a wild card. She gave off the vibe that she didn't care what anyone said about her or thought.

"Just forget it. You've seen my house."

"You don't bring any of your gentleman callers back home?"

"I can't say that I ever have."

That made him feel satisfied for some reason. Like he had an edge on those guys, even though he hadn't slept with her. He had been to her house. So there. And they were going on a date, which was something. It just was.

"Well. One of these days, you're going to let me in."

He took his eyes off the road for moment, and his gaze clashed with hers. He realized the double meaning in what he had just said. And he felt the impact of it way down low in his gut. Down even lower. He had never been so affected by a woman in his life. There was just something about her. And there always had been. Despite her vibe, she really did care what other people thought. She worried about it. Because she felt different?

Was that all it was? Did he feel that maybe he understood Jessie Jane and she understood him because they were both odd birds?

He had never considered that. But then, he did his very best to wear his disenfranchisement like a second skin. To act as if he didn't give a shit what anybody thought about him. When in reality, he felt sidelined by his family, and he had embraced the label of outlaw because at least then he was alienating them on purpose. There was something that scratched the back of his brain, something to do with Jessie. Some quality he recognized. He couldn't exactly nail it down, he only knew that it was closer to who he was than he had ever anticipated. But that wasn't the only reason he was attracted to her. The other reasons were visible and obvious, particularly right now, when she was looking more polished and done up than he had ever seen her. Particularly now, when she was close to him in his truck, and he could smell her perfume. Or maybe it wasn't even perfume. Maybe it was just soap and her skin. Either way, her scent attacked his senses in a way he couldn't call unpleasant.

"You know what it's like to grow up in a home that looks totally different from all the ones around you," she said softly.

"Yeah," he said. "I do. When you don't have a mom and dad."

"Or a front yard," she said.

"You have a giant piece of property."

"Sure. But it's more carnival than home."

"Did you ever even try to have anyone over?"

She shook her head. "No. Never. Did you?"

"Dalton. He's one of those people that doesn't . . . I don't know. His family moved here from out of town, and he's never much seemed to care. Who my parents were or what the house was like, you know?"

"I just never met a Dalton. The Wilders and the Hancocks—our families could've been allies, but we weren't."

That made him feel guilty. It shouldn't. It wasn't his fault . . . Except, he hadn't done anything to fix the enmity between their families when they were kids. But why would he?

Kids inherited prejudices from their parents, and didn't really question them until they were given a reason to. But it did stick in his gut that the Wilder family had experienced hardship in town because of their name, and the Hancocks had too, and rather than banding together, they had put up barriers. It was a helluva thing. Not necessarily a good thing.

He had made a friend; she never had. Well, not when she was younger.

"You got invited places, though. When you were older."

"Yes. I did. Thank you for the concern."

"Good. I just . . . don't like the thought of you being totally by yourself."

"Thank you. I didn't think there would ever come a day when Flynn Wilder was worried about my social calendar. Obviously, I'm fine."

"Yeah. Well. You definitely figured it out."

"Something."

They didn't speak the rest of the way into town, and when they pulled up to the front of the restaurant, he parked against the curb and got out. He held his finger up when she started to undo her seat belt, indicating that he wanted her to wait. When she acted as if she was going to try to race him, he moved quickly to the door and opened it before she could. "Don't be a brat," he said.

She looked shocked and offended. "I'm not a brat."

"You're a brat," he said, leaning in. Why was he playing this game? He was torturing himself. Torturing her. Her eyes dropped to his mouth. Her cheeks turned pink, but she didn't tell him to move. Didn't say that she wasn't attracted to him.

"For what it's worth," he added, "I don't hold anything against your family. That was an Austin Wilder special."

"I know. I don't really blame him. Not really. You were never mean to me. I mean, your family never was. We weren't friendly, that's for sure, but we weren't mortal enemies either. At least you didn't run around calling me Contagion."

She got out of the truck then and he closed the door behind her. "Contagion?"

"Don't you remember that? I guess not. You were probably in middle school. I had lice. And I got sent home. So some of the boys called me that for a while."

"Shit," he said. He didn't like that at all. He had never really thought of her as a human being with frailties. That was his fault. He'd been shortsighted. He'd thought of her as an emblem of something rather than a human being. People hadn't been mean to him in school because they had always known that Austin or Carson would beat them up. And once he got older, he would've done it.

"Why didn't West beat the shit out of them?" he asked.

"I didn't tell him."

"Why didn't you tell him?"

"West is four years older than me. He had his own life. He had his own stuff going on. I was never going to go whining to him whenever I had a difficulty. That's just . . . it's silly. It wasn't something that I needed to do. So I didn't do it."

"He should have. He should've known, and he should've beaten them up."

She laughed and rested her head against the back of the seat. "Appreciated."

There was something soft about her then. And it evoked something in his chest. Because now he was looking at her and seeing something other than all that brash attitude she put on display; now he was looking at her and he was seeing someone softer. Someone who had been treated badly in this life.

Someone who wasn't all that different from him.

They were seated at the table, and he knew that everyone was paying attention to them. That people were fascinated by seeing them together. Especially because word of Jessie Jane's candidacy was now common knowledge in the area. But also because not only were the two of them never seen at nicer establishments, but the two of them were never intentionally seen together. Not before this past week. Jessie tossed her head, her glossy brown hair shimmering over her shoulders. She smiled as she looked at the menu. She slipped back into that cocky ease. That ease he was beginning to realize was a mask, and an important one.

A defense against being wounded.

She looked down at the wine list. "I don't really know anything about wine."

He saw her bravado falter just a little bit then.

"Do you like it?"

"I guess. I favor a bottle of Two Buck Chuck, if I ever have it."

"I'll choose something for you."

"You don't have to do that."

"Let me."

He reached out and put his hand over hers. It wasn't sexual. It wasn't part of this game they were playing. The back-and-forth dares, the tit for tat. He wanted to reassure her. His intention wasn't sexual, but it didn't stop him from feeling all the heat and fire he always felt whenever she was near.

Her cheeks turned pink, and she looked down.

"I've got it," he said. "What are you interested in for dinner?"

"I like pasta," she said.

"Good. I'll choose a wine that I think would go well with your pasta."

"How did you learn that?"

"Oh, I have at different times in my life tried to figure out what the hell I might talk to my family about. You know, that family."

"Oh."

The waiter, *Bradley*—Flynn took a dislike to him immediately, though he wasn't sure why—came to the table. He was one of those servers who didn't write anything down, and Flynn was never a huge fan of that.

But, as long as the guy got their order right, he supposed he would be impressed, rather than annoyed.

But then he saw Bradley look down Jessie's dress, and he decided his initial irritation was justified.

But Bradley wasn't here with Jessie, and Flynn was.

Flynn ordered some fancy-sounding appetizers. Then he chose two different pasta dishes, and glasses of wine he thought would complement them both, so that he and Jessie could split the meal and get some variety.

"Wow. I didn't know you could pass for civilized."

"Like I said, at times in my life I tried to figure out how to be the kind of person who could sit at dinner with my mom's family. Especially my grandpa. He was a good man."

"He used to be the mayor," she said. "When I was almost too young to remember."

"Yes," he said. "He was. And he was a good one. I think my mom was rebelling against her family, against the idea of having to be perfect, when she hooked up with my dad. You know they were never married or anything. But my grandpa never held that against me. I don't know what things were like between the two of them, and I'm not foolish enough to think that everything is as simple as it looks on the surface, but he was good to me. He used to take me to dinner sometimes, and we would talk about wine that he liked, music he liked. You know, he left me that property, and his sweaters."

"His sweaters?"

"Yeah. They're ugly. Loud-patterned knit things that I would never wear. But they remind me of him, and they smell like his pipe tobacco. So I have them in the closet at my house."

"I didn't realize that you had a good relationship with him."

"Well, it's strange. Because having me was so difficult for my mom. And you would think maybe that was in part because of how difficult her parents made it. I don't really remember my grandmother. She died when I was young. I don't know what she thought about me. I don't know that she was as enamored of me as my grandfather was. He was good to me from the beginning."

He wanted Jessie to keep on softening up. Wanted her to continue to share things with him. He was fascinated by her. By the realization that there was more to her than met the eye. He had a feeling that if he was gentle with her, he could continue to draw her out. It was the one thing he'd never tried to be with her. Because he had been locking horns with her forever, he hadn't realized her toughness was all a facade.

"There are probably some really important parts of me that wouldn't be there without him. This is where things have always been complicated. I can't hate them."

"I get it." She looked down at her hands. And he covered them with his own.

Chapter 10

*I saw him in town today and told him that if he was going to
stare, he might have to pay like everyone else.
I'm sure he'll never look my way again.*

—Belle Martin's Diary, April 1868

Jessie didn't know what was happening. And she wasn't exactly sure
why she was allowing it to continue. He was being so nice to her.
He was touching her, but not in a heated way, not with that same
kind of electric energy as in the bar bathroom, or even when he had
kissed her for show the other day.

His hands were rough, his touch was gentle.

She didn't know what to do with that. She didn't let men get
close to her, but they sure as hell never treated her like this.

She looked up at him, and those green eyes touched something
inside. Her inclination was to try to run from it, from him. To do
what she always did: make some kind of distancing comment.

His look made her chest feel sore and her body feel things that
she couldn't ever recall feeling before. It made her feel like telling
him. Who she was and why. The way her childhood hurt. Because
he seemed to understand complicated, even if his brand of complicated was different from hers.

But then the waiter came back and set their appetizers down between them, and she was distracted by the smoke coming from the
herbs at the center of the olives. "What is that?"

"Fine dining," Flynn said.

She laughed and admitted to herself privately that it smelled
good, and she was enjoying herself. Maybe she should tell him. But

then that would be like showing him another part of herself, and she had already shown him quite a bit.

So she ate the warm olives, and did her best not to close her eyes and groan at how good they tasted. Same for the deviled eggs, with their little pickled onions on top. She could only be grateful that this wasn't a real date, so they weren't actually going to kiss at the end of it, because that would be adventurous.

Except now she had thought about kissing him.

Without her permission, she found herself looking at his mouth.

"Yes?" He looked at her in a way that made her feel as if he absolutely knew what she was thinking.

"Nothing."

"That isn't the face of a woman thinking about nothing."

"It would be pretty amazing if I became mayor." Somehow, that topic seemed safer than admitting she was looking at his lips and thinking about kissing him. "Because I . . . I used to feel I didn't belong here. But of course there's nowhere else for me to go either. I think that's the weirdest part about being baked into the history of this town, even on the negative side of it. You know how that is. There is nowhere else that you are as rooted to, and yet nobody likes your roots."

"Yeah. Though I always had fun with being an outlaw."

"You said it gets you laid," she said, regretting throwing that word out into the middle of the table.

"Yeah. Because there's something sexy about a rebel. You should know."

His green eyes were hot, and a spark ignited in response at the center of her chest. She supposed she did know that, even if she had never acted on it. Because men were attracted to her. And there was the whole thing about getting to be with her—all lies, but lies she never bothered to correct.

"Yeah. I suppose so. But don't you feel it keeps people from . . ." She stopped herself. Because she wasn't sure she wanted to have this conversation at all.

"What?"

"Nothing." She was breaking her own cardinal rule. Making it too obvious she was putting up a wall. She knew better than that. This was the point where you should just acquiesce and give in. This was the point where protesting too much made you look silly.

"It's not nothing."

She took a breath, trying to dislodge the frozen, pressured feeling at the center of her chest. "When people only know the reputation, they don't really know you, right?" It was such a disingenuous thing for her to say, because she had built her reputation by design. But then, she had to wonder if he did too. If to an extent he leaned in to all that outlaw stuff so that people just saw the legend and not the person.

She didn't want to admit that's what she did. But if there was one person who would understand without her explaining, it was probably him. The whole conversation was risky. But so was letting him touch her hand. So was being here with him. Hell, it had been a risky game from the moment she had approached him, because there wasn't nothing between them. It had always been something. Always.

"I suppose that's true," he said. "But I've had to live so many different ways. There was getting by in my father's house, which meant being self-sufficient. It meant not being precious about things, not caring too much. My father was fun, but he didn't take care of things. Didn't take care of us, not really. He was wedded to alcohol and one-night stands, and that was way more important to him than being a father. Then at my mother's house, there was a new language to learn. Being civil. Table manners and all that. I was a little more myself with my grandfather, I suppose, because he seemed interested in who I was. But then you go out to a bar, and some girl wants to know all about those outlaw Wilders, and I know how to play that up too."

She only had the one mask. She wore it everywhere. She didn't do what he was talking about: changing with the wind, learning to blend in depending on the venue. "Are they all pieces of yourself?"

"I guess they become pieces of you," he said. "Because all of those people are part of my life. I mean, I definitely play up some of it. My half brother Mike is about eleven months younger than me. When my mom decided to make something different of her life, she really went for it. And it always felt like he was her real son. I could never compete with him. Not when he was being raised in the civilized environment one hundred percent of the time. So I made him envy me. I think he still does. Because he's trapped in a nine-to-five, in this relentless grind, sort of hand-shackled by his own relentless need for approval. There's a certain point where if you can't assimilate, it's almost more fun to make the ones that can wish they were you."

She nodded slowly. "Yeah. I guess that's one way of coping."

"Is that what you do, Jessie? All those silly girls that were so mean to you . . . Do you think they envy you? Because they're not brave. Because they care so much about what other people think, and you walk around doing what you want, when you want, saying whatever you want."

He was so close to the bone. To the truth of it all. "Yes. And no. You know what's funny about the two of us, Flynn Wilder? We probably know more about human nature than most people. Every good con man does."

"Is that what you think I am?"

"It's in your blood. I don't think there's anything wrong with it either. People like us, it's only fair that we get a little bit of a cheat code, don't you think? Some way that we can navigate our lives. We didn't choose them." She looked at the back wall. "What I've noticed is that people are almost paralyzed by their desperate need to be liked, to fit in. Paradoxically, the minute I stopped acting like I cared about that, people liked me a whole lot more. They can smell fear, and they could smell desperation. But if you act as if you don't need their approval, as if you don't need them to like you, well then, they want to know why. They want to know what makes you so special. And maybe the secret is that there's nothing special. Nothing at all. But they don't know that."

"I think there's something special," he said, his voice rough.

She just sat there, frozen, feeling he had demolished a wall inside her, and she didn't know how she would ever get it back up. She didn't know how she would ever get herself together. How she would ever hide herself from him again.

But then, thank God, their appetizers were cleared, and their pasta was brought out.

"He's checking you out," Flynn said, gesturing back toward their waiter.

She hadn't even noticed the waiter. Much less whether or not he was checking her out.

"Oh?"

"It's a great dress."

"Thank you. But you know men will check out basically anything. I don't get any satisfaction from that."

She wondered if that was true. Because she definitely got a little something out of it. Especially . . .

The reason she never stopped the rumors about herself was that the idea of men tying themselves in knots and lying about sleeping with her was sort of an ego fix. That they would lie, that there were bragging rights associated with it. And she didn't even have to risk herself to get it.

Maybe there was something wrong with her.

But then she kind of already knew she was messed up.

She took a bite of her pasta, and for a moment she couldn't think of anything but how good it was. "This is amazing," she moaned as the creamy carbonara sauce overtook her.

"Share with me," he said.

"No."

"Hey, that's why we got two different kinds."

"I don't date, and I don't share food."

"We just shared appetizers."

"It's different."

"Come on," he said, taking a swirl of the spaghetti marinara on his plate and holding the fork up in front of her. "Taste it."

She leaned in and took a bite off his fork, too late realizing what an intimate move it was. Realizing too late that it was going to affect her.

Being here, being on a date, was just so normal. But for her, it was entirely abnormal. What if she became mayor? Would it change that?

Would it make things like this feel normal?

Would she feel she could just come into a restaurant like this? Would she go on dates?

It wouldn't be with Flynn. Because after her candidacy, it would be over. And what would that be like? To not be with Flynn anymore. To not see him all the time.

That didn't feel right, and yet . . .

Maybe this was the problem. Flynn had always been something. He made her feel things, in spite of herself. She wanted to be hostile to him, but could never quite pull it off.

Maybe this was part of her journey. Maybe Flynn really was a mountain that she had to climb.

That made her throat dry, made her body feel warm.

Flynn.

He had always been there. This man who inspired feelings inside her that no other man ever had. And after this, maybe she would be mayor. Maybe she would go to upscale restaurants, and maybe she wouldn't spend all her time at The Watering Hole. Maybe she would want a real relationship, because maybe she would be closer to being the real person she had wanted to be so badly when she was younger.

But she would still be a virgin. She would still have to have a first. She would still have to admit that she was afraid, and that intimacy had always frightened her.

She realized then with stunning clarity that she could never admit that, not to anybody but Flynn.

He was the man who was meant to be the first. She knew it with as much clarity as she'd ever had in her entire life.

She only knew one way to go about things like this. She took a bite of her pasta. "I'll share with you."

"Thanks," he said, reaching over and starting to take a bite from her plate.

"And after dinner, maybe we should fuck."

His fork scratched against the plate, and he looked up at her as if she had grown an extra head. He didn't say anything. He just stared at her. Her heart began to pound hard. She had said it. Oh, she had really said it.

"Just, you know, I think it's actually starting to get a little bit undignified, the way we're avoiding it."

She said that like she wasn't about to come apart at the seams. Like it didn't terrify her. It did. God damn, it did.

But this was the only way. The only way forward. Not just to deal with the ridiculous hold Flynn Wilder had had on her for all these years, but with living on the outskirts. Living behind a mask.

"I can't talk to you about this here," he said, his voice low and rough.

"Well, damn. Now I suspect I'm not going to get dessert."

Those green eyes went hard, like cut emeralds. "You'll get it."

He was actually going to do it. She had known that he would. And now her brain was tripping over itself trying to plan it all out. She could grab him. Kiss him in the truck, maybe they could just do it there. He was the kind of guy who would have condoms in his wallet, probably. The kind of guy who would be prepared, so that she didn't have to be. Maybe he wouldn't even notice. She rode horses, after all. The likelihood of her having a hymen was very low. Maybe if she brazened her way through this the way she did every-thing, he would never know that she was a fraud.

And then it would be done. Well, probably they would do it a few times.

But he had already seen her house. He had already seen her.

She had told him more about her experiences growing up than she had even told her own family.

She could do this.

"Well. Good." She took a big bite of pasta. "Do you have breath mints?"

He looked at her and shook his head. "I do. But I'm not sure that either of us is going to care."

Excitement shot through her veins, all the way down her limbs. Collected at the apex of her thighs.

She had always thought of sex as a terrifying, exposing thing. But maybe she should think of it as an adrenaline-fueled ride. After all, everything with Flynn was like that.

Kissing him had left her buzzing. It had been one of the most incredible experiences of her life. Sex with him would probably be like that too. It didn't have to be ponderous or sweet.

She thought about the way he had put his hand over hers on the table. How that gesture had, to an extent, spurred these thoughts.

She dismissed them.

It could be the thing that she had turned away from in the bathroom at The Watering Hole. It could be all those sparks and electric currents. Maybe it would be like a final metamorphosis, not because she thought he was a man with the power to make her a woman, but because this was like scaling a cliffside. Doing the terrifying thing.

Though it wasn't only terrifying.

Suddenly, she wasn't hungry, which really was a shame, because it was a beautiful meal. Flynn, for his part, powered through the rest of his pasta, and half of hers. As if he was determined not to let her totally derail this moment.

He was so stubborn. And so beautiful. Maybe after this she would finally unpack the way she had always felt about him. Maybe once the damage was done, she would go over all the moments in her life when Flynn Wilder had made her heart leap in her chest. All the moments when he had made her feel breathless.

When bantering with him had left her with rosy cheeks and bright eyes.

All the things she avoided, and wow, did she avoid them.

"Can I get you anything else?" their waiter asked as he began to clear their plates away.

"Just the check," Flynn said.

There was a finality to his voice that made her shiver.

The look on his face was a warning, and she felt she'd been given notice.

She glanced outside and saw that it had started to rain. She felt as if God was making fun of her. Because she had told Flynn that she wasn't attracted to him, and she had also told him that it wasn't going to rain. Here she was, wrong on all counts.

And a liar on at least one.

Every step seemed to last forever. Waiting for the check, Flynn paying the check, signing the receipt. Wasted time. Anticipation. She didn't like anticipation. She preferred to tear the Band-Aid off.

Tear the Band-Aid off.

That would be her motto.

She could imagine it. As soon as they got to the front door of her trailer, she would kiss him. He wouldn't have time to look around. She would get him naked as quickly as possible. Her pulse picked up, her heart hammering hard.

Yes. That was exactly what she would do. Like learning a new trick routine. She was agile, and she was fearless. Just because she hadn't done something before didn't mean she didn't have the necessary skills to do it well.

Finally, finally, he was finished with all the things he needed to do to wrap this date thing up, and when they stood, he took her hand.

It was for show. This sweet gesture had nothing to do with what she had said to him a few minutes ago.

His fingers twined in hers, and the way he held her made her feel steady, stable. That was not what she was looking for right now.

They walked out of the restaurant and into the pouring rain. And then he wrapped his arm around her waist, turned her around, and backed her up against the side of the truck, his mouth crashing down on hers. He kissed her, and it was nothing like the kiss he'd given her at the library that day. Tonight, he kissed her as if he was starving and they hadn't just eaten dinner.

And he was right. She didn't think for one moment about breath mints.

All she thought about was him. The rain cascaded over them,

and she didn't care. The truck was wet against her back, and she didn't care.

This was the fierce, hot kiss that she had always wanted with him. That she had always known was possible.

This was everything. His hands were on her face, large and rough and hot, skimming over her skin, which was slick with raindrops.

His tongue swept against her lips, and she parted them for him, hoping that she was doing it right. He didn't seem to have any complaints.

His hold was strong, his body hot and firm in front of her.

When they parted, he pressed his forehead to hers, his breathing ragged, just like hers.

"Is that what you had in mind?" he asked.

"Well. I was thinking maybe it would go further than that."

He chuckled. He raised his hand and slid his thumb along her lower lip. "Not on the street."

"Oh. We *are* on the street."

She hadn't really given any thought to that. She supposed if there were any rumors floating around that they weren't actually together, they would be cleared up by the sight of them making out against his truck. But this wasn't about the election. It wasn't about convincing anyone of anything. It was about her.

She couldn't remember how long it had been since something was just about her.

"You a little dizzy?" he asked.

She looked up into his green eyes and lied. "No."

"We'll drive back up to your place."

She didn't argue. It made sense. They would go back up there, and then he could leave afterward. There would be no awkward morning after; there would be no spending the night. He wouldn't have to drive her home after they dressed.

And her family wouldn't care. If they were even home to notice.

They already thought she and Flynn were together, so it wouldn't even signify.

"Okay."

He pulled her away from the truck, opened the door for her, and deposited her inside.

When he closed the door, she shivered just slightly. But she wouldn't let him see her nervousness.

No. She wasn't going to be nervous. She wasn't going to be like that.

This was going to be great.

And she was going to be good at it.

She knew that he would be good at it. She wasn't worried about that at all.

When he got in the truck, she could hear that he was breathing hard, and she was gratified by the fact that she had affected him in the way he had affected her.

"I'm sorry," she said, because just as she realized that, she realized what lying to him had done.

"About what?"

"Saying that I didn't want you. Making you feel you were alone in this."

He chuckled as he pulled the truck away from the curb. "Jessie Jane, I always knew I wasn't alone in it. You're not that good a liar."

"It bothered you, though."

"Sure. Nobody likes to be lied to, even if the lie isn't a bad one."

She was glad he didn't ask why they hadn't done this before. She wasn't going to ask him either. He was no virgin, so he certainly didn't have the same excuse she did. But they had avoided this. Mutually.

For a very long time.

She didn't know how to act. How to make conversation as they drove out of town.

She remembered that she had told him she didn't bring men back to her place, but then also, she hadn't protested when he had suggested they go back to the trailer.

She wondered what he thought of that.

Whether he noticed the discrepancy, or whether he was just as on edge as she was, and therefore not thinking about it one way or the other. Did people normally make conversation when they were on their way to have sex? What were you supposed to say? Should she be saying erotic things? Talking about it as if they were in one of the romance novels Millie liked to read? Should she say that she wanted to lick him or something?

The very idea made her wish she were dead.

Not the idea of licking him. She liked that idea. She just didn't want to . . .

When they got to the action part, she was going to be able to do it. But she couldn't do any kind of verbal foreplay beforehand. That was above her pay grade.

Luckily the rain provided a soundtrack for the drive, the drops hitting the windshield, the water on the road splashing against the tires. She looked outside, the view blurry from the rivulets of water running down the passenger side window. Making the trees an impressionist blur.

Finally, they pulled up to her house. Finally.

And as soon as they parked, just behind a little copse of trees that would keep the truck from being visible to anyone in her family, he pulled her onto his lap, or rather he tried. She flailed around until she managed to free herself from her seat belt and then went willingly into his arms. He enveloped her. His frame was so large, his kiss so deep, so intense. He moved his hands through her hair, and suddenly she forgot about everything but how much she wanted this. Because nothing else mattered. Nothing but him. Nothing but this.

Flynn.

The whiskers on his face were rough, his mouth hot. His hands were sure and certain as they moved down her back, as he urged her against him. She wanted to strip him naked then and there. Wanted to free him and hike her dress up and just have it be done. She needed relief. From this desperate desire for him. From her nervous anticipation.

He kissed her lips, her neck. His mouth. Oh God, his mouth. It was so good. So perfect. Just like him. How had she gone so long without it? How had she resisted this? She hadn't known what she was missing, that was how. His hands . . .

They moved over her curves. It wasn't enough. She wanted more. She wanted his hands on her skin. And logistically, doing it in the truck probably wasn't a great idea.

"Inside," she moaned. She wasn't entirely sure she meant that she wanted him inside her, or that they needed to get inside her house. She had a feeling that one would lead to the other.

He opened the driver's side door and lifted her out. His arm was still around her waist as he urged her forward into the house. She didn't have time to be embarrassed about his seeing her personal space. This soft inner sanctum that seemed perfect when she was the only one who ever saw it exposed too much now that he was here.

Her pink bedspread, the stuffed animals that rested against her pillow. But for now, he was kissing her. Then he lifted her up and set her down on the edge of her kitchen counter, moving between her thighs, the hard thrust of his arousal settling there, letting her feel how much he wanted this too.

She could feel how wet she was, how much she wanted it. Needed it. She pushed her hands beneath the hem of his shirt, her fingertips grazing his stomach muscles and the crisp hair there. She was desperate to see him. She urged his shirt up over his head, and he accommodated. Her jaw just about hit the floor when she saw what a perfect specimen he was.

She moved her hand up his chest, back down over his ridged abdomen. She was obsessed. Obsessed.

He was just . . . everything.

And what about her? What would he think? She had never been insecure about her looks before; she wore a very specific armor that worked for her. Men liked the way she looked, but they never got too close. That suited her. Now she was on the verge of living out every fantasy she'd ever had with Flynn Wilder—what would he think?

Suddenly, that mattered so much. Suddenly, she was terrified.

The rain was loud on the roof of the trailer, their breathing heavy. "Take me," she whispered.

"Not quite yet," he said, and he kissed her again, deep and maddeningly slow.

"Come on," she said, moving her hands to his belt. "We don't have to make a meal out of this."

"We absolutely do," he said, putting his hand over the top of hers. "I've wanted to do this for years. And I will take my damn time, Jessie Jane Hancock. You said you wanted to fuck. And I want that too. But we'll do it on my terms."

"I didn't agree to that."

He moved his hand around to the back of her head, held her steady as he looked into her eyes. "What are you in such a hurry for?"

She wanted to look away from him. She didn't want to feel this. Not this deep. Not this real. "I . . ."

"Don't be scared of me, Jessie. We both knew this was inevitable. We were silly to try to fight it for so long."

Maybe he thought it was inevitable. But she never had. She had thought maybe she could stay protected in a cocoon of her own for years and years.

Forever.

And suddenly she was shivering, shaking. On the verge of something she didn't have words for.

"Jessie?"

She closed her eyes and grabbed his face, went back in for a kiss. She kissed him so fiercely, she couldn't think. Yes. This was what she wanted. What she needed. Fast and hard. She needed to not think about it. She needed to not feel.

He pulled back, and he was breathing hard and heavy. "What's wrong?"

"You're talking too much," she said. Her mouth felt foreign to her, like a stranger's. Her lips were swollen from kissing him. From desire.

"What's wrong?"

"I'm just impatient."

"You look scared. And I don't want to have sex with a woman who's afraid of me."

"I'm not scared."

"Jessie . . ."

And suddenly, the truth bubbled up inside her. Because she had brazened things out all her life. If a person persisted, kept on pressing, you just had to admit it. And act as if it wasn't a big deal.

"I've never done this before," she said. "But I'm impatient, so let's get it going."

"Stop," he said, putting his hand over hers, square in the center of his chest. "What do you mean you've never done this before?"

"Sex. I've never had it before. But that's not a big deal. I'm ready to have it now."

"That . . . that's not possible," he said.

He looked dizzy and disoriented. The one thing she could say about her admission was that she had definitely taken some of the power back here, because he obviously had no idea what to say.

No idea what to do.

She might have just dumped a bucket of ice water over what had been a very pleasant encounter.

"Yes, it is. Because I haven't."

"I've seen you leave The Watering Hole with men before."

"Have you?"

The thing about her legend was that it was so secure, nobody ever really questioned it. What they saw versus what they thought they saw; the truth versus what they thought they knew. It hurt her a little bit to know that Flynn was the same, that he didn't magically see her in a way no one else had. But it didn't matter. Not really.

"I . . . I was sure I had."

"A lot of people are sure they have. And there are plenty of men who like to brag to their friends that they've done it with me. I kind of let the rumors go on. Mainly because I think they're funny."

"Jessie . . . you're beautiful."

"I know. Not having sex is my choice. It isn't because nobody wanted me."

And that, at least, was true. Not any kind of false bravado.

This wall of protection she had built around herself was entirely of her own making. She had been comfortable with it. Happy with it.

Until Flynn. Until this whole thing had become inevitable. Until she had decided that there was no point avoiding it anymore.

"I don't understand."

"Well, does it put you off?"

He stared at her for a long moment. "No. As long as you're clear that you want to do this, it doesn't put me off at all."

"I'm the one who said I wanted to do it, aren't I?"

"Yes. You are."

"I want to. You're the one who didn't know I was a virgin, not me." Using the word in front of him made her want to curl into a ball and hide. But she wasn't going to do that. She was going to be bold. She was going to be that version of herself she knew worked well. "We don't need to go slow or anything."

"I want to do this," he said. "But I need you to realize something. I'm the expert. So you don't get to tell me what to do. If you want me to be your first time, then you let me show you."

"Well, what if you don't do what I like?"

"Then you tell me. Me being in charge doesn't mean you don't get a say in what feels good and what doesn't. In fact, it's very important that you tell me exactly what feels good, and anything that might not. But we can't go fast. We need to take our time. You only get to do this for the first time once, Jessie, and I am not going to waste that."

A lump began to form in her throat, a feeling of panic. Of fear. She wanted to push him away. Or pull him close. She didn't want to have him stand there like that looking her dead in the eye. She didn't want him to hold her the way he was, so gentle. Why couldn't it just be hard and fast and done? They could have finished by now, she could already not be a virgin, but he insisted on talking.

On making it special. Making her feel special.

"I want to talk about this," he said. "But after."

She closed her eyes. Okay. She was good with that. They didn't need to talk about it now. And maybe they could avoid it altogether.

He leaned in and he kissed her. But it was slow this time. Achingly so. Deep and reverent. And part of her wanted to pull away, but she couldn't. Because it felt too good.

He cupped her face, sifted his fingers through her hair, as if she was a treasure. As if she was something sweet to be savored, something worth taking his time over.

And it was like balm for her very weary soul. She had never felt particularly special. Not until she had decided to act special. But still, there was a part of her that could never really believe it. A part of her that didn't fully think she deserved anything. That was still convinced she was a contagion. A sad, strange little girl who didn't have any friends, and who never could as long as she was being herself.

But that thought, that part of herself, began to melt away with his kisses. He trailed his fingertips down her spine, moving to the tab of her zipper and taking it down slowly. "Can I take this off?"

She let out a shaking laugh. "Haven't you been listening? I want you to."

"Don't rush me."

"I thought men liked to go fast."

"It doesn't matter what men like. It doesn't even matter what I usually do. What matters is this. What matters is us."

She looked down, and he cupped her chin, holding her face steady. "Look at me."

She was powerless to ignore the command. She had to look at him. She had to.

What she saw shocked her all the way down to her soul.

Because he was looking at her as if he didn't ever want to look anywhere else.

He slipped the straps of her dress down and then let the bodice fall to her waist. She hadn't worn a bra that was meant to be seen.

She hadn't anticipated that he would see her. So it was just simple, black and lacy, the right foundation for the dress, but not revealing or anything.

The breath that he let out in response was slow and shaky. "You are so beautiful. And I am the luckiest man in the world."

"Why do you think that?" Her voice sounded so thin. "You thought you were getting a girl who knew what she was doing."

"No. Because all those men tell stories. They convince themselves maybe even that they got to see this, but only I have. No other man in the world. That automatically makes me the luckiest. No competition. Damn, Jessie."

It was like a prayer, not a curse. He moved to kiss her neck, down her collarbone, to the curve of her breasts, just where the cup met her skin. She let her head fall back, let her body surrender to him.

"Damn," he whispered. His breath was hot against her skin. And still she shivered.

He reached around and unhooked her bra, letting it loosen on her arms. Then he pulled it off, and she found herself fighting the urge to cover herself. Which just seemed ridiculous. She had never considered herself shy or modest, but it wasn't about that. It was about being worried that she wouldn't measure up. But the expression on his face eased that concern pretty damn quickly. She had never seen that look on a man's face before.

Let alone on his.

"Beautiful," he whispered. He moved his hand to cup her breast, sliding his thumb over her nipple. The sensation was so glorious, she couldn't hold back her sound of pleasure as he stroked her.

"All good?"

She nodded. "Can't you tell from context clues?"

"Oh, don't worry. I'm very confident in my abilities. But this is your first time. And it's my first time with you. Which means I'm not taking anything for granted. I want you. I want this. And I need it to be the best experience you've ever had."

"Ever?"

"Yes. Ever. Better than Christmas morning, better than learning a new trick-riding routine, better than hustling a whole slew of people at the bar in a pool game."

"Tall order."

Except it wasn't. Because already this was better than anything. But she didn't want to give him the satisfaction of knowing that. "I need to taste you."

She was about to say yes, but then he lowered his head and traced a circle around her nipple with his tongue before sucking it deep into his mouth.

Her hands shot to his shoulders, her nails digging into his skin. She did say yes then. Repeatedly. Over and over again.

"This is better . . . It's better than I imagined."

How? They had barely done anything. Well, to her they had done a whole lot, but to him this must be nothing.

"Don't look so worried. I've got you."

In spite of herself, she felt some of the tension leave her body. He had her. It was Flynn Wilder. The one man she could trust with this.

The man she had spent so many years convincing herself she didn't like.

He wrapped his arm around her waist, crushing her breasts to his bare chest, and carried her across the trailer to her bed. He laid her down in the center of the mattress, looming over her, his eyes searching hers. He kissed her, and she melted. Every time his mouth touched hers, she melted a little bit more.

He pulled her dress off the rest of the way, took her underwear down with it. Then her shoes. Throwing it all on the floor. She was naked in front of him, but she couldn't feel embarrassed, not anymore, not with the open appreciation on his face.

"Trust me," he said, his voice rough. He leaned in and kissed her hipbone. She jumped. Oh, he was going to . . . Oh.

He kissed his way down the top of her thigh, and her heart was pounding so hard in her head, it almost eclipsed the sound of the rain on the roof. He pressed her thighs apart, and her skin got hot. All the way up, her ears burning.

But then he kissed the inside of her thigh, and she gripped the bedspread, trying to find something to hold her in place.

"Trust me," he whispered again as he moved his mouth to the center of her thighs. As he began to lick her. Kiss her the way that he had just done her mouth. His tongue was even more effective here. The way he teased her. Tormented her. Her hips arched up off the bed, and he took that as an invitation to grab her rear and hold her tightly to his mouth, as he ate deeper and deeper into the intimate heart of her. She felt pleasure building in her stomach, felt tension stretching tighter and tighter. She was a virgin, but she knew what an orgasm felt like. And this one was coming on strong.

She wanted to hang on, wanted to stop it. Because suddenly the idea of losing herself like this in front of somebody else made her feel more than naked. But she couldn't hold back. He slicked his tongue once more over that sensitive bundle of nerves there, and she shattered. Crying out his name, clinging to his shoulders. He was everything.

This was everything.

"Good," he said. He kissed her thigh again, her stomach, back up to her mouth. He claimed her even as he put his hand between her thighs and began to slick her wetness over the place she was most sensitive. He angled his hand, pushing one finger inside her. She gasped. It was unfamiliar, but it didn't hurt.

"Good?" he asked against her lips.

"Yes," she whispered.

He teased her like that, before adding a second finger. "We're going to take this part really slow," he said.

"I'm a horse rider. It's not going to hurt."

"We're going to make sure it doesn't hurt," he said. "To the very best of my ability."

"It won't."

"You haven't seen me naked yet, don't forget."

"Oh." In many ways that was very good news. Because she wouldn't want the glorious Flynn Wilder to be a disappointment in that department. But now she felt a little bit of trepidation.

Just a little bit.

"Still good?" he asked, as he stroked her gently.

"So good," she said, her head arching back on the pillows.

"You're so gorgeous, Jessie. I've never wanted anyone like I want you. And it's been so many years. You have any idea how many times I thought about it?" He moved a third finger inside her, and this time the stretch was a little bit uncomfortable. But she trusted him. Relaxed into it. "I've thought about being with you so many times. Even if it wasn't quite like this. This is better, though. I want you to know that. You're better. I never could've imagined you exactly as you are. You're even more perfect."

What she really didn't expect was for his words to affect her so profoundly. What she really didn't expect was for those words to be the thing that carried her straight over the edge into her second orgasm. Her internal muscles gripped his fingers tight as she helplessly shuddered out a release that left her feeling spent and breathless. "Flynn," she whispered.

"That's right, good girl."

She wanted to lean against him. Wanted to rest herself on him. *Good girl.* That was going to echo inside her for longer than it should. She had never dreamed about being Flynn Wilder's good girl. But she could get used to it. She was usually difficult. Usually kind of bad. And she didn't mind that either. But this was something only the two of them shared.

Just them.

This was something special.

He withdrew his fingers, but kept on stroking her, kept her on the edge of another climax. Even though she felt wrung out. She also wanted to keep on going. She wanted more. She wanted everything. He stood up, took his wallet out, and threw it next to her on the mattress. Then he undid his belt, his pants, and kicked his shoes off as he removed the rest of his clothes.

Her heart stopped.

Well. She understood his point now. He was . . . glorious. And very big. But somehow, she just knew that he would be perfect for her. Because hadn't he been? Everything he had done had been great. She expected him to get a condom out and thrust home, but that wasn't what he did. Instead, he got onto the mattress, lay next to her on the bed and stroked her face. It made her heart feel as if it was going to explode. "Are you ready?"

She nodded wordlessly. He moved his hand along her cheek, and she turned her head, biting his thumb.

He chuckled. "You're a whole thing."

"So are you."

He grabbed his wallet, and then he did take out a condom.

They were really going to do this. But in some way, she felt they already had. They had already achieved the kind of intimacy she had always been afraid of.

She wasn't afraid of him. She wasn't. But he did make her chest ache. He did make her heart beat faster. She didn't quite know what to do with that. Because he made her want things.

And wanting things went against her better judgment. Wanting things when she couldn't hide that she wanted them was even worse.

But then he was kissing her, and she couldn't think. Even as the blunt head of his arousal pressed against her, she couldn't think.

And when he filled her, it was everything. He was everything. She was wrong about one thing. Everything that had come before this was nothing like this. Flynn was deep inside her, so deep that it took her breath away. Flynn was moving inside her, and she could feel him. Every glorious inch.

He was shuddering in pleasure now, and the look on his face was almost like pain, except she knew it wasn't. She knew exactly what it was, because she had felt it.

"I want you," she said. Because she was trying to blot out the lie she had told. How had she ever told Flynn that she didn't want him? She was an idiot. She wanted him.

Of course she did.

He was Flynn.

She had never wanted anyone else.

He thrust deep, hard, and his eyes clashed with hers. Suddenly she couldn't breathe. Terror streaked through her, just for a moment, because that instant felt too big to be contained. It felt too big for her to hold onto.

This felt like something dangerous. Lightning in a bottle, and if that bottle shattered, they were cooked.

But she couldn't pull away from him. Didn't want to. She had to see it through to the end, and oh, how she wanted it.

But it was every bit as big as she had always been scared it would be. Every bit as profound.

His movements began to take them both to heaven. She had been so certain there was no way she was going to be able to have another orgasm. But as pleasure chased them both, as it caught up with him, as he began to lose control, she found herself closer to the brink too.

Because she had done this to him. It made her feel like she mattered. Like she was special.

It was that feeling that sent her over. She clung to him, arching against him, even as he shook, calling her name like a curse and a prayer all rolled into one.

She clung to him. She didn't want it to be over. She didn't want him to pull away from her. Not now.

"Flynn," she whispered.

He kissed her cheek. "Thank you," he said.

"For what?" she asked.

"For giving that to me."

She wanted to say it wasn't a big deal. But it was. It was a huge deal. And she couldn't pretend. It was in her nature to push people away. But doing that with him now would just seem silly. "You were the only one," she said because it was true. "The only one I could've done that with." He looked as if he had been hit in the head. "Not because I'm in love with you or anything," she said quickly. And immediately felt stupid. "It's because . . . there's always been something between us. And when we were talking tonight, I knew that you're like me. You actually understand."

He leaned in and kissed her, and suddenly she felt overcome.

"I'm staying," he said.

"You don't need to do that," she responded.

"I want to."

Jessie started to move slowly underneath the covers, climbing beneath them entirely so he couldn't look at her anymore.

"Jessie," he said from outside her cocoon.

"I'm hiding."

"I see that."

He lifted the blankets up and got under them with her. It was dim, but not entirely dark, and being this close to him was making her dizzy.

"What's wrong?"

"You can never underestimate how embarrassing it will be to lose your virginity at twenty-eight."

"Well. You've got me there. I don't actually know what that's like."

"Clearly."

"Talk to me."

"But it's so much easier to keep pushing you away."

He gripped her arm and dragged her up above the covers again, settling in beside her. "No. That was easier to a point. But it's not easier now. Now you might as well just tell me everything. Because I already know."

He presented a winning argument with that. He did already know. He was the only person who knew. Consequently, maybe he was the only reasonable person to have this discussion with. He was the one who had to do this. Had to be the one to . . . Well.

"I learned a really great trick when I was in middle school," she said. "If you act like you have it all, then people believe you. And so I did that. I started acting like I didn't care about them. What they thought. I dressed the way that I wanted to, and I acted confident about it. I acted like I didn't want to go to their birthday parties. Like I didn't need them at mine. And suddenly everyone got a lot more interested in being my friend. It worked so well I carried it into everything. But . . . if anybody actually knew me, then they would know . . ." She looked around the room. "This is who I am."

"Stuffed animals and a pink bedspread?"

"Yes. And baking and actually caring quite a lot what people think about me, and about this community. I didn't want to let anyone in. And the longer all this went on, the harder it was to explain."

"Why me?"

"It had to be you. Because . . ." She was going to have to be honest. Not just with him, but with herself. "I'm attracted to you. I have been for a long time."

"When? Tell me about the first time."

"You tell me," she said. "I think I've given up quite enough, don't you?"

He let out a long, slow breath, lifted his arm up and rested it under his head, and her eyes went to his bicep. Because he really was hot, even now that they were doing this whole intimacy thing. Even now that she felt exposed and a little bit threadbare.

"You snuck into the bar with a fake ID. I think you were probably twenty. I remembered you from high school, of course. You were always pretty. But two years younger than me, which seemed like a lot in those days."

"True."

"So when you walked into the bar, it was like . . . I realized we were basically the same age. But mainly, I looked at you and . . . my heart just about jumped through my chest. You were wearing white jeans. A white tank top. Your belt was sparkly, and your boots were bright blue."

"You remember all that?"

"I do. I remember you turned your head, and you smiled at Gus. I think you were giving him a hard time about your ID. Your hair caught the light. Everything about you just sparkled."

"That was eight years ago."

"Yeah. It was. And I don't do abstinence, Jessie. I don't hold back from what I want, not physically. But there was always something else wrapped around you. I told myself that it was your family name, and mine. They don't mix. Like oil and water."

"No. They don't. At least, they never have."

"But things are changing."

She wished he would go away. Because she wanted to curl up in her bed and take everything he had told her and unwrap it like a special present for her to look at in private. She wanted to do that for the whole night. She felt inundated with change. And she wanted a moment by herself, but he wouldn't give it to her. Damn Flynn Wilder.

That he remembered that moment . . . She didn't quite know what to make of it.

"Your turn," he said.

She made a huffing sound. "Well, when you're in high school, and the boy's two years older, it doesn't actually seem like that big a deal."

"Did you have a crush on me in high school, Jessie?"

"This is why I didn't want to tell you. Because you're going to go romanticizing it."

"That's me. Hopeless romantic."

She growled. "No, I just . . . You know I thought it was really sad that you were so handsome, because your family hates mine so much. I knew I could never go on a date with you. And so I was mean to you sometimes."

"You were mean to me in high school?"

"You didn't even notice? That's kind of insulting. I ignored you."

"I mean, I was ignoring you because I was a senior and you were a sophomore."

"Right. Well. You noticed eventually."

"That you were mean? True. I did."

"Well, that's why. Because that's what I've learned. You don't act like you want something. Once you do, you just feel bad. And acting like I do isn't necessarily a way to get what you want . . . I did, though. It just took a while."

"Are you telling me this was a long con? Are you even running for mayor, or were you just trying to get in my pants?"

She laughed. Grateful that he was being ridiculous. Because if their talk got any more serious, she was going to chew her own arm off. "You caught me. It was all an elaborate ruse."

"I really hate to tell you this, but all you had to do was ask."

"Well, I like to do things the hard way."

She lay there for a long moment, and she really did want to push him a little bit. Ask why he hadn't made a move on her, since he liked her and all.

But the words stuck in her throat. Because everything felt a little bit raw, and she wasn't sure how deep into the conversation she wanted to get.

Instead, she didn't say anything.

"Your family is going to know I spent the night," he said, pulling her close.

"My family already thinks we are sleeping together."

"Why didn't you tell West that it wasn't real?"

"I don't know. I guess because it was embarrassing."

"My family knew."

"Yeah . . . I love my brother, but we don't share things with each other, really. We perform together. The show is such a big part of our lives. But there are certain things we don't talk about. I think that's true for the whole family. It's funny, because my parents don't actually care what we do. You'd think that would mean we talk about everything. But instead it just . . . It's like a facade. Of being open and sharing our feelings, but we never really do."

"Why is that?"

She curled her fingers into fists underneath the blanket. She didn't want to say. She didn't want to tell him that half her problem was that even though her parents could be wonderful people, she felt really angry at them. If she were truly honest, she would have to get into all that stuff, and she just didn't want to.

So instead she grabbed hold of his arm and rubbed her face against his skin.

He chuckled and wrapped his arm around her, pulling her close. "I'm tired," she said.

"Then you want to get some rest," he said.

"Agreed."

She was exhausted. She felt different. She definitely needed to sleep that off.

And in the morning Flynn would still be here. That was a sobering thought.

Chapter 11

I was wrong. He asked to take a walk with me today, and I told him he could. I expected him to offer money, to ask for my body. He took my arm instead. He walked me to the end of the lane and told me he'd like to do it again. Like I was a lady.

—Belle Martin's Diary, April 1868

Early in the morning, Flynn woke up before Jessie, who was curled into a little ball on her stomach. He got up, went over to her coffee maker, and started fiddling with it until he managed to get a pot going. He was still reeling from the night before. From all the revelations.

He tapped his fingers in time with the sound of the percolating coffee. Her first time. Damn. He never would've guessed that in a million years, and he wasn't sure what he would've done if he'd known prior to their actually . . . getting to that point.

By the time they were actually in the trailer, by the time she had confessed, he was past the point of no return. So he had decided that he would be as gallant and skilled as possible. Sure, if she had told him to stop, he would have, but she had said she wanted him. Maybe if his head weren't swimming with need for her, he would've made a different decision. Maybe if she'd said at the restaurant, *I want you to take my virginity* . . .

Yeah. He still would've done it. He was lying to himself. He had wanted Jessie for so long that he would never have turned down the chance to have her, no matter what the circumstances.

His stomach tightened. Maybe this was what had kept him away from her all those years. Maybe some kind of instinct.

Because now it wasn't just sex. Knowing that it had taken a

whole lot of trust for her to tell him the truth. Yeah. It was complicated now.

And when he was a young man, he would've run from complicated.

He had never exactly run toward it as an older man. But when
it had looked him in the face, he had been brave enough not to run.

You were horny.

Whatever.

He clattered around the kitchen looking for a mug and poured
himself a generous portion of brew.

Jessie still didn't stir.

He moved over to the bed and looked at her. Her hair was in
her face, and she looked . . . He wondered if this was how she would
look all the time if she wasn't so dedicated to maintaining her facade.
He had never spent the night with a woman before. It was almost
more intimate than sex. He put his hand on her face and rubbed her
cheek. And she sat bolt upright, windmilling her arms. Letting the
blankets fall to her waist, exposing her breasts. Then she looked at
him, and her mouth dropped open. "Oh, right."

He laughed. "Did you forget?"

"I was sleeping," she said, drawing her knees up, but not the
blankets.

"I know. It's getting late."

"It's not late," she said.

"I'm a rancher. It's late for me."

"Oh. Do you have to go see to your animals or whatever?"

"Elk are pretty self-sufficient. There's general maintenance, but
they're fine for the morning."

"I have rehearsal," she said.

"And the show tonight, right?"

She nodded. "You can watch the rehearsal if you want."

"I'm not going to get interrogated by your family?"

She laughed. "I mean, they might be a little bit interested that
you're here. Considering I've never . . . Well, you know. I've never
brought a man home before. Though they don't know why."

"So your family doesn't know that you . . ."

"Oh, no. That's horrifying. Can you imagine?"

"I don't know. I just . . . It's not like we talked about it in my family, but I guess assumptions are made past a certain point."

"Exactly," she said, her syllables crisp. "Assumptions are made past a certain point. And I have quite the reputation."

"You mentioned last night that you were happy to let men all lie about it. But they know they're lying."

"Sure. But they don't all know that the other guy is lying. They think everyone but them is telling the truth. That's how ridiculous rumors grow. And that's how my whole reputation grew."

"Why didn't it bother you?"

"I get it. I'm supposed to be bothered by it because I'm a woman, and there's all kinds of slut-shaming undertones to talk like that usually. But the version of myself that I've always been in public is so much braver than I am. And I think part of me liked that. To imagine that there was a version of myself who could do all those things."

He sort of understood that. Because it was a lot like the way he had split himself apart to try to fit into two very different families. To try to hurt different people.

It was easy to lose yourself when you did stuff like that. But that was something he wasn't ready to talk about. And maybe it was best if neither of them said it.

"Can I have some coffee?" she asked. She looked soft. And he wanted to kiss her. Instead, he just turned and got her a mug, poured her a cup.

She curled her fingers around it and started drinking slowly. "Thank you."

"It's your house. Your coffee."

"I know. But you made it for me. Nobody's ever done that."

Of course they hadn't. He hadn't spent the night with a woman before, and she hadn't spent the night with a man. Except they'd had a literal sleepover a couple of weeks ago now, and he had made her coffee then. For some reason, the memory made his heart feel just a little bit tender.

"You know, adult life isn't middle school. You don't have to pretend."

She took a sip of her coffee. "We both know that isn't true. Look at how hard Austin worked to be taken seriously. To get people to recognize what a good guy he is. This town is absolutely still middle school. In a lot of ways."

"I guess so. But maybe it's time that other people were ashamed about it, instead of us."

"I guess that's kind of the whole point of all this, isn't it?"

"I guess so." He let a beat pass. "Except, what happened last night wasn't about that. I just want to be clear. It wasn't about making anyone jealous. It wasn't about the campaign. It was just about us."

"You know, I know that. Because, actually, what I know about you is that you're a pretty decent man, Flynn. Regardless of what they say."

"And what is it they say?"

"That you're an outlaw."

"Well. Both things can be true," he said. "I can be an outlaw and a pretty good guy."

She ducked her head, and he could see that she was blushing. He wanted to have her again, but he didn't know the protocol with virgins, and he suspected he should probably give her body a break.

"This is going to happen again," he said.

"Totally," she agreed easily. "There's no way the two of us can keep spending time together like this and not do that again. It was great. Sorry for not saying that already."

"I know it was," he said, taking a sip of coffee.

"How?"

"Because," he said, "only fucking idiot men can't tell when an orgasm isn't real."

"Really?"

"Yes. I could feel how hard you were squeezing me. My fingers and . . ."

Her face went cherry-red. "Oh."

"You came hard."

He was starting to feel hard again. On edge. But in a good way.

"I did," she whispered. And then a little smile curved her lips. "I really did."

"You're a legend, Jessie Jane."

"I fucking am."

He drove her over to the arena for practice, and just as she said, her family didn't make a big deal out of his presence. He had never actually met William Hancock before. But when he took his seat in the front row of the bleachers, the older man came to where he sat and stuck out his hand. "The name's William."

"Flynn," he said, standing as he shook the other man's hand. "Flynn Wilder."

"Nice of you to come by and watch the practice."

"I've been wanting to see the routine."

"I know you Wilders generally frown on the show. Don't like the spectacle."

"That is my oldest brother," Flynn said. "Though we did all come to a show last year. He's softening in his old age."

"Well, that's good to know. We've never meant any harm. But we like the sensationalized version of the story. The sensationalized version of the Wild West. Sure, in reality, it was grim and gritty and there was a lot of dysentery. But there were heroes too. And sharp-shooters. There were incredible horse riders and feats of derring-do. There were also villains, and I know our family was among them. Both our families were. I don't really mind that they pulled off stage-coach robberies. But it never sat right with me that Butch Hancock betrayed members of his own gang. There should be honor among thieves."

Jessie was right. Her dad was a showman.

He looked past William at Jessie, who was on her horse in the arena, staring over at them and looking very worried.

He smiled, just to make sure Jessie knew that he was fine.

"You know, if one of you ever wanted to join the show . . ."

"That might be a bridge too far," Flynn said, "though never say never. Maybe when Jessie is mayor."

William chuckled. "Oh. I appreciate her courage in running, but they'll never elect her. This town is too boring."

Flynn wanted to defend Jessie, because he thought she would be great at the job, actually. But it wasn't his daughter that William didn't believe in. It was the town. And he imagined that just like Flynn, he had plenty of reasons to doubt his neighbors.

"Rehearsal begins," William said, tipping his hat and moving away from Flynn toward the arena. He stood up on a platform, and music began to play. Flynn had the impression that rather than running through William's whole spiel, they were timing certain things. Jessie started to ride in a circle, keeping a slow pace. And then she stood up on the back of her horse, dropped down, flipped upside down, and hung beneath the running beast.

Flynn's heart climbed up into his throat. And it didn't leave the entire time she was riding. He kept telling himself the routine was designed to look as if she needed help. And at the climax of the music, West rode up beside her and helped her onto his horse, which was also running. Then she stood up behind her brother, held onto his shoulders, and the two of them rode off.

"Perfect!" He heard West's shout across the arena, and Jessie cheered.

What happened when they messed up? They seemed awfully excited about getting it *right*.

It hadn't really occurred to him how dangerous Jessie's work could be. Hell, he had seen the show a year ago and it hadn't occurred to him. He had just assumed the act would all work out fine because they rehearsed it.

But he hadn't known her then. Not really. He had thought she was beautiful, sure, but it wasn't like this.

No. It wasn't like this.

They were setting up card tables in the middle of the arena, and Jessie walked behind the stables. He got up from his seat and went to where she was standing. "That's a new routine?"

"Yeah. It's . . . it's hard work. My muscles are kind of sore." She said that last part in a low voice. Right. Her muscles were sore because of him.

Normally, he might feel a little bit proud of that, but he was still recovering from the surge of adrenaline he'd gotten watching her routine.

"You guys do this all the time?"

"Yes. Well. This is a new act, like I said, but this and things like it."

"It's like acrobatics."

"Yes. It is. A little bit gymnastics, a little bit trapeze."

"A lot of flipping upside down on the back of a running horse."

"You sound tense."

"I feel a little tense."

"Well, don't. My trick riding is not a facade. I'm actually very good at it."

"Is that where the other act comes from?"

She nodded slowly. "Yeah. Well, look at my dad." William was back on the podium, making gestures and introducing the next event. "Is anyone in town all that close to him? No. But if you were going to ask around, you would get the sense that he's well liked. The thing he does . . . Everyone responds to it."

He had to admit, her dad was pretty charming.

"I decided to copy him."

"What does your mom do?"

"She makes costumes. She helps a little with the choreography of the routines. She doesn't like to be in front of people much, so when I got old enough to ride, she decided not to do it anymore."

"She used to do that stuff?"

"Yes. But I don't think it was ever fun for her. Oh, the tricks were. She still does all that. And sometimes she still drops in to perform. She just doesn't want to do it all the time. She kind of likes keeping to herself and being left alone with her different collections."

"Collections?"

"She has a lot of them—crystals, houseplants, spurs. She actually has a whole trailer in our little circle dedicated to them."

"I see."

"We're all weird," she said. "She's not a hoarder. Everything is very organized."

"Somehow I imagined that."

"My mom will probably be at the show tonight."

The *you could meet her* was silent, but he felt it hanging in the air. And then he could see Jessie grow a little insecure. A little nervous. But hell, he supposed they were becoming enmeshed in a way they hadn't intended to be. She had come to his house. She knew that side of his family. Hell, she was running for mayor against the other side. It made sense for him to meet hers.

"Well, I'll look forward to that."

Jessie jumped, then reached into her pocket and took her phone out. "It's Millie."

She put the phone on speaker. "Hi."

"I just wanted to let you know that Danielle has reserved town hall next week for a debate. I imagine you're going to find out, but I don't know when she's going to tell you."

"Oh."

"Yeah. But I keep an eye on the schedule."

"Well, thanks. I don't think Danielle has my number, so I wonder how I was supposed to find out."

"I wouldn't be surprised if you were supposed to find out when it got posted around town. Or went up on the community board online. Somehow, I don't think she wants this to be fair, exactly."

"Well, thank you, Millie," Jessie said. And then her face took on a determined look. "I'll be ready."

She ended the call and looked directly at Flynn. "I'm going to need your help preparing for this. You know the kind of person your sister is."

"So do you. I have a feeling you've got this." He was irritated, though. That Danielle was taking every opportunity to be as underhanded as possible. Maybe William was wrong. Maybe the town of

Rustler Mountain wasn't the problem. Maybe the problem was people like Danielle, people like Sheriff Lee Talbot, who had conspired with Butch Hancock all those years ago to betray Austin Wilder so that he would look like a good person. A hero. Even though he was taking bribes and doing all manner of unsavory things.

Maybe the whole town just needed the opportunity to see who they all really were. All of them. From Danielle to Jessie Jane.

"You're going to be amazing," he said. "I know it. And I'm going to help you with whatever you need."

Because for a while there, he had been Team Revenge.

But at this point, he was unapologetically Team Jessie Jane.

Chapter 12

He walks with me most days. He never asks me for a thing.

—Belle Martin's Diary, May 1868

She had glitter all over her face, and in her hair. She was wearing a prairie dress, which wasn't her normal garb for the shows, but it seemed to fit the new routine tonight. All she could think of was the fact that Flynn was in the audience. It made her heart beat just a little bit faster. He had watched her perform earlier, and she was almost certain she had done better because he was there.

Don't go getting attached to him.

She really *didn't* want to do that. Because that was the whole reason she had put off sex in the first place. Not wanting to be vulnerable. Not wanting to get . . .

To get to the point she wanted something she couldn't have.

Enjoying his company was one thing. Getting overly emotional about it was another.

"Your man is here," West said as he walked by her.

"I know." She responded as if she hadn't just been thinking about him. As if she hadn't just been wondering.

She had butterflies in her stomach, which was unlike her. But maybe it was okay that he gave her butterflies.

Just maybe. She mounted her horse and took a deep breath.

"Don't drop me," she said to West.

"Don't drop *yourself*, sis."

"You're so encouraging."

"Hey. I'm here as backup. But you'd better not need the backup."

"Oh blah blah blah."

She took her position in the stall.

Her dad was welcoming the crowd. The first team of horses would ride out for the national anthem and "God Bless America," and then her dad would introduce West and her.

She waited, keeping the reins taut, adrenaline making her hands sweaty.

But this was something she knew how to do. Well.

Last night she had done something totally out of her comfort zone.

Last night she had done Flynn.

She smiled softly.

"Head out of the clouds," West said, his eyes severe and blue through the slats of the stall.

She stuck her tongue out at him. But she heeded his admonishment. They were great at what they did, but there was a high level of skill involved.

She probably shouldn't be fantasizing about her fake boyfriend.

Was he her real boyfriend because they'd had sex?

She swallowed hard.

She didn't think so.

Because there was no future for them.

There couldn't be.

He was Flynn, and she was . . . just trying to figure herself out.

One thing at a time. And if she won the election, that was going to be a big thing to figure out.

She shrugged off her worries and listened to the music. Let the familiar anthem wash over her. For better or worse, this was her life. This was what had made her.

Very quickly, the moment of uncertainty passed.

And she was being announced.

"And before the lady knew it, her horse was running away."

On cue, the gate opened, and Jessie burst out on the back of her horse. Running full tilt through the arena. She started her acrobatic routine, hanging upside down. For some reason it brought back memories of Flynn. Flynn's hands. The euphoria she felt. But the memories didn't distract her from what she was doing. Far from it. They made everything feel electrified.

She felt more in touch with every part of her body. Was aware of every muscle as she moved on the back of the horse.

She felt . . . beautiful. Maybe it was just because she knew Flynn was watching. But it was an extraordinary feeling.

She still felt all the adrenaline she was used to. But there was something else she had never felt before.

As she moved into the last trick, just before West was supposed to ride up beside her, she realized what it was.

She was in her own body. She was herself.

She wasn't hiding. She wasn't conscious of needing to look a certain way. Just being herself felt like enough.

She hadn't even thought about her mask. Hadn't thought about looking confident, looking at ease. She hadn't thought about projecting a thing. She had only thought about her movements. The way she felt. How happy she was to be doing the routine, and how much it suited her.

"I'll save you!" West shouted, and she pulled up into position, leaping from her mount to his, right behind his saddle, where she stood up and waved to the crowd as they did a final circuit. Her horse ran back into her stable, and she and West went back into his.

She hopped off the horse, laughing, her cheeks pink.

"Perfect," she said.

"You were something else out there," he said. "I thought you were going to kill yourself."

"I did great."

"Oh, it *looks* great. But I'm just saying you were overextending."

She frowned. "I was not overextending. I was getting full extension. I know what I can handle. I don't need you in my face."

"What are you going to do when I'm not helping you with these routines anymore?"

She stared at him, totally unable to figure out what he was saying. "You're not leaving."

"I am. This is Dad's thing, not mine. And I've only stayed so long because of you. But now you're doing the mayor thing and . . ."

"What happened to you being my backup?"

He sighed heavily. "You don't need it."

She did, though. What was she supposed to do without West? They were the only ones who understood this life, *their* life. He had always been there for her, and, no, they didn't verbally share everything with each other the way Flynn and his brothers seemed to, but . . .

He was her brother.

She was used to living near him, working with him. What was she supposed to do when he was gone?

"I might not win," she pointed out.

"You might not. But you're not going to just stay here after this either. You're with Flynn, and you've already figured out that you could do more. I've never wanted to leave you here."

"West . . ."

How was this happening? How was he telling her this right now when he was going on again in just five minutes?

"But you love this," she said. She knew he didn't. She knew that he participated in the show because of their family, and for no other reason.

He wasn't a showman. Not in his soul.

"But where you going to go?"

"I have to get ready. We'll talk more about this later, okay? But you're going to be just fine. I know you are. Because you're amazing. And because you did it. You're not stuck here anymore."

"What do you mean 'stuck here'?"

"You already know, Jessie. Even if you don't want to say it."

She wanted to smack her brother on the back of the head, because they had never talked about this before, and he was acting as if she already knew what he meant.

Or maybe, just maybe, West knew her better than she had ever given him credit for.

That thought sat uncomfortably in the pit of her stomach. But her brother had to get ready for the next event, and she peered through the slats and watched as he pretended to play poker and dodged an angry bull.

All right, it was easy to see why West didn't necessarily want to stay here.

She didn't want to leave. Not entirely. She always felt torn. That was the thing. Between her desire for a more normal existence and . . .

Being afraid that she couldn't actually have it.

She watched the rest of the show until it was time for her to do the final routine with the whole crew. A montage of the best tricks from the night as everybody rode through the arena quickly and did a little exhibition to some rollicking country music.

And then, it was time for the shoot-out, which was essentially a finely tuned stunt show.

Her brother was playing the part of Austin Wilder tonight, which she thought might be weird for Flynn. West stood up at the very top of a second-story building facade that was made to look like the main street of town.

"You'll never take me alive, Sheriff."

The sheriff had been altered in their little show, and was now a mustache-twirling villain, while Austin was painted as a heroic figure.

"You'll have to shoot me dead if you think you're going to take me."

"That can be arranged."

Their stunt gun popped off several shots, and West clutched his chest, falling straight out of the window, onto some dust-colored mats below.

The whole crowd cheered, and Jessie rode her horse back into the arena along with another line of riders, doing some rapid-fire stunts. And then West's horse trotted out to him, and he got on the back of it, standing and waving at the crowd. "Legends never die."

And then he rode off into the sunset. Just as it should be.

It made her sad to think he meant to leave this behind. Made her feel lonely.

She needed to talk to him.

But she looked into the crowd and saw Flynn, standing there in the front row, clapping for her.

And her heart leapt up into her throat.

Oh, Flynn.

She put her horse away and then hurried out the back exit, into the crowd.

She never mixed with the audience. Usually, she avoided crowds. But this time, she was meeting potential constituents. And this time, Flynn was waiting for her.

She had to stop and talk to all the people who recognized her from her announcement and from her campaign signs. She hadn't expected this response. But it was enthusiastic. To say the least.

"All I can say," she quipped, signing a hat for a small child, "is it's much cooler to have a mayor who can do trick riding, isn't it?"

Then Flynn came to her side and kissed her on the cheek. And she thought her heart might burst through her chest. When they finally broke away from the crowd, her heart was pounding hard. "I meant all of that," she said.

"What do you mean?" he asked.

"I meant all the things I said to everybody. I wasn't doing a bit. I just feel . . . I feel confident. I feel like myself tonight in a way that I can't really explain. I'm just . . . I feel different. And it isn't because you 'made me a woman,'" she said.

He looked a little bit as if she had hit him in the side of the face with a two-by-four. And then he recovered. "I did, though," he said.

"Absolutely not. None of that caveman stuff."

"Oh, please. You're walking around with a new pep in your step, and you were foolish enough to tell me about it. You must want me to be a little bit of a caveman about it."

She thought about it. "Yeah. I guess I do. A little."

Because while she had been a secret virgin, Flynn definitely wasn't. So maybe she did like the fact that he might feel a little pleased about the way they had come together. Possessive even.

When he wrapped his arm around her and walked with her toward the staging area at the back of the arena where her family was standing, she felt small. Feminine and protected. Which was different from feeling lusted over. It was just different.

"Great show," Flynn said.

"Thank you," her dad said, clapping Flynn on the back.

She looked on, feeling uneasy for some reason. She knew her whole family couldn't tell that she and Flynn had just had sex for the first time last night. In fact, they would assume that they had been doing it all along.

"We're having a bonfire. You want to join us?" her dad said.

"Sure. If Jessie wants me to."

"Of course I want you to," she said.

Actually, what she wanted to do was squirrel him away from everybody so that she could have him to herself. But they hadn't really discussed the particulars of when they would do it again, or where.

Maybe he would want to make rules. Maybe she would want to make rules. She didn't really know yet.

Last night had opened up the door to a whole bunch of things she had never thought about before. And there was still the whole situation with West.

"Then yes. I'd be happy to join the bonfire."

The crew always got together after the show, but she didn't always join in. Tonight, though, it seemed especially appropriate.

Her mom popped her head out from behind the tall, painted fence. "Is this Flynn Wilder?" she asked, in that soft, monotone voice of hers.

"Yes, Mom. This is Flynn."

"You're her boyfriend?" she asked.

Cutting straight to the chase, also a Lucinda Hancock special.

"Yes, ma'am," Flynn said.

She felt a little bit itchy about his lying to her mom, but she had started the charade. So she had no right to be testy about it. She knew that.

"That's good. I think Jessie is lonely."

"I'm not lonely," Jessie said.

"You are," her mom said, patting her on the shoulder.

"How are your crystals?"

"Great. I got three new amethysts. Now I have thirty-seven."

"Well, I look forward to seeing them."

"Okay."

Then her mom abruptly turned away and went to sit in a chair near the blazing bonfire.

"That's my mom. She's . . . her."

"I can see that," he said.

"I love her. Very much. But . . ."

"What?"

"She couldn't exactly teach me how to make friends."

"Right. Gotcha."

"Well, my dad couldn't really either."

"He's a friendly guy," Flynn said.

"Oh, he's a very friendly guy. But whether or not you can actually know him is something else entirely."

"Well, this is pretty great, though," he said, gesturing to the gathering around the fire.

"It is," she agreed readily. Because it was. As unorthodox as it was, this was her family. Some of the performers had been with the show since she was a child, and even the newer ones were friends she worked with every day. She wasn't lonely.

Her mom was wrong about that. She had taken steps to remedy her loneliness, and she had done a damn fine job of it, thank you. She wasn't lonely.

West came by and thrust beers into her and Flynn's hands. "If you survive this, then you might actually have the fortitude to become one of us."

"He's not taking my last name," Jessie said.

Flynn guffawed. "Okay. Austin is being pretty cool about all of this, but that would be a bridge too far for him."

Jessie laughed. "Yeah. I can just imagine."

And what scared her was how real it all felt. That she knew Austin, that it made her feel a little warm with affection because he was still so prickly about his brother associating with a Hancock.

"What did you think of the shoot-out reenactment?" West asked.

"It's an impressive stunt. I'm not like my brother. I don't have a chip on my shoulder about all that."

"No," West said. "Your chip is about your sister being mayor."

Flynn forced out a hard laugh. "Yeah. That would be the one."

"Well, we all have our things."

Her mother drifted over to their group and put her hand on Flynn's shoulder. "Did Jessie tell you about my collections?"

Flynn smiled. "She did."

"Oh, good. They're very important to me. I can tell you about them."

Jessie wanted to put herself between Flynn and her mom. She wanted to protect her mom from Flynn's judgment. Why hadn't she done a better job of explaining her mom?

"I'd love to hear about them. Every single one."

He didn't miss a beat.

West took Jessie's arm and moved her slightly away from that conversation. "Well, he's pretty great."

"That's the nicest thing I've ever heard you say about another person."

"I don't see people do a lot of nice things. But . . . anyone who can jump right into Mom's collections . . ."

"Yeah."

"Sorry I ambushed you with the stuff about me leaving."

"Yeah," she said. "Me too. Why didn't you tell me? And what is your plan?"

"I have money, Jessie."

"From where?"

"Investments. Farm futures. I'm good at it. Some of the guys who ride for the rodeo are into that kind of thing, and when we started doing events, I started talking to them about it. I started taking all the money I had and investing. I have enough now to buy my own ranch. And that's what I want to do. I don't want to stay here. I have . . . I've actually put in an offer on a plot of land."

"Why didn't you tell me any of this?"

"We don't talk about that kind of stuff. We just shove it down."

"Well . . . that's how we get by. But a big change like this . . ."

"Jessie, come on. You know growing up here was . . . not ideal. It didn't do either of us any favors. And the only reason I stayed for as long as I did was . . . to protect my family. You and them. Everything. They can't survive out in the real world. Can you imagine? If Mom and Dad had to have nine-to-five jobs? If I didn't make him pay his taxes every year, he wouldn't. He would forget. They live in another time, or in a made-up place in their heads—I don't know."

"Yeah. And we're their kids. So why should we have to . . . Never mind."

"It's a very good point. We shouldn't have to. But we have. Always. Some of it's not their fault. They did the best they could. They did. But some of it . . ."

"I love them," Jessie said.

"Me too. A hell of a lot. They're our parents. And I can't say that I would trade them. But I also know that I'm not fixing to live my whole life in a carnival."

"I didn't realize," she said. "I mean, I always knew that you didn't love this. You don't . . . You're not necessarily the kind of person who enjoys all this attention."

"No," he agreed.

"But I didn't realize you were doing it to protect them."

"I was. And no, I never did as good a job as you did. I couldn't organize all this stuff. I can't sit still that long. I can remind Bill to do his taxes, but I sure as hell can't do them for him. But . . . I don't know. Forgetting things and being disorganized has made me extra careful. It doesn't seem to have done that to Dad."

"No. I would say not."

"Ranching is something I can do. And I'll be happy doing it. It's not a desk job, but it's one that will keep me busy. And I'll probably continue to invest."

"I had no idea you did that."

"It's like a video game."

"With real money."

"Yeah. But there are patterns . . . You just have to pay attention. And sometimes you have to be ballsy. But I'm good at both."

Her brother was not always good at paying attention. Unless he was really, really interested in something, and then he could focus on it forever. Apparently, finance focused him.

She wanted to be happy for him. But she just felt . . . sad, that he hadn't told her. Weird that things were changing.

Well, she was changing them, honestly. But she wasn't leaving.

"You don't have to stay forever," he said.

"But I'm good at this."

It came out small and kind of sad.

"Jessie, you're good at a lot of things. Look at you. You organize this place. You really keep it moving. And on top of that, you're running for office."

"I know. But . . . if I don't keep everything together for them, then who will?"

"They can hire somebody. When we were kids, we didn't have any choice but to live here. We didn't any choice but to participate in all this, but we have a choice now."

"I didn't know that you . . . I mean, when we were kids . . ."

"I'm older than you. I wasn't going to complain to you. And yeah, we had a lot of freedom. So there were certain things that it felt silly to complain about. But it was . . . it just wasn't our choice."

He wasn't wrong. And when she was younger, she would've given anything to have a life that was more stable. More normal.

She had figured out a way to cope. But what did she actually want? For her life? For her future? She was running for mayor because she cared about Rustler Mountain—that much was true. She wanted to do right by everyone in town. She wasn't running just to poke at Danielle. Petty revenge wasn't enough. It also just wasn't her. Maybe she wanted to prove that she was smart. That she could fix things. That she mattered. But she also wanted to actually do the fixing, so that had to matter for something.

"We'll just see how everything goes," she said.

"You might win," he said.

Her stomach swooped. "Maybe."

"But whatever happens, you have him."

Except she didn't actually have Flynn. Although, she had had Flynn. And now she couldn't imagine . . . It was difficult to imagine life without him. At least in some capacity. Maybe they were friends now. Maybe.

Her mom walked away from Flynn rather abruptly, which was just how her mom was, and Flynn turned toward her and West. "Great bonfire," he said.

"Just wait until my dad starts telling stories," she said. And she kind of meant it.

They sat down in lawn chairs near the fire and made s'mores. Her dad started telling tall tales, Western myths and legends.

"You want to go back to my place?" he asked when she yawned.

"Yeah," she said. "I'd like that."

It felt right. His place tonight. She could spend the night. And she could see his bedroom. The idea thrilled her.

"When you're ready," he said.

"Oh, I'm ready," she said. "Drive me back to my place. So that I have my truck. I'll follow you over there."

He looked a little bit reluctant to do that, but it was just common sense.

"All right."

They said goodbye to everyone at the bonfire, but they didn't talk as he drove Jessie to her truck.

She got in and started the engine.

She didn't play any music on her way over to Flynn's. She just replayed everything that had happened in the last twenty-four hours.

And it seemed more like a movie than real life.

Chapter 13

I thought there was nothing left to discover in this world. I know
every hard truth there is, but I didn't know this joy.

—Belle Martin's Diary, April 1869

Jessie Jane pulled right in behind him when he parked in front of
his house. He had been a little worried she was going to make a run
for it. She was in a strange mood, and he couldn't entirely sort out
what it was.

She had seemed to enjoy tonight, but this evening, she had been
a little distant.

It had been interesting meeting her parents. They were definitely
unique. But they were kind people. That much was easy to see.

In fact, the whole troop was comprised of some of the nicest
people he'd met. Yet again, he thought it was a shame that his family
had judged them so harshly. The Hancocks had a way of infusing a
lot of joy into this outlaw thing.

He could only respect them.

He opened his truck door, and she did the same; they closed
them in unison. He walked straight over to her, wrapped his arms
around her, and pulled her in for a kiss. He had been behaving himself the whole time they were in public.

"That was great," he said, and he meant it. "Your family is . . ."

"Weird?"

"Yeah. They are. But in a very fun way."

"Or something."

"I like your parents," he said.

"And West?"

"He might take a little longer to warm up to."

She huffed a laugh. "He likes you."

"Does he? Well. That's nice."

He kind of meant it. After all, who was harder to win over than the brother of the woman you were . . .

Well. *Sleeping* with.

"How did your parents meet?"

He was curious about that. Because William Hancock was very charming. And Lucinda had her own charm, for certain. But she was definitely the sort of person people would call quirky rather than personable.

"Oh, they went to school together. My mom is from here too. But not part of any notorious family. Her parents moved away a while ago. I don't remember them. My dad called her his sparrow. Like she had fallen out of the nest, and he picked her up. He just always wanted to take care of her. He always says he really likes how easy it is to know what she wants. Because she speaks her mind. You got a little bit of that."

"Yeah. That is true."

"It was hard for her, though. Having to take care of the house and kids. Participating in the chaos of the show. But not all of the glamor around it."

He opened the front door and gestured for her to go in.

"I see."

"When they were trying to get the show off the ground, we didn't have any money. I mean none. It's been in our family for several generations, but when I say it has gone through feast and famine many times in those years . . . I mean it. My dad isn't the best businessman. He has big dreams and big ideas, but it's hard for him to execute them. He's interested for five seconds, and then he moves on to something else. Conversely, my mother can't let go of anything. So that's always interesting. Between the two of them, it's . . . amazing that they get anything done. But they do. And I'm proud of them. Truly."

"You said that you do a lot of the behind-the-scenes organizing."

"Yes. I do. And actually, West handles a lot of things. My parents are dreams people, idea people. The doing part, though . . ."

"Got it."

They were both silent for a moment, standing there in the entryway of his house. He flicked the lights on. "My dad was really imperfect. Like, really. He was kind of a mess. And definitely more than a little bit self-serving. I really miss him. If you'd asked me when I was thirteen what my life would be like without him, I would have said that he didn't matter. He would forget to pay the electric bill, and the lights would get turned off. He would forget to buy us food. Three teenage boys up at a house that only had beer in the fridge. He was doing his best, though, I think. It just wasn't good enough. And he never got the chance to become good enough, because he died. Because his bullshit killed him. I know what it's like to have a parent who actually loves you quite a bit, but isn't like everyone else's parent." He paused for a moment. "Though your parents seem a little bit more together than my dad."

"Oh, we had some adventures. Sometimes the power got turned off, and we had to pretend we were camping."

He laughed. "Well, we have that in common."

He didn't judge, because he'd experienced many of the same things. She didn't judge him either. They just knew how it was. Other than his family, he couldn't remember ever connecting in the same way with another person.

"We always had food, though. Even if we had to go down to the Wesleyan Church to use the food pantry. My parents always took care of that."

She wrapped her arms around herself. "Embarrassing, though, when we would see classmates who were volunteering with their parents at the food pantry, and we had to use it."

He nodded slowly. "Yeah, you know this kind of stuff is hard enough without everybody else making it harder. Your dad said something to me earlier today. Just that he thought the town might let us down in regard to the election. And I've been thinking on that. My dad is at fault for some things—but not everything bad that happened to me. Some of it was the small-minded people in this town who made everything worse. Who want to rub things in your face."

"Well," she said. "That is true enough."

It was a very strange realization that maybe Jessie Jane understood him best of all. They could've been having these conversations for years, but hadn't. Because he had pushed her away. And she had pushed him away.

He'd only known one way of doing things, and it wasn't this. It wasn't talking to the woman he'd slept with. Sharing deep emotional wounds.

But then, Jessie wasn't like anyone else, and she didn't do things the way anyone else did. She was an anomaly and a contradiction. A woman who seemed so at ease and yet had the deepest part of herself on lockdown.

A woman who acted as if she hated him and yet was drawn to him like a magnet. Just as he was to her. Maybe they were both full of contradictions. Because he was an outlaw. He wasn't supposed to give a shit. But he did. So much. That was the problem.

If he could hate his family, things would be simpler. And the companion piece to caring, to not hating them, was loving them and wishing they accepted him the way he was.

Because he would've accepted them.

He had come into their house open. Wanting to fit in. Wanting to be like them.

It was only years of being pushed away that had created the resentment inside him.

Love was just so much work.

And Jessie knew that same truth. Her family was great in many ways, but her parents looked like a lot of work. They had created a lot of extra work for her.

So had the people in town.

He felt cocooned here. With her. With this woman who defied everything he had ever believed about himself.

About the world.

And so, in the entryway of his house, with trauma still on their lips, he kissed her. Because it was the thing he wanted most of all.

She whimpered, and leaned into him, wrapping her arms around his neck.

How had it taken this many years to do this? To taste her. Touch her. Talk to her. Share a bed with her?

She was extraordinary. Beautiful. Strong.

"I want to see your room now," she said, her eyes alight. Then it occurred to him for the first time that he had never brought a woman back here. Well, except for her. She had slept in his guest bedroom. But he hadn't let her into his room.

Tonight would be different.

"It's not that exciting," he said, taking her hand and leading her down the hall.

"I imagine we'll find a few exciting things in it."

"You," he said. "It's going to be you."

She turned pink, all the way up to the roots of her hair, and he had to admit he liked that. He wouldn't have thought Jessie Jane Hancock was the blushing type, and the fact that he could make her blush sent an unreasonable thrill surging through his veins.

He hadn't lied to her—his room was simple. But she moved away from him and began to look around, opening up his closet door and peering inside.

"No interesting secrets, I'm afraid," he said.

"Can I open your nightstand drawer?"

"Sure," he said.

He stood back with his arms crossed. When she opened it and found it empty, she frowned.

"There's nothing there."

"Did you think maybe the Gideons had put a Bible in there?"

She huffed. "No. But I was expecting condoms. Lube. A couple of sex toys."

"I don't bring women back here," he said.

"Oh. Well. Don't you need lube for when you . . ."

"Oh, I *have* it," he said. "Don't worry. And sometimes I even bring it out with me, because I am a gentleman."

"I won't need it," she said, her cheeks getting pink.

"No. You won't. But some women do. And that's fine too."

He probably shouldn't have said anything about other women, but she'd brought it up.

"*Do* you have sex toys?" she asked.

"I might, Jessie. Play your cards right, and maybe I'll show everything to you."

"Where are the condoms?"

She was insatiable.

"My bathroom," he said. "Because I grab them when I get ready to go out."

He went into the bathroom, opened up the medicine cabinet, and took the box of condoms out. When he returned to the bedroom, Jessie was perched on the edge of the bed with her hands on her knees, staring at him. He held the box up and shook it. "See?"

"I'm intrigued."

"By what?"

"You really don't bring women back here."

"I said that I didn't."

"I know. But I mean, you really don't. Here's the evidence and all of that. It's fascinating."

"Why is that?"

"I suppose for the same reason you were so interested in my virginity."

All right. He couldn't argue with that. "Well. This has been different from moment one. I know you. I . . . I like you. And it doesn't feel weird to have you here."

"Wow," she said, suppressing a grin. "It doesn't feel weird to have me here."

"Well. It just . . . It never felt right. The idea of bringing someone back here. My place. Where . . ."

"You can be yourself."

She said it so simply. So directly, a straight dagger through his heart. Because he was so many different people in so many different places. But not here. On this lonesome ridge that his grandfather had given him. The only person who maybe knew him and understood him exactly the way he was.

"Good point."

"Well. It's only fair that you let me up here. Because you're the one person who's been in my house. Who knows me." She stood up and closed the distance between them, wrapping her arms around his neck. "I really like you, Flynn."

Her words warmed his heart. Which was a sentence he had never thought of in his life.

Nothing and no one had ever warmed him before. This felt like Thanksgiving and Christmas, if he were someone else. Someone with a family who wasn't quite as dysfunctional as his.

Her kiss turned savage, and he loved it. Wanted to revel in it. In everything Jessie Jane.

She moved her fingers through his hair, ran her hands down his face, and he felt a growl rise in his throat.

She was perfect.

"Jessie," he said.

"Flynn."

She pulled away from him, and she smiled. "I can't believe it. I still can't."

"That we're finally doing this?"

"Yes. And that I'm brave enough. Finally."

She went back to him, claiming him with another hot kiss. Then she pulled her shirt up over her head and revealed a simple white bra that honestly drove him insane. This was the kind of thing he didn't get because he didn't do intimacy. He got going-out lingerie, underwear that was meant to be seen, and there was definitely something hot about that, but her plain white T-shirt bra was doing things to him that he didn't think he could ever explain.

She licked her lips, moved her hands to her belt buckle, and stripped her jeans off. And there she was, white cotton bra, white cotton underwear. Her arms were toned, her midsection firm, her thighs well defined from all that trick riding she did.

She was a specimen, was Jessie Jane. He had always thought she was beautiful. Hot. Had always known that sex with her would be incredible.

But that fantasy sex was with the woman he'd thought she was. Sex with the real Jessie Jane was better than he could've ever imagined. And there were aspects of it he could never have anticipated.

She reached around behind her back and unhooked her bra, let it fall loose before casting it to the ground.

She was bold, keeping eye contact with him as she took her underwear off too, leaving her entirely naked while he wore way too many clothes.

She moved to him and planted her hand in the center of his chest, pushing him back toward the mattress, and he went willingly. Which was how he found himself, still wearing boots, jeans, a shirt, and hat, lying flat on his back with a naked woman over him.

He could die happy. Honestly.

She raked her fingernails down his clothed chest, and he arched his hips upward, searching for some kind of relief for the need that flooded him.

"Don't try to buck me off, cowboy. You know that doesn't work with me."

Yeah. He did know. He also knew he wanted this woman to ride him.

Badly.

"You're a quick learner," he said.

"I just know what to do. Because it's you."

He didn't want to question that. Didn't want to dig into it too deeply. He just wanted to keep it. Hold it close. "Undress me," he said.

"You're bossy," she said.

"We both are. So let's make the most of it." He moved his hand, cupped her rear, then gave it a smack. "Take my shirt off."

Her breath was coming in short, hard gasps as she pushed his shirt upward and eventually off.

She leaned down, her nipples skimming his chest as she kissed him, and he growled through clenched teeth. "Lord have mercy," he groaned.

She got off him, then turned her focus to his belt and his jeans. He flicked his hat off his head, and he heard it hit the wall next to the bed and bounce onto the floor. He didn't care.

She took his jeans and underwear down, tugging them lower and lower, and when she got to his ankles, she took his boots off along with everything else. Then she moved back up into position and stopped.

She looked at him, mischief shining bright her eyes, and then she leaned over and took his cock in her mouth. "Dammit," he said, his breath hissing through his teeth. He moved his hands up to grab her hair, fistfuls of that gorgeous silk, and she took him in as deep as he had ever been taken. He was weak.

Her lips were like salvation, her tongue an incantation. And the sure glide of her mouth over him was a hallelujah chorus. He was undone.

He had never thought much of God, but he was sure right then that he saw him.

In vivid detail.

He tried to keep his eyes open, so that he could watch her. That familiar, beautiful face doing those things to him.

Jessie Jane.

Jessie Jane Hancock.

"I need . . . no more of that," he ground out he pushed her away from him with great effort. He deserved a medal of honor for that.

"I was enjoying myself," she said.

"Me too. Too much. That's not how I want it."

"What about how I want it?"

"I don't think that's how you want it."

Her cheeks went pink, and he reached over and grabbed a condom out of the box. Then he moved toward her and put his hands between her legs, stroking her until she was whimpering, until she was moving her hips in time with his rhythm. Until he knew she was right on the edge.

Then he lay down on his back, grabbed her hips, and brought her down over the top of him. "Ride me."

"Flynn I . . . I don't really know what I'm doing."

"Judging by what you just did to me, you absolutely know what you're doing. You know what I want. I want you. Get on me and ride."

She bit her lower lip, and he gripped the base of his shaft, angling it upward as she lowered herself slowly onto him, and took him in inch by devastating inch.

He nearly blacked out.

Judging by the way she was digging crescent moons into his shoulders with her nails, she was close too.

"That's right," he said. "You might be kind of a bad girl, but you're a good girl for me, Jessie Jane. So make it good."

She moaned and began to rock her hips back and forth, the subtle movement driving him crazy. Then she began to move, establishing a rhythm that was both too slow and too fast all at once. Too much.

She cried out, and her internal muscles pulsed around him, and he gripped her hips, driving her up and down on his length for a moment before he reversed their positions, completely out of control now, just following the beat of his own pleasure. She cried out again, and he let go. Her name on his lips, desire a beast that grabbed his throat and wrung him out completely.

Left him damn near dead.

He lay on his back, his forearm thrown over his face, and Jessie moved up to him, snuggling her face into his neck. They were lying sideways on the bed, and he realized his feet were hanging off. He didn't care.

"Wow," she said.

"Damn straight," he responded.

"That was . . . that was incredible, actually."

"Well, thank you."

"I can stay the night?"

"You have to stay the night," he said.

"You don't have to be bossy," she said.

"I'm bossy," he responded. "As we just covered."

"Well then, in that case . . ."

She slipped away from him and moved up to the top of the bed, sliding beneath the covers, and snuggling into his pillow. She was on his side of the bed. But then, he had always slept in this bed alone, so he supposed he didn't really have a dedicated side.

So that could be hers.

He sat up, then went into the bathroom to dispose of the condom before coming back out and joining her in bed.

"I have to prepare for that damn debate," she said.

He turned toward her, and his lips were right there, next to her temple, so it seemed totally logical that he ought to kiss it. "You're going to be great."

"I'm afraid this is where people are going to find out that I'm kind of a fraud? And you know what, I never minded being a fraud. But I do now."

"Why do you think you're a fraud?"

"Because I . . . I don't know . . . I don't know anything about policy, really. I mean, I have read up on a lot of things, and I know the city code pretty well."

"Of course you do. You run a business here. You're part of the town. And maybe you can't play the game in quite the same way that Danielle does, but I think that's a plus. You're one of us. And you want things to move in favor of those of us who own businesses in this town. Who work here. Who live here."

"You would think that Danielle would too."

"No. You know how she is. She thinks she's better than everyone else. She thinks she can make this place better than it is. But her version of better is . . . it's just snobby. She thinks she's fancier than Rustler Mountain. But if she moved into a bigger pond, she would never have this kind of power. It's why she stays here. Not for the love of it, but for the love of the status she has in this place."

"Wow. Well, when you put it like that . . ."

"She doesn't have to be exceptional here. She's coasting on the legacy of our grandfather, and she is not doing him proud."

"I guess . . . not."

"Very not. Trust me."

"Well, I do want to do what's right for the town. I also would really like to ride in one of those cool convertibles in the Christmas parade."

He laughed. "Well, I think that could be arranged."

"Who doesn't secretly want to be a parade princess?"

"I don't. But I'm happy for you."

She laughed, and he thought that he could maybe die happy if her laugh was the last thing he ever heard.

"Tomorrow, let's go into town and do some shopping. We'll visit all the businesses, and we'll make sure everybody knows about the debate. Make sure all the people you want to know about the debate know about it."

"You're brilliant, do you know that? I could've had you be my campaign manager instead of being my fake boyfriend."

He chuckled. And yet, *fake* just seemed like a weird word to use here. Because nothing between them felt especially fake.

He didn't say that, though.

"Well, we created more gossip this way. And you did want that."

"Definitely." She pursed her lips. "I do know how to create a spectacle. I'm very good at that."

"Yes, ma'am."

She let out a long, slow breath. "Do I seem different to you?"

"How do you mean?"

"I don't know. I just feel different."

"I guess I just . . . I've always felt I've known you. Granted, I know you better now than I did. But you don't seem different to me. You seem like a woman who knows what she wants. And is on the right track to get it. And for that, you ought to be damn proud of yourself."

There was silence in the room. "I am," she said finally.

Flynn fell asleep with a smile on his face.

Chapter 14

I fear hope will make a fool of me.

—Belle Martin's Diary, June 1869

Flynn was such an early riser, it really was irritating. But she got to climb up into his truck with a thermos full of coffee and ride around Lonesome Ridge with him, having a look at his ranching spread. And best of all, at his elk herds.

They parked on the edge of one of the fields where the elk liked to hang out, and she looked out at all the majestic animals, her heart beating hard.

"They're beautiful," she said. There was a large bull lying in a patch of grass, his massive rack of antlers branching out high above his head. Elk really were preposterous creatures. They had long faces, long necks with dark shaggy hair, and large bodies, with a light tan patch on their rear shaped like a heart.

"When you hunt for them, that's what you see," he said, gesturing toward one cow that had her back turned away from them. "Those heart-shaped butts."

"They're so majestic. It's kind of sad to think about hunting them."

"Don't worry. They're smarter than most hunters. There's actually a reason they call it hunting and not catching."

She laughed. "Did your dad take you hunting?"

"Sometimes. Not here. There are rumors that there's a wild elk herd out here, but I've certainly never seen it. We would go over to the coast mainly. Did it a few times. When Dad could get all the paperwork done and get his shit together for the license. I can still remember standing in the woods, and suddenly there was all this crashing going on around us, and the little whistling noise the elk make. And then there they were. Thirty of them, running through the trees. And just like that"—he snapped his fingers—"they were gone. Completely silent. No evidence that they were ever there. It's like magic. There's a reason elk used to be called the Ghosts of the Forest."

"Wow."

"My dad used to say that elk are where you find them."

"What does that mean?"

"Exactly."

She shook her head. She felt a strange, expanding sense of pride that this place belonged to Flynn. That he had taken up a different sort of ranching. That he'd set himself apart from his brothers.

"My brother is going to ranch," she said. "Apparently he bought a plot of land."

"No kidding," he said.

"Yeah. I . . . I had no idea. But it's something he wants to do. I mean, I did always have the sense that the Wild West Show wasn't his one true love or anything, but I never thought he would leave."

"It seems like the two of you don't really share much with each other."

It was an observation devoid of judgment, but it felt painful anyway. Because he wasn't wrong. She and West didn't share that much with each other. And she didn't really know why.

"I wonder if it's a side effect of hiding the reality of our life. We never wanted our parents to get in trouble for anything. And I think also we never wanted to really say anything bad about them. Because we love them. I don't think they could function outside the life they've made for themselves, and when you really think about it, it's brilliant. To fashion a different life for yourself when you can't fit. They did so much well, so much right. It feels disloyal to complain. And still, in my heart, I find it all really complicated."

"You're both practiced at keeping up a barrier so that you never have to talk about your parents' shortcomings."

"That's exactly it. We're just too good at it. We're both . . . trying to protect them, trying to protect each other. Not burden each other, but then it all comes out in weird ways. Like him telling me he's doing this without there being any lead up to it."

"You've got a good family," he said. "And I'm not saying you have to be grateful for them all the time. You can have complicated feelings. I'm just saying, they do love you an awful lot, and that's obvious. I think your dad is really proud of you; I think your mom is proud of you."

"She's maybe a little bit prouder of all the different spurs she's collected."

"Maybe. But I suspect you are equal to the spurs. She said a lot of nice things about you. She also said you never brought a man home before, so she was surprised to meet me. She understood maybe I was special."

Those words made her chest feel as if it was caving in on itself.

"Well, I guess that is true."

"Nice to be somewhat special," he said.

"*Somewhat*," she said, elbowing him in the side.

"You're ruthless."

"Very. But you should take me to get a sweet coffee."

So then they drove down into town, making Scallywag's their first stop. It was crowded, but she didn't mind. They found a table in the corner, and she had a different variety of coffee and a croissant. She took a deep breath. "I hardly ever come here or buy fancy coffee because I still have this really intense scarcity mindset. I have money squirreled away. Enough for a down payment on a house. I could start a business; I could do a lot of different things."

"Really?"

"Yes. Really. But I just stay at the Wild West Show because I don't know what else to do with myself."

"You're running for mayor."

She nodded. "Yeah. It's really the first big thing I've done. I

want to make a difference. I want to change things. I want to matter. I don't want to be the girl everybody laughed at. I want to prove
to them that they were stupid to do that. By doing an amazing job
as mayor."

"You already have my vote. But if you didn't, you'd have it
again."

"Thanks."

They finished up at the coffee shop and then walked out onto
Main Street, committed to going up and down both sides and visiting all the shops. They went to The Pot Rack, where they chatted
with the owner of the store about the handmade knives in the display case, and then about the upcoming debate. Then they moved
on to The Laughing Bison.

"Jessie is very much keeping in mind all the concerns of the local
business owners. So if you can think of any . . ."

"That damned dining tax," the owner said. "It's going to keep
people from coming out here. We are already so far off the beaten
path, and if it's more expensive to come out here than it is to eat
other places, no one's going to make the drive. Remember, Jacksonville tried to do something like that, and the ordinance got shot
down. Well, now we'll be next to them, farther up the road, and
with higher prices. No one will ever bother to make the rest of the
trip."

Jessie couldn't deny that.

"Well, don't worry. What I'm mayor, that proposal is gone. I'm
killing it at the outset."

"Then you definitely have my vote."

They were met with similar enthusiasm by a lot of different business owners. They were worried about changes that affected them.
Changes that could cost them their bottom line. And any policies
that weren't compatible with running a small business were deeply
unpopular. But of course, Danielle hadn't imagined that someone
would oppose her, so she hadn't been paying attention to what was
popular.

"It would be different if it was for schools or something like that."

They were in Perry's florist shop, watching her make a bouquet. "I could get behind that. Something that really benefited the community. But she's earmarked some of the money for landscaping? And that still leaves a lot of what we can theoretically assume we would get in revenue from that tax unaccounted for. Particularly since she wants to cut some of our programs and services, what is it even for?"

"Well, it might make sense for another kind of town," Jessie said. "One that gets heavier traffic. But it's so much work to drive to ours."

"That's what I've been saying," Perry said. "People have to drive an hour out of Medford to get here. And there's a lot to distract them along the way."

"Come to the debate. And you can hear me challenge Danielle on all of this."

"I will. Happily."

By two thirty, they were at The Watering Hole. It wasn't as crowded as usual, but some of the regulars were there already.

"I just need to make sure you all know that there's a debate coming up at town hall between Danielle LeFevre and myself."

"They don't want us there," said Richard, one of the more ragtag regulars.

"I don't care what they want. *I* want you there. I want you there to raise the issues that you care about. You can force Danielle to engage with them. And ask me nicely to do it. And I promise you I will."

"That was amazing," she said, buzzing as they drove out of town. "Agreed."

"I bet you are ready to have me get out of your hair."

"Not at all. Come up for dinner tonight at Austin's."

"Oh."

His family would know. That was the thing. They would figure it out immediately, because she and Flynn had been honest with them from the start. So they would see the difference.

"I don't care if they know," he said.

"Really?"

She was amazed that he had read her quite so accurately.

"Yes. Really. Anyway, Carson and Austin are going to harass me no matter what my circumstances are. So they might as well harass me for this."

"What about Cassidy?"

"Well, she's the worst."

Jessie smiled. She liked Cassidy a lot.

"I'm going to have to go back up to my place and get some clothes."

He nodded. "Fair. Maybe you should bring a bag down?"

He was inviting her to stay with him.

"I mean, I have rehearsals, and . . . Yeah. Okay."

He laughed. And he didn't tell her how much to bring. Didn't put any parameters on her stay. So when they got back to his place, she climbed in her truck and made the trek back to her house. She went inside and grabbed her little turquoise carry-on-size suitcase and began to fill it with some of her favorite things.

She wished she had sexier underwear. Not that he had made any complaints.

She got all packed up and drove up toward Flynn's house, but took the turn that would take her to Austin's instead.

The parking spaces in front of the house were filled with cars, and she wondered who was here tonight. Probably just his family. And he had invited her.

She swallowed hard, the realization making her throat scratchy.

It was . . . nice. That he had invited her. And she had to wonder if it was just about sex or the mayoral race or . . . She wasn't sure.

When she walked into the house, the women were seated in the living room: Perry, Millie, and Cassidy. She could hear the sounds of the men talking from the kitchen.

"Hi," Jessie said.

"Jessie!" Millie said. "Sit down."

"Oh, I . . ."

"The men are cooking," Perry said.

"Fuck the patriarchy," said Cassidy.

Well. Jessie was certainly doing that lately.

"Right on," she said.

"Did Flynn tell you that I was . . ."

"He actually did. He was such a grown-up."

Perry had a wicked little grin on her face. "It was nice to see the two of you this morning."

"Oh. It was nice to see you too."

Austin came in, with baby Emma strapped to his chest. "Can I get you something to drink, Jessie?"

"Oh that's . . . that's very nice. Just a beer."

"Coming right up."

She had the sense that this wasn't at all the way Flynn's home life had been when he was a kid. That this was an entirely different version of this house. Of their family life.

He had talked about his father being disorganized. It was difficult to imagine Austin being anything of the kind. The house was incredibly neat, always well ordered. A simple, meticulously kept cabin with enough room to host family gatherings like this. Nothing fancy, which was funny, because she knew that Austin could afford whatever he wanted now. He could've added on or done all kinds of things after the success of his best-selling book, but he hadn't done that. The house was still the same homey, welcoming space.

Austin disappeared, then returned a moment later with a bottle of beer in his hand and Flynn behind him. "Hi," Flynn said.

She waved at him, and she could feel herself blushing.

"I still need him," Austin said.

They disappeared back into the kitchen again, and all of the women fixed Jessie with a look. "Yes?" Jessie asked.

"You wouldn't happen to be for-real dating my brother now, would you?" Cassidy asked.

She laughed, a nervous sound. "I . . . No. I don't think so. I . . ."

"You like him," Perry said.

Well, Jessie could hardly deny that.

"What's not to like?"

"I didn't think that you and Flynn would ever say such nice things about each other. But he's been saying a lot of nice things about you," Millie said.

She was being ambushed in a very soft, loving manner, and she didn't quite know what to do about it. She realized that this was one thing her life had been absolutely missing for a very long time. She didn't have many woman friends. That was the problem with her bravado and the facade she kept up. She could slip behind that facade. She could push them away with it. She could absolutely tell them and herself that nothing was going on with Flynn. Or it was just sex, or something shocking.

She decided to try honesty.

"Well, he's . . . I've gotten to know him. So of course I like him more now than I did."

"Well, we like you for him," Millie said, smiling broadly.

"You . . . like me for him?"

"Yes. Flynn is hard to pin down," Perry said.

"Very," said Cassidy. "But he's also the best. Like absolutely, really the best. Just the greatest older brother. He has always taken care of me and picked on me in equal measure. And I really like that he's finally . . . found someone."

That made Jessie's heart flutter in a sort of panicky way. Had he found someone? Had she? She had honestly never thought about the concept. Finding someone.

Falling in love or whatever else.

She'd never even had sex. Why would she have entertained the idea of a lasting romantic relationship? It would simply be beyond her. It always had seemed that way.

"We also love you for the town," Millie said. "And we're very excited about the possibility of your being our next mayor. We'll do any canvassing you want."

"Well. I'm probably going to need a lot of canvassing." This was slightly more comfortable territory. But still it was foreign to her. Sitting with a group of people who actually seemed to want her around? Usually that happened in a bar or at the Wild West Show. But the sense of camaraderie she felt here was something else.

"You should come to the holiday bazaar," Perry said. "I'm going to have a booth with dried flowers. Actually, if you want to set up in my booth, that would be great. I have a really big space, and I don't need it all."

The holiday bazaar was held every year on the main street of town. Traffic was blocked off so people could walk between booths and see all the Christmas decorations for the upcoming season. "It's after the debate. It'll be the final push before the election."

"Well . . . thank you. I would love that. It's a great idea. I . . ." It sounded so . . . festive. And warm. And exactly like the kind of thing she actually wanted to be at.

"Yay," said Perry. "It's settled. You can canvass at the holiday bazaar. And in the meantime, feel free to put a sign up in my flower shop."

"What about . . . If I lose, do you think Danielle is going to retaliate?"

"We're all guilty by association." Perry smiled happily. "We are all associated with Flynn. There's absolutely nothing we can do to escape her evil eye if she decides that she's going to be big mad about it."

"Well, I really appreciate the offer. Even if you do incur her wrath."

"I'm not afraid of her," Perry said. "I could absolutely take her in a fight."

Millie, who was small but rather ferocious, looked at Perry with glittering eyes. "I already cursed her. Effectively. She's stuck with Michael."

Everybody laughed at that.

Then the men came into the room, promising a glorious feast. They all trooped into the kitchen to find the table laden with a feast: corn on the cob and fluffy rolls, baby back ribs and potato salad.

"You Wilder men don't mess around," she said.

"We never do anything by halves," Flynn said. And immediately her mind was in the gutter. Unavoidable.

He didn't do anything by half.

She was appreciative of that.

They ate dinner, and the easy conversation washed over her. She even found herself participating in it. Not dominating it. Not feeling the need to do her Wild West Show bit.

After dinner, there was pie—which Austin confessed to buying from the store.

They ate it happily, and chatted, and then when it was time for her and Flynn to drive back to his house, she followed him closely on the road.

Her suitcase ended up being left by his front door, and he grabbed her and ravished her almost immediately. And when they were naked, lying in his bed, she traced shapes on his bicep. "I was thinking how different your house probably is now compared to when you grew up there."

"That's a loaded topic," he said.

"I know. But . . . your family really is so lovely and functional."

"It was a fight to get there. Austin . . . Millie definitely tamed him. But so did resolving some of those issues with our family's reputation. The feeling that he was just going to repeat history, that he was an outlaw, no different from any of our predecessors, no different from our dad, that was hard on him. And then there's Carson. He lost his first wife. And then he and Perry practically broke every bone in each other's body trying to sort out how to be in love. So yeah, now they look functional. But Austin has always kept the place clean."

"They seem to really . . . You all care for each other. Cassidy says that you're the best big brother in the world."

He got a faraway look in his eye. "Well, that's nice of her. Honestly. She's a good kid, and I . . . Her mom just left her, you know. Left her on the doorstep and didn't even bother to check what was going on with us. Our dad had just died the month before. She didn't even know that. When Austin called to tell her, she didn't care. She was on to greener pastures. She wanted to date some new guy who didn't want anything to do with kids. Cassidy had to acclimate to Oregon ranch life after living in Florida."

"Really? I didn't realize she came all the way from Florida."

"Yep. Apparently, her mom was willing to go to a lot of trouble to abandon her. I feel for her. I really do. Because I know all that stuff is sharp."

"Didn't Austin and Carson lose their mom too?"

"Yeah. She left. But they don't remember her. I know what it's like to remember a mom who doesn't especially want you around."

"No wonder Cassidy feels so close to you."

"I wish she didn't. Not for that reason."

"It's all so complicated. But you guys make it look easy. You make it look like family."

"Well, so does yours."

That they appreciated each other's version of family felt special in a way she couldn't quite articulate. But tonight had been about the closest thing she'd ever had to a sleepover. One where she felt included and welcome.

A strong, terrible thought hit her. When all of this was over, she wouldn't only lose Flynn, but the closeness she had built up with his family.

That made it almost impossible to sleep.

Chapter 15

He's talking about a future for us, and I haven't let myself dream of the future for a very long time.

—Belle Martin's Diary, January 1870

Jessie and Flynn prepared mercilessly for the debate. As it drew closer, she actually felt real calm descending over her. She had this. She just did. She knew what she wanted to say, she had done a lot of preparation, a lot of reading, and most of all she had spent a lot of time talking to people in town.

Flynn encouraged her to dress in one of her Wild West Show outfits—all rhinestones and fringe, big hair, her. Because she wasn't trying to be Danielle.

She wasn't.

The last week had been intense, but wonderful. She had spent every night at Flynn's house, and though her brother had raised questioning eyebrows at her a few times, he had never commented.

On debate night, all the Wilders and all the Hancocks filed into the redbrick town hall building. They walked right into that large, white-trimmed room, leaving dusty boot prints on the dark walnut floor, and took up a whole section of seating in the very front. She felt, right then, that she had two families. Even if it wasn't entirely true.

It was harder and harder for her to remember that she and Flynn were playing a part. They were. That's all it was. They were playing a part.

Except the sex between them was very real, and so was the way her heart beat faster when she looked at him.

But right now, she needed to get that out of her mind.

Danielle hadn't arrived yet, and Jessie was trying to figure out exactly what sort of power move she was making when her opponent walked into the room, her blond hair swept back into a neat, low bun. She was wearing black. A black jacket and black pants. She looked like a woman who was running for a real political office, not just mayor of a town so small it was barely a town.

Millie's friend Heather was acting as moderator. Which had apparently been a little bit of a knock-down, drag-out fight with the town council. But Heather had been rated as someone who was neutral, and as a member of one of the founding families, she had a right to speak her mind.

But she also didn't own a business in town, and neither did her husband, which put her in the neutral category. Even so, Jessie knew that Heather didn't care for Danielle.

The knowledge made her heart shiver with glee.

"If everyone can please take their seats, and the candidates can come up to their podiums," Heather said, speaking into a microphone from a small table that was facing the stage. "This debate will be conducted in a town-hall style. We will be taking questions and comments from citizens in the audience, with each candidate having two minutes to answer a question. I will act as moderator."

There was polite clapping for Heather, and then slightly louder clapping when Jessie Jane and Danielle took the stage. She wondered which of them the audience was clapping for. But of course, the most uproarious clapping was coming from her section. And so she did what she knew she had to. She put her hand up and pumped a fist.

"Some decorum," Danielle said.

"I'll allow it," said Heather.

But then, the doors opened again, and in filed some of Jessie's favorites from the bar. Including Gus, who took a seat all the way in the back. The turnout was huge. She didn't frequent town meetings, but she knew for a fact that she had never seen this room so full.

"We're going to start things off with a couple of pre-submitted questions. And this one question was asked the most frequently, so I decided to make sure it was the first thing we covered. It's about the restaurant tax."

Heather launched into a question about the reasoning behind the restaurant tax, the allocation of funds, and what both candidates intended to do with the measure.

Danielle obfuscated, saying that it was impossible to know exactly how they would allocate a budget when they didn't yet know how much revenue they would be bringing in with the tax.

"I'm not having it," Jessie said. That earned her a round of cheers. Even from people she wouldn't have normally expected to support her. "I'm not having it because I don't think it's good for the town." She launched into all the concerns that the different shop owners had voiced to her. And especially the concerns the restaurant owners had.

"The bottom line is, if it's bad for tourism, it's bad for all of us."

"Tourists who are able to bring more substantial money into the community won't mind a tax," Danielle said.

"And regular people will. They'll go somewhere else. I'm aware you don't care about that, that you like the idea of filtering out the people you don't think have as much value or merit, by your standards. I'm not."

"You have a conflict of interest."

"Your time to speak has lapsed, Miss LeFevre," Heather said.

"I think I should have time for a rebuttal," Danielle said.

"We'll move on," Heather said. "The next question is about the historic-colors ordinance."

The historic-colors ordinance meant that only certain flowers, certain types of plants, and certain paint colors could be used on homes in the town proper. Jessie had always thought it was stupid. And when it was her turn to speak, she said as much.

Her answer was clearly very much less popular than her first response had been.

She felt slightly stung and a little bit foolish. There were several questions like that. Issues that no one she had talked to had brought up, but that clearly mattered quite a bit to certain people in town.

Sometimes she was thrusting; other times she parried. Sometimes she was definitely on the winning end of an argument, and other times she missed a beat.

And when it came time to give their final statements, she was feeling a lot more uncertain than she'd expected to feel.

"The way I see it," Danielle began, "we can continue to refine our town. We can continue to bring in the right kind of tourists, and we can continue to have the best and brightest of us representing the community, or we can descend into anarchy. I understand that noise ordinances and taxes on diners are not necessarily popular choices. But for the most part, a dining tax makes sense because it brings money in from outside our community, rather than putting an undue burden on citizens.

"Change is good. But with caution. And precision. That's what I bring to the table. You know me. You know how I handle myself, and when it comes right down to it, my opponent is a wild card." Danielle took a breath. "Thank you for your time."

The word branded itself on Jessie's spirit. A wild card. Yeah. She was. She sure as hell was a wild card.

"My opponent is right," she said. "I am a wild card. And I don't think our town needs to be more exclusive. If we've learned anything from our history it's that when we exclude people, we lose real, valuable contributions to society, to our home. The *right kind of tourist* implies there's a wrong kind. Well, I'm sure to Ms. LeFevre half of us here would be the wrong kind. I welcome any tourist who wants to come and enjoy this place, not just somebody who wants to go on a wine trail. I welcome people who want to come and enjoy the Wild West Show. Eat a fine dinner or go to a dive bar. People who want to go to concerts in the park, or hike in the mountains, just enjoy the views. People who want to come to the lake and drink beer all day, and yes, people who want to go wine tasting. And just like there's no right kind of tourist, there's no right kind of citizen. This outlaws-and-lawman thing has gone on for so long, and it permeates everything we do, despite the brilliant book Austin Wilder wrote that told people we're a lot more complicated than we ever really want to believe. We are. I know I am. I'd like to think you all are. Danielle is certainly a choice you can make. One you've made before. She feels safe, but if you really listen to what she says you'll hear the hidden message in her words—she thinks she's better than all of you, and she thinks she has the right to decide what and *who's* best. I pledge to be a wild card. To listen. To do the unexpected. To make this town a place for everybody. Whether they're visiting, or they live here. That's what the outlaw ticket is all about. I'm free to be me. You're free to be you. And we all live together. Work together. Enjoy this town, this life, together. There's no need to regulate the joy to be found in this town. Thank you very much for your time."

The applause she got was thunderous. And it wasn't only because of her family.

In that moment she thought she might actually win. Lord. She might've actually done it. And it wasn't by creating a spectacle. It was actually by being herself. Maybe she hadn't needed Flynn at all . . .

Her eyes went to him, to the proud smile on his face.

No. She needed Flynn. She absolutely needed Flynn. Because he had given her this confidence.

She stepped down from the stage, and he closed the distance between them, drawing her close and kissing her.

She looked over at Danielle, who was standing with Michael, her boyfriend, and Michael, her brother. Flynn's mother was standing next to Danielle too. And she was looking between the groups of people, clearly undone by the whole thing.

"Do you want to go say something to her?"

"She can come say something to me," Flynn said.

She knew that wasn't going to happen, and it made her heart hurt for him.

"Hey," she said. "All of my supporters, come back to the Wild West Show, and we'll have a bonfire."

The announcement earned her a riotous cheer from the crowd. Her dad's face suddenly lit up. "That's right. Come to the Wild West Show. Home of Jessie Jane Hancock, your future mayor. Everyone who comes tonight will get ten percent off the next performance."

Her mom drifted over to her and patted her on the arm. "You did a good job."

"Thanks, Mom."

She wrapped her arm around Lucinda's shoulders, but only for a minute. Because her mother tensed up when there was too much unexpected touching.

"I appreciate you coming."

"Of course I did," she said, looking past Jessie's shoulder. "I would never miss something so important."

She wouldn't. That was true. Mom had difficulty with certain things, but she was always there to support her kids as best she could. It didn't always look like the way other people's mothers supported their children, but it didn't mean that her love was any less. It didn't mean that she meant it less. Hell, she had been involved in the Wild West Show for all those years even though it was hard for her. Hard for her to be in front of people, hard for her to perform just because it was time.

But she did it. Every time. And it really was an incredible testament to how much she loved Jessie and West and their dad.

"You're a good mom," Jessie said.

"Thank you," Lucinda said. And Jessie couldn't tell if that was something her mom had ever worried about. If it was something she had been waiting to hear. She couldn't tell much of anything from the interaction, so she would just have to accept it for what it was.

She had ridden over with Flynn, and she got into his truck to go over to the Wild West Show.

"Sorry about your mom," she said.

"Really? That's the first thing you have to say to me after that amazing debate performance? You did great, Jess. We don't need to talk about my mom."

"But this is hard for you. And it's a lot. And . . ."

"All of the above. But I knew it would be."

He forced a smile at her.

"Did you?" she asked.

"I maybe didn't know all the ways that it would be hard. But I knew it would be. Because that's just . . . family."

"My mom does her best," Jessie said. "I don't know if I ever really appreciated that until tonight. She came out even though it was hard. She was there with everyone, and she'll probably even come to the bonfire for a while. I wanted her to be like other moms. She's not. She's her. That doesn't mean she doesn't love me, though."

"But you were probably still hurt by some of her . . . the way she is."

"Well, yes. It's hard when you're sort of at the mercy of your parents' choices. But you know, I would rather have an unorthodox upbringing with people who loved me than . . ."

"Whatever the hell is going on with my mom?"

"I think she loves you. I wasn't even actually meaning your mom. It's just . . . I can't imagine being a parent. Can you? Have you ever thought about it?"

He snorted. "No. I can't say that I have."

"Well, maybe I would be terrible at it. Maybe trying to do the best thing for me would be the worst thing for my kid. Because in my head, I would want to do everything super normal. I would want them to have a nice house on a nice street. I would want them to go to school in brand-new clothes. But what if they turn out to like vintage? And what if they aren't made for regular schooling, and they really wish they were homeschooled or something? I bet my mom was suffering a lot from her own childhood."

"She could've told you that."

"I guess. And I could've also told her when I was uncomfortable. Or didn't like something."

"Jessie, you were caught between a home life that was pretty happy and a world that treated you like there was something wrong with the house you grew up in. I don't know how you were supposed to feel about any of it. Or how you were supposed to navigate it. It's unfair to be too hard on yourself. You were a kid. People were mean to you. It's as simple as that."

She nodded slowly. "They were the enemy. Like we talked about. If other people had been willing to make life outside of my house softer on me, home would have been fine. Good, even. It was the people that insisted on making everything about me wrong. Just because I was different. I don't know that I innately wanted to fit in. I think I just wanted to have friends."

"Sorry this town sucks," he said.

"Well, me too. I'm sorry that the LeFevres are so . . . them."

"Me too."

They didn't speak for the rest of the drive, and when they pulled in, the number of cars in the lot just about made Jessie dizzy. There were so many people who'd come out to celebrate.

They started calling for a speech, and she got ready to stand up, but Flynn did it first. "This is a great turnout tonight. But remember, you have to show up on Election Day. Drop that ballot in the box, folks. And elect Jessie Jane as your new mayor. For all the reasons that you heard tonight, and all the reasons you have yet to discover. And also, because my sister sucks."

That earned him an appreciative roar from the crowd.

He sat down, and Jessie hung onto his arm, burying her face in his bicep.

There was drunken singing, and some acrobatics from people in the show. Poker games broke out around the bonfire, and about the time it started getting really rowdy, Carson, Perry, and Cassidy excused themselves. Austin and Millie had already taken Emma home.

"This was great," Perry said, yawning.

"Fantastic," agreed Cassidy. "I love this place."

"Don't get any ideas," Carson said, jabbing his sister on the shoulder. "You're not doing any trick riding or anything like that."

"You can't tell me what to do," Cassidy said.

"I can," said Flynn.

"Unfair. If it's good enough for your girlfriend, it ought to be good enough for me," she said.

His girlfriend. Flynn's response got lost in that label echoing in Jessie's head.

His girlfriend. That seemed so . . .

Well, actually, it seemed far too tame for what they were. And it also seemed way too permanent. Way too intentional. They were just doing this thing until the election wrapped up. That was all.

Except the idea of a relationship didn't seem quite as ridiculous as it had before. Because she knew him now.

But the idea of . . . of putting herself out there like that made her want to die. Because she had known so much rejection in her life. So, so much. And the idea of having any more . . . Especially from him.

Well, she wasn't going to think about it. That was all. She was simply going to live in the moment. Because she had never felt quite so good living in the moment as she did now.

"Your place?" he asked when they were alone.

"I would love that," she said.

She missed her little camper. Her little camper with all her frilly little things. Flynn looked so large and masculine in it. She couldn't help but notice when they closed themselves inside. She moved to him and kissed him. It felt different. It felt as if things were shifting. It had been easy to define the early shifts. When she had gone from having never been kissed to having been kissed by Flynn.

From that kiss to another. From never having had sex, to having sex with him.

Now she had lost track of the number of times they had been intimate, but things still kept changing. It was just harder and harder to explain how. To herself, and especially to Flynn.

What were these feelings inside her? She didn't have a language for it. But she could kiss him. Kiss him and know him, both physically and through conversation.

He was hurting tonight; she could feel it. He was also genuinely proud of her.

It was complicated. Just as everything was always. So she kissed him, and he kissed her back.

His arms were tight around her, and he backed her up against the trailer wall, making the whole thing shake. She pulled off his clothes, and he tore off hers.

She let him lay her on the bed, and she knew what was coming would be fast and furious. She welcomed it.

He protected them both, then thrust deep inside her, the race to completion making her dizzy.

When she finally cried out his name, he was only a few seconds behind her.

And then everything was still. Reality crept back in.

"People are just really disappointing sometimes," she said.

And she meant his family. Wholeheartedly.

"Are you still thinking about them?"

"Yes. I am. Because how can you be in the same room as your family, and they don't even talk to you?"

He let out a husky laugh. "That's sort of an encapsulation of my entire childhood, actually. Never knowing when they were going to include me, or when they weren't. But . . . I don't wonder anymore. Not really."

"It doesn't mean it doesn't hurt."

"No. It hurts. But it's an old wound. And all too familiar."

"Well, I think it's stupid. That they treat you that way."

"Thanks."

"You were the person in the room I wanted to talk to most of all. I'd never ignore you."

"Thanks, Jessie."

"I'm glad we're . . . friends."

"Friends?"

"Hey. I've never had a close friend before. Not really. Will you be my friend?"

She felt like she had really put herself out there. It wasn't a declaration like the kind that had been hovering in the back of her mind earlier. But it was still a lot. Certainly more than she had ever asked of another person before.

"Yeah," he said, his voice scratchy. "I'll be your friend."

"Oh good. I'm really glad. Because I'm a lot happier with you in my life."

He didn't say anything for a long moment, but then his hand covered hers. "Me too."

That was going to fuel her for a long while.

Chapter 16

I understand more things about men than I'd like to. But the one thing I never learned was how to let one love me. What a foolish thing, to have found someone good and to feel like the one thing standing between myself and happiness is that I simply don't know how to hold love in my hand.

—Belle Martin's Diary, February 1870

The town was abuzz with excitement about the election, which was rare. Because usually it was a mere formality. This time, there was the potential for exciting change on the horizon. Flynn certainly felt changed. He could never have imagined willingly going to this craft-fair thing under any other circumstances. But now he was unpacking campaign merch from his truck, and ferrying it over to Perry's booth so that Jessie Jane could put her makeup on before things got started.

"You're very supportive," Perry said, patting him on the arm as he placed a big sign on the outside of the booth.

"You don't have to say that like it's surprising."

"It's not surprising. I mean, if Carson can get ahold of himself, you certainly can."

"I appreciate that you think I'm a little bit less messed up than Carson. That I could get my stuff together this many years sooner in my life."

She laughed. "Don't tell him I said that."

Of course, he thought Perry might be reading too much into the situation. Jessie was his friend. She'd said that to him a couple of weeks ago right after the debate, and he had decided he liked the term a lot. Because it meant this wasn't just a temporary thing that would automatically stop at the end of the election. But it also meant that it was something manageable. Something he had experience with. He knew how to be a friend. So he was being friendly.

Jessie appeared a moment later, in all her cowgirl glory. She looked up at him with large eyes, lifted her hands, and started to shake them out. He grabbed hold of them and held her still for a moment, his gaze holding hers. "You're good," he said.

"The election is so close."

"Yes. And you have done everything you possibly can do."

"What if it's not enough?"

"That's on the town, not you."

"Isn't that how it always is?"

"Yeah. I suppose so. Because things are easier for some people. And harder for others. Here you are. You tried. You've done absolutely all the best things. And you did it because you care."

She leaned in. "And for revenge." She said that part in a whisper. And she was so cute, he had to kiss her on the nose.

"Right. But we don't need to tell everybody that. That's an inside thought." He tapped the side of her head.

"You're ridiculous," she said.

"You too, sweetie."

The whole interaction made his heart do something strange in his chest, and he didn't quite know how to categorize it. So he didn't.

But he loved to watch Jessie work.

She was so dynamic. So great with everyone that came to the booth to talk to her.

He couldn't escape the feeling that he was utterly superfluous. But he didn't actually care.

It felt good to support her. To watch her do her thing. Which made him question himself.

Why exactly was he here? What was this? Was it really just a ruse they were engaging in? Or was it something more?

It didn't really matter. He was here. They were together.

He took a step away from the booth after they'd been at it for about an hour and looked down the street at all the different displays.

There was a coffee cart with baked goods, and he decided he would walk down that way and get something for Jessie.

She didn't treat herself all that often—she'd said so herself—but he had noticed how much she enjoyed having a fancy coffee and a pastry.

He had the sudden, strange thought that if he could give her little treats every day for the rest of her life, it might actually make him happier than anything else.

He was blindsided by that notion. Didn't know what the fuck it meant. He actually didn't know what was happening to him.

But something was shifting. Changing inside him.

He was just about to reach the coffee cart when a hand reached out and grabbed his shoulder.

He turned sharply and came face-to-face with his half brother. They had the exact same color green eyes, and he always found it alarming. To look at those eyes, which were so familiar, set into a face that was a sort of distorted version of his own. A bit softer and rounder. And always with hard resentment glittering right at the surface. He wondered if he appeared just as resentful when he looked back at Michael. But he didn't envy Michael. So he didn't think so.

"You're such an asshole, do you know that?"

"For real?" He turned away from his brother and decided to try to keep on walking.

"I'm talking to you, Flynn."

"Why? It's not Christmas."

"Don't act like that. Your supporting this dog and pony show just to get back at us is ridiculous."

"Why would anything I do have something to do with you?"

That question would've been completely disingenuous at the beginning of the race, but not now. It was about Jessie Jane now. It was about the fact that he thought she was the best person for the job. The fact that he thought she deserved to achieve every hope and dream she had ever had. He thought about his family less and less.

He didn't care what they thought. Not about her candidacy. Not about anything.

"I'm supporting my girlfriend."

"Are you? Blood should be thicker than water."

"Oh well, then. How convenient that suddenly I'm blood, Michael, because generally speaking, you can take me or leave me. And so I guess this time I made the decision myself. Is that what bothers you?"

"It's because you're jealous of Danielle and me, and you always have been. Why wouldn't you be? We grew up in town in a beautiful house and you grew up in that shithole with that crazy old man of yours. We had both of our parents. I understand why you wanted to be part of our family."

"You really don't."

Because he couldn't deny that he had. But it just wasn't for the reason Michael thought.

"Well, you got something out of it. You got Grandpa to leave you that land."

"Don't," he said. "I had a relationship with him. I loved him. That he left the land to me wasn't anything I expected."

"I have a hard time believing that."

"Of course you do. Because scheming to get the land is what you would do. It's what you would care about. I don't care about the same things. We are not the same. You love that I'm different from you. An outsider." He tried to turn away again.

"She just didn't want you. You realize that, right? But Mom is a good person, so she felt guilty about it. She was always trying to include you in family things, but you were just too much of a mess. You don't fit. And you never did."

Flynn felt dizzy, as if he was in some kind of time warp. This was the most juvenile tantrum he had ever witnessed in his life. The worst thing was that it hurt. It really did. It hit him right between the ribs, slid right where he was most vulnerable. Got at the thing he had always been afraid of. He just wasn't wanted. He wasn't enough. No matter how hard he tried, that love would always be out of his reach.

"Okay," he said.

"What?"

"Okay. There's nothing I can do about it, Michael. Do you want me to cry over it? Two people fucked thirty-one years ago, and I've been paying for it ever since. I didn't ask for it. I didn't ask to have to deal with you. I didn't ask to have to deal with your sister. I don't deserve your resentment. I sure as hell don't deserve this tirade. This is bullshit."

Nothing had ever brought him more clarity than this moment. Part of him had always feared it.

To have the truth shoved in his face. So that there was no more plausible deniability. To have the thin veneer of resentment pulled back so that he actually had to hear how much everyone hated him. How much of an imposition he was.

But the truth was, he hadn't asked to be born. And the two people who should have been the adults had done a piss-poor job of dealing with the situation. Maybe his mother hadn't wanted him, but then she should have been clear on that. Signed away her parental rights, or something. Or maybe just have been a better mother. Because the simple truth was, she couldn't have hated him when he was a baby.

He was the consequence of his parents' mistakes, but they had made him live with the consequences, instead of paying the price themselves. His dad had done the same with all his children. And his mother had simply run away, taking no responsibility for him.

Only Austin had done that. Carson.

And here was Michael, acting as if Flynn's existence was some kind of burden, when it had never really affected him. He'd grown up in a beautiful house. He had both of his parents.

"If I have so little, then why the hell are you so obsessed with me?" Flynn asked. He turned away again, this time decisively, and got in line for coffee. His brother did not follow him.

Rage churned through his veins.

And churned and churned.

He brought the coffee cup over to Jessie, along with a bag that had a donut in it.

"You don't look so great," she said.

"I'm fine," he growled.

"You sound like you're ready to commit murder. But okay."

He worked on smiling again. On getting his head back in the game. He was here for Jessie. This had nothing to do with his stupid brother.

"I'm not going to commit murder. If I was going to murder that little weasel, I would've done it years ago."

"Who?" asked Perry, poking her head around Jessie to look at him.

"My stupid half brother. He's a dick. There's no reason to get wound up about it."

Even if he did feel wound up.

"What did he say?" Jessie Jane asked, looking at him with sympathy. Well. Jessie looking at him so softly . . . It made his chest ache, and he didn't need his chest to ache right now.

"Nothing. Just the usual kind of vitriol you expect from people like him."

"We'll talk about it later," she said.

Which was maybe the most relationship thing the woman had ever said to him. Soothed, he turned his focus back to handing out flyers, buttons, and other Jessie Jane–related paraphernalia. Until the street started to get less and less crowded, and darkness began to fall, and a chill settled in the air.

Perry had sold almost all her dried flower bunches, and there was very little to clean up except the booth itself, which was being handled by some volunteer organizers for the event.

Jessie had given out most of her literature, and they started packing up what was left.

"You're an idiot, you know."

Flynn turned sharply, and there was his brother again, right in his face.

"Here you are. Obsessed with me. It's very weird."

That seemed to enrage Michael. He took a step forward, his chipmunk cheeks red and his eyes glittering. "They're not going to vote for some woman trying to use her rack to get votes."

Jessie looked down at her shirt and then back up. And Flynn saw red. He was beyond himself. He stepped out of the booth and punched his younger brother in the face.

"Don't you ever, ever talk about her or any other woman like that."

Michael was holding his face, down on the ground, shouting and cussing.

"I'll . . . I'll ruin you," he said.

"Ruin me how? I'm already at the bottom of the well in this town. You can't get me *fired*—I work for myself. You, on the other hand, might lose some clients." He reached down and lifted his brother up, bringing him back onto his feet. "Maybe some of this is my fault. Maybe I wasn't the older brother you should've had. So let me tell you something, but it's not man-to-man, because you're no kind of man. If you ever talk about a woman like that, you should expect to get hit. Because no real man is going to stand by and let it happen. And you're sure as hell not going to win any points with it. Not with anyone who has a shred of integrity. You can critique the policies that Jessie is running on, but the minute you start talking like that, you've already lost." He shook his head. "I don't envy you. Because whatever happened in your life, you came out like this. And I would rather be me every day of the goddamned week."

He shoved his brother back. Michael stumbled a little but righted himself.

"I should call the police," Michael said.

"Go right ahead. You're going to look like the biggest crybaby in the world. You called the cops because your big brother punched you in your ugly mug for running your mouth about his girlfriend. You know what the real problem is, Michael? You envy me. Because you're stuck being whatever it is you are. And I'm me."

He felt hands on his shoulder, and then Jessie wrapped her arms around him. "You really didn't have to do that. You know men have said way worse things to me."

"Not in front of me," he said. "And I'm not going to stand for it."

The incident had drawn a small crowd, and as Michael slinked away about three-quarters of the people stepped forward and started to take brochures out of the box Jessie had been packing up.

Everyone had heard what had been said, and certainly no one seemed to think that the punch was unjustified. "Anyway, that was probably good for my campaign," she said.

"He's disgusting," Flynn growled.

"Well. People often are. Why was he harassing you today?"

"He feels threatened. He's such a small man, anything that threatens his power enrages him. But really, all the power belongs to Danielle. It doesn't belong to him. He's always felt insignificant. I could have been there for him, but they never wanted me. That's what he said. My mom never wanted me there."

"Flynn . . ."

"It makes sense. She felt guilty, so she kept inviting me, but she didn't actually want to deal with me. It would've been more convenient for her if I could've just disappeared from her life. I've always felt that, but it . . . Yeah. It's something to get confirmation."

"Please don't listen to him."

"Why not? It's actually good. I have confirmation. It's something I always knew was probably true, and now I just . . . It's fine."

He ignored the stabbing feeling in his chest and kept packing things up. Perry was looking on, clearly uncertain what to say.

"You know how dysfunctional families are," he said to his sister-in-law.

"Well, yeah."

"It's nothing."

Except she looked as if she wanted to cry for him, and he really didn't need that. He didn't need any of this.

Because his dysfunctional family was something that was always part of his life. Always. Michael talking about it didn't mean that it hadn't been there all along.

And hearing the truth in front of everybody didn't mean it was news to him.

Jessie shot Perry a look, and Perry nodded, then vanished inside her store. He had the very distinct feeling he was being managed.

"What?" he asked.

"I've thought we should talk and . . ."

"I don't have anything to say, Jessie. There's nothing *to* say. He's a prick, and that was unfortunate. I'm sorry he talked trash about you."

"Like I said, it's not a big deal. Men are like that sometimes. I'm not hurt."

"That's how I feel," he said. "I wish our confrontation hadn't played out on the street, but my family is like that. It's not my fault."

Except he felt it might be. It was the strangest thing. Because he'd had this moment of clarity, but the follow-up sensation was just gross. Maybe all of his initial thoughts were just wrong, and maybe the conversation hadn't actually gone down exactly the way he was remembering it even now.

Now that the adrenaline had worn off, he felt that somehow he had lost because Michael had succeeded in making him act like the person his whole family already thought he was.

Maybe that shouldn't bother him. Maybe he should be fine with it. With himself. But he just felt like shit, and he had been in this position before. He never knew what to say. He never knew what to do. He was swamped by a complete and utter sensation of being inadequate. In every way.

They loaded up the truck, and the silence in the cab was sharp.

He had never had to contend with another person while he was going through family trauma, and Jessie's truck was at his house, where she had been staying with him. So it was all just . . . great.

"It really isn't you. It's not," she said, when they were about ten minutes down the road. "You're right. He's jealous of you. Because you have a better life. And you're a better person."

"He doesn't think I'm a better person, though. He thinks I'm trash."

"Maybe he does, but I think deep down he must know better."

"Just don't," he said. "There's no point having a conversation. There's no point trying to make me feel better. This is just stupid."

"It's not stupid. You're allowed to have feelings about the fact that your family is a bunch of assholes. I'm sorry I dragged you into all of this, honestly. I feel like the dynamics are just so . . . toxic. I feel really awful about it."

"I don't need your guilt on top of everything else, Jessie. Don't make it about you."

He felt her shrink over to her side of the car, and he felt like a dick. Because now here he was being mean to the person who was trying to be nice to him. "I didn't mean that."

"You probably did a little," she said. "And that's fair. I don't want you to be upset, because I . . . want you to be happy. I like it when you're happy, and I guess that's a bit self-serving."

"It's not. It's probably normal. But what would you and I know about normal? We're both maladjusted."

She huffed a laugh. "Well. That's true. But today gave me a lot of clarity. Because my family does want me. And they do love me. And I'm sorry there are people in your family tree that act like Michael. It's really not fair."

"Life's not fair."

He didn't know why, but the sympathy was making him prickly. And he was starting to get frustrated.

"Flynn, I don't want to fight."

"I'm not fighting with you," he said, his voice rising just slightly. He let out a long, slow breath and relented. "I'm sorry. I'm fighting a little bit. And I don't mean to. I'm just frustrated. I'm frustrated that they have the ability to get to me. Because they shouldn't. I'm frustrated because I know it's not my fault, but it feels like my fault."

"Fair."

She didn't say anything else. Finally, they pulled into the driveway of his house. He just wanted to get away from the discussion, from the thoughts in his head. From everything.

"Maybe you should go home," he said.

He looked at her. At the stubborn set of her chin, and he really thought she was going to argue. "Sure," she said. "If that's what you want."

"Yeah. It's what I want. I need some time by myself."

"I get it."

"Maybe if this was . . . if this was something real. Maybe then it would make sense for you to stay, but it's just for the election."

He knew that was a terrible thing to say. He didn't even think he meant it. But she could tell him he was wrong. She could tell him she did want him, their being together had nothing to do with the election. She could . . .

No. There was no point in that. He had to deal with it by himself because that was the way he had to deal with everything. What they had wasn't real. It was true. It might hurt her to hear it said like that, but they both knew it. They were dysfunctional.

They weren't going to work out their dysfunction together.

They'd had some moments that felt really good. But they were just moments.

They had great sex. He liked her. They were friends, even, but it didn't go beyond that. If he was ever going to share his pain with somebody, if he was ever going to experience it with someone, it would be someone who was more than a friend. It would be . . . something else.

"Oh," she said. "Well. Of course. You did punch him in the face, though. For me."

"I would've done that for any woman."

Of course, hearing it said about any other woman wouldn't have made his blood boil that hot that quickly. "I mean, he shouldn't have said it about you. It did make me extra mad. But it's just . . . You're my friend. You are my friend."

"Yeah," she said. "I'm your friend. I really appreciate that, Flynn. I do. But . . . if I'm your friend, maybe we shouldn't sleep together. Because it's been a little bit intense, with me here at your house. It's fine that you want me to leave. It really is. It makes sense. It actually makes way more sense than the amount of time I've been spending here. Especially with the election being just a few days away."

"Exactly. So you get it. Because I haven't had any time alone, and this whole thing just kind of caved my head in. And I really need just some time . . ."

"You have it," she said, a shrill note to her voice. "You have all the time you need. Fuck. Great. Take time."

She was mad. Her words weren't angry, but they sounded angry. And there was a strange kind of panicked feeling in his chest even though he knew what he had said was totally reasonable, because it was everything they had agreed upon. Because dammit, they were outlaws. They were lone wolves. They both were. And it wasn't just that he was committed to his facade and she was committed to hers. It wasn't just that he didn't know how to let down his guard, and he didn't know what to do right now because everything inside him felt like it was bleeding. No. It couldn't be that. He was just being damned reasonable.

"I'll probably call you tomorrow."

"You could also not. Because we've done all the work we need to do for the election. But you have to vote. You still have to vote—you know that, right? And so does your whole family."

"Of course I'm going to vote. I'm not going to let Danielle win now. I'm all in. I punched my brother in the damned face. In fact, no one on that side of my family will probably ever speak to me again. Which is fine. It's better that way. Can you imagine? My mom had to pretend she wanted me around for my whole life, because she didn't want to look like a terrible person. I'm glad I could be the worse person. The smaller person. I'm glad I could be the one to finally cut the cord. Honestly, best decision I ever made."

"Yeah. It is. It's a good decision. Just like this one. I'll see you. On Election Day."

"Yeah. I'll see you."

She got into her truck, and she didn't kiss him goodbye. Which was fine.

He walked up the steps into the house, and he put his hand on his chest. He felt like he was having a heart attack. His whole body hurt. And he was alone. Which was exactly how it should be. Because he deserved to be alone. He fucking did. He deserved to be without Jessie. Without his mom.

Because he had never really fit. And so he had to be good at this isolation thing. It was really the only thing.

It was fine.

But he felt for some reason as if he had just severely broken something, and if he thought about it, he had a feeling he would figure out exactly what and why. But he hadn't asked for this. He hadn't asked for any of it. He hadn't asked to be born; he hadn't asked for his half siblings to resent him. He hadn't even asked for this whole election debacle.

He growled and threw his elbow against the hard side of the wall, cursing when he left a dent in the drywall. Why was this so fucking hard?

Living. Being a human.

About the only thing that hadn't been hard was being with Jessie. It was all the surrounding things. It was . . .

He thought of her face. Of the hurt in her eyes when he had sent her on her way.

He wasn't going to dwell on that. He just wasn't.

He hadn't said anything that wasn't true.

But then, maybe Michael hadn't said anything that wasn't true.

Chapter 17

I ran again, to another town. Another life. Because I couldn't trust what Benjamin offered me. All this time I wouldn't write his name. Now it's all I can do. I didn't want to hope. But now I've let fear take the best thing I've ever had away from me.

—Belle Martin's Diary, June 1870

Jessie cried all the way home. And she couldn't even say why. They were sticking to their agreement. So what was she supposed to say back to him?

It was going to be over after the election. She knew that. She had known it the whole time. There was no doubt about it. There was no question. There was no reason to be upset.

But it *hurt*.

Because being with him felt like it was something different. Had felt like it was something different for days now. Maybe even weeks.

But he had just said he needed time alone.

And you just left.

Of course. Because pushing back would mean dropping her mask. Because pushing back would be opening up her chest and revealing truths she wasn't even certain of herself.

She pulled up to the front of her trailer and curled her hands tightly around the steering wheel. She was in love with him.

No. She didn't want it to be true. She didn't want to be that big a cliché. She didn't want to be that sad.

She loved him.

How long had she loved him?

Well. Not all that long. She hadn't known him before. Maybe she'd had a crush on him, maybe she'd been attracted to him, but the love thing . . . That had built over the course of the last month and a half. When he had surprised her at absolutely every turn by being a more wonderful, sensitive human being than she'd ever imagined him to be.

He was smart. He was just wonderful.

He was great in bed. He taught her how to be herself. Gave her the strength to do it.

Except today, when she had needed to do it most, she had faltered.

She had not stood her ground.

But she had been doing so much of it lately.

Campaigning for office and fighting. Finding ways to be herself in public and not feel she had to put on such a show.

But this felt like a bridge too far. It felt like too much. Like too big an ask.

What should she have done? Looked him right in the eye while he was telling her he didn't want her around and tell him that she was in love with him? That it wasn't a show for her. That it was real. That it was everything.

She had stopped herself from admitting it before because she hadn't been sure of what she wanted.

She knew the answer now. She wanted him. However that looked.

She had never really thought much about getting married. Having children. She hadn't imagined her future taking the shape of anything so traditional.

She had worried, when she ever did think about marriage, that she might be bad at it.

But she had been finding her way with Flynn, hadn't she?

She didn't just have to be a reaction to her parents—she could be her own person. She could be the woman she had become. She could shape herself around him, just as he would with her if . . .

If he loved her. But he didn't.

Or maybe he needed her to say it first.

And that brought her back to the fact that she was just too afraid to reveal her feelings.

Because she had been rejected already. She knew what it was like to want something, to know it was out of reach.

Why did she have to open herself to rejection again?

She thought about his family.

His father was dead, his mother didn't want him. He didn't have love. And she did.

She hadn't been lying to him when she had said that Michael's harsh words had given her something to think about.

Because her own parents were different, and they had done things that had messed her up, but they did love her. And she would rather have that than a seemingly normal family that disdained her.

She put her truck in reverse, and she found herself driving toward her parents' home. More specifically, straight to her mother's archival trailer, where she housed all her collections.

There was a light on in the living room, and she could see Lucinda standing in front of the bookcase, shuffling things around.

She got out of the truck, walked up to the door, and knocked.

It took a moment, but Mom came to the door and opened it. "Jessie."

If she was surprised, her tone didn't betray it.

"I wanted to talk to you about something."

"Sure."

She stood away from the door and gestured for Jessie to come inside.

She did, and as her mother closed the door, Jessie looked around the space. It was filled with curiosities. Display cases with spurs, crystals hanging from the ceiling in front of the windows; she knew that during the day when the sun came, the whole trailer sparkled. There were potted plants everywhere—the place awash in greenery. Books and little origami figures. Little things everywhere.

She suddenly remembered what Dad had said about Mom. About how easy it was to give her what she wanted. Jessie suddenly thought all this was beautiful. Because these things were little pieces of her mother's heart, on display for everyone to see. It made it a lot easier to know her than Jessie had realized. She felt a momentary surge of gratitude, especially in light of what had just happened with Flynn's brother.

"I wanted to ask you about . . . Dad. And I don't want to hurt your feelings."

Her mom frowned. "Why would it hurt my feelings?"

"Because I just . . ." Oh, she was really going to do this. Break the unspoken rule she and West had made all those years ago: to always pretend that everything was normal and fine. She couldn't anymore. She needed answers. "You and Dad are really different. But you know that, right? That you're different from other people?"

Her mom blinked. "I would hope so. Everyone is supposed to be different from other people. That's what makes you special."

Jessie smiled slightly. "Well. Yeah. But I mean . . . unconventional."

"Yes. We are." Mom was so unbothered.

Jessie wasn't sure what reaction she wanted, honestly. So she decided to just ask about love.

"Does that make being in love easier or harder?"

"I don't know. I don't know what it's like to be somebody else."

"Okay." Jessie almost laughed. Because her mother's answers were so simple, and it was hard to believe it was that simple. To just not compare yourself. To just be as you were. "But I mean, when you were falling in love, did you have to fight for it? Did you feel there was a pattern you could follow, or did you feel you were starting from scratch? Did you . . . did you worry about losing him? Were you afraid for him to see all your collections? For him to see *you*."

Jessie swallowed hard. "People don't like me, Mom. Or they didn't, not when I was little. They thought we were weird. And they thought I was weird. I got so tired of being rejected. I'm scared of being rejected again."

Lucinda was silent for a long moment, and then she went over to her bookshelf and started touching the spines of the books. In a rhythmic pattern, sort of a soothing motion. "I was rejected all the time. But I never understood why I should hide myself. I wasn't the one who was being mean or unkind. People didn't like it when I talked too much about the things I enjoyed, but I thought they were boring. Why wouldn't you want to talk about interesting things? But that doesn't mean it didn't hurt."

Of course her mother had experienced a lifetime of rejection. Of course she had. Jessie had felt protective of her multiple times in the present, but she had never thought about what her mom's life might've looked like in the past. She had never realized, not fully, that of course her mom had been a kid who was often alienated from the people around her.

"But how did you find the courage to tell Dad how you felt?"

"I couldn't hide it. No other man was ever interested in me. But he liked the way I was. He never asked me to change. He never asked me to talk about different things. He likes things to move quickly, and he's very brave—in ways that I've never been. He's different from me, but I don't need him to be different from himself. Just as he's never needed me to be someone I wasn't. But yes, telling him how I felt was scary."

"Did you tell him first?"

She nodded. "Yes. I've never been very good at lying. And there was a point where I knew I wanted to be with him forever. So I thought I'd better just say it."

"I'm just afraid. I love Flynn. I love Flynn, but I don't know what he wants. I don't know if he feels the same way. I don't know . . . I don't know. And I'm so worried that I'll do the wrong thing and ruin it."

"If it's love, then saying the wrong thing won't ruin it. It might be like a train that gets kicked off the tracks for a while. But it won't be ruined."

They were such simple words. And yet Jessie could feel a lot of wisdom in them. She and her mother weren't exactly the same. Jessie had learned to hide herself. Jessie had learned to protect the woman she was in her deepest heart.

Her mom had never learned that. Instead, she had accepted rejection as an immutable part of life. Jessie wondered if in some ways her mother's response was better.

Because the stakes felt so very high. Flynn was the first person to see her. He was the first person to really know her and like her.

She had given more of her real self to him than she had given to her family, and . . .

Maybe that was why it felt so frightening.

Because if he rejected her, it was the real her. The very real, very vulnerable Jessie Jane with her pink bedspread and her baked goods. With her squishy heart that just wanted to be accepted.

And maybe he should be the one to make the first move, except fundamentally, one of the reasons Jessie was so angry was that she felt she deserved to be accepted.

She didn't know if Flynn believed that he did.

Her mom grabbed hold of a small, red book, then turned around and handed it to her. "I have a collection of old letters and diaries. This one belonged to our Belle. One of your ancestors. A prostitute."

Jessie looked down at the book. "I know who she is." She turned it over in her hands. "I didn't know you had her diary."

"You never asked."

"I . . ." She looked down at the book and felt a tug of connection. "She must've been rejected a lot. People aren't very nice to prostitutes."

"They're not very nice to women in general. Especially when you're not doing exactly what they want you to. If you're just a little bit different."

Jessie felt her eyes fill with tears. "Yeah. You're right, Mom. That's true."

"It's an incredible thing when you can make it through life being yourself. Because we're all different, but people don't want us to be. You're special, Jessie. You always have been. You're strong. And talented. I would never be brave enough to run for office, because you can't just decide that you don't want to talk to people today. And some days I really don't want to talk to people."

"I know," said Jessie.

"But I don't know if you realize how special you are. You are.

And I'm very sorry I didn't know that people were being mean to you when you were a child. It's just . . . I looked at you and I saw the most beautiful girl in the whole world. I thought everybody was being nice to you. Because you are so funny and so clever. And the most fun to be around."

Jessie felt a tear slide down her cheek. It had honestly never occurred to her that Mom just didn't realize that not everybody loved her the way she did. And she had never really thought about how much Mom loved her. She'd had the deep acceptance she had always wanted right here. She hadn't seen it. Because it didn't look the way it did in movies. Because it wasn't conventional.

But God, it was real.

Jessie closed the distance between her and her mom. "Can I hug you?"

"Yes."

Jessie hugged her, even though she knew it wasn't Mom's favorite. She let her go before she wanted to, for that reason too.

"You are the best mom," she said. "Just the very best. You love me exactly the way a mom should love her daughter."

She clung to the diary. She had a feeling she was going to find something in it that she really needed. Because her mom knew her well enough to give it to her.

"You're the best daughter." Lucinda reached out and smoothed Jessie's hair, the simple contact healing in ways Jessie would never be able to articulate to someone who didn't understand her mom.

She didn't need them to understand.

She did.

Jessie decided to hold that realization close, even as she walked out of the trailer, then drove herself back to her home.

She opened up Belle's diary and started reading.

About a woman who had always wanted to be a lady but had simply never had the chance. It was a sad story. Belle had been doomed to fail from the start.

But it wasn't that she was never a lady; it was that the world wouldn't *let* her be. And then there was a man who saw her as a lady, no matter her circumstances. A man who saw her exactly as she was and loved her.

Belle rejected him, because she was scared. Jessie couldn't blame her. It was terrifying when you had spent your whole life being told you weren't good enough.

It was just the most terrifying thing.

Jessie read all the way to the end. Then she pressed her face into her pillow and cried.

He felt like shit.

He felt like shit, and it was the day of the election. He took his ballot and filled it out, and dropped it in the box the very first thing. When his pen hovered over Jessie Jane's name, he felt a deep longing reverberate in his chest. He filled the bubble in without hesitation.

Now the vote was cast, and it really was over. Unless . . .

What was he doing? What the fuck was wrong with him?

He didn't want it to be over. He just didn't know what else to do. He didn't know how else to be.

He didn't know how to . . . want something better.

For a brief moment, he had.

His grandfather had loved him, invested in him, and he had given him that land. God damn, Flynn had felt honor bound to do something with it. Something great. Something interesting.

Because that old man had believed in him.

But as far as his personal life went, he had just never . . . Love seemed to take so much work. Just so much work. And that was why he told himself he and Jessie weren't in love.

Because he really didn't want to go through all that.

The ache in his chest intensified.

He decided to drive a different route home than he normally did. At least it wasn't love. At least.

He kept on repeating the words to himself, but something felt wrong. Felt like a lie. He turned off the street he was on, onto a residential street, and it took him a minute and a half to realize that he had driven to his mother's house.

She was standing in the front yard, watering her flowers. Flynn stopped his car in the street. Then he pulled over, getting out before he could decide what he even wanted to say.

"Morning," he said.

"Oh," she said, starting and putting her hand on her chest. "Good morning. I'm surprised to see you here."

"Because I punched Michael?"

"Yes."

"I suppose he didn't tell you why."

She shook her head. "I'm sure he deserved it."

Her words stopped Flynn in his tracks. "Are you?"

"He can be . . . abrasive. He gets that from his father."

Flynn held himself back. *Oh, your husband's not perfect? Your precious son isn't perfect?*

No. He didn't say that.

"I didn't realize," he said again. "I mean, I realize I don't have a great relationship with them, but I thought that was me."

"I don't think it's you."

Flynn swallowed and took a step toward her. "Mom. I have to ask you something. I don't want you to lie to me, even if it's hard. Just please don't lie to me."

"Okay," she said, "I'll try to be honest."

He was on one side of the fence, and she was on the other, and it felt like a damned metaphor. "Is it true that you didn't want me?"

She drew in a sharp breath. "Is that what Michael said?"

"It's not why I punched him. But yeah. It's one of the things he said."

"I've never said that in front of him. I've never said that."

"But did you?"

Her lip wobbled, and her eyes filled with tears. "I didn't want you. I didn't know how to have you. I made a mistake, going off with your dad. And I made a mistake leaving you behind. But I was young, and I was afraid. I thought I would never be able to start over if I had a child. It felt like too much baggage. And your dad already had kids. You were so close to your brothers, and I just thought you would be okay. But I missed you. I got married to the first man who wanted me, because I was trying to justify leaving you. I didn't want to be alone. I made a lot of very poor decisions. And by the time I realized how bad they were, it was too late to fix them. I never felt I had a right to you, Flynn. By then, I did want you, but I was worried about where you would fit in. And the older I get, the angrier I am at myself for that. For caring about what other people thought. For . . . I love my kids. All of them. But I didn't love you very well. And whenever I see you . . . I'm afraid you're going to tell me that."

He felt as if he'd been punched in the stomach. Because he had finally gotten the courage to face down his worst fear, and his mom had confessed her own. And the truth was close to what he had always thought. That she wanted to believe he was more okay than he was. That she didn't want to fully accept the ways in which her absence had hurt.

"I basically didn't have anyone. Austin and Carson raised me. And now I don't . . . I don't fucking know how to love anybody. Because the only thing I know is that I worked my whole life to try to make you love me. And it just felt like you didn't. No matter what I did. No matter what I did, you didn't love me. And I don't know what to do with that. I'm screwing myself over right now. Ruining my own life because I don't know . . . I don't know what love is supposed to feel like."

Tears spilled down her cheeks, and he was shocked that they were actually having this moment. That there was honesty between them. He barely knew what to do.

"I'm so sorry. I'm so sorry, Flynn. I knew that you were going to need to say this to me one day. And I just . . . I have been trying to outrun my bad decisions. Trying to make myself feel better. But you . . ."

"I love you. That's the thing. I've never hated you. That's why it hurts so much."

"It was like that for me too."

"But I didn't have any control," he said, and he couldn't worry about whether or not it hurt her feelings. "I was a kid. And the only person who ever made me feel like I was good enough was Grandpa. Nobody else did that for me. I didn't fit in the family picture, so . . . I didn't fit."

"I know it doesn't mean anything now. I know it's too little, too late. But I know that I made the wrong choice."

She wasn't wrong. And he was going to live with the damage of her decision forever. There was no easy fix. His childhood was a mess because of her. But as for its being too little, too late for them, he realized there was a choice. She'd had all the power when he was a kid, but he had it now. Their relationship could be what he wanted it to be. It could be what he needed it to be.

He got to decide how hard he was going to make it for her.

And he realized he just didn't have the energy for any more hard. More than that, he didn't want it.

"It's not too late," he said. "Because I don't want it to be."

"But . . ."

"I know. I blew things up. But if we're going to have a relationship, everybody else has to stop treating me like I'm invading their lives. They invaded mine."

His mom couldn't quite laugh at that, but it was true.

"I can talk to them."

"And it's going to be especially hard to do now. Because of Jessie and the election."

"Probably," his mom said. "She ran a hell of a campaign, that girl. She's really something."

"Thanks. I think she is too. But I . . ."

At least it isn't love.

Why did he think it wasn't love? Because it didn't hurt?

Because being with her felt easy? Because she felt like an extension of him, his other half? Because he didn't have to be all sorts of different things to make her want him?

That was . . .

He was letting his messed-up family define love.

And that realization really did blow his mind.

"Mom I . . . I have to go. I have to think about some things."

"I really do want to fix this. As much as you'll let me. As much as I can."

"I'm not going to make it hard." He took a deep breath. For the first time, he felt he was taking a full breath. "Because it just shouldn't be."

He got into his truck, drove all the way to the top of Lonesome Ridge. And he stood there, a man apart from everything. Even himself, just for a moment, as he let this new revelation wash through him. As he thought about his grandfather. About Austin, Carson, and Cassidy. The people who loved him. The people he loved.

Jessie Jane.

Yeah. He loved her. It hadn't been a fight. It had been a fight to stay away from her. For far too many years.

He . . . he fucking loved her.

And he had been too stupid to recognize it because it hadn't been a knock-down, drag-out fight. Because in the end, it had been a fight not to love her.

But he'd hurt her. When he'd sent her away. What a dick he'd been. She was so afraid of being rejected, and then he had gone and done exactly that.

He hated himself for it.

He loved her. Like breathing. It was second nature to him. Something he didn't have to try to do, something he couldn't help but do.

All he had to do was grab on.

All he had to do was take the step.

And he damn well would.

Chapter 18

There were so many things I didn't understand until Benjamin. That love can be stronger than fear, that forgiveness is better than anger. That hope is not foolish at all, not even in the slightest. At our wedding, I thought of my mother, and how she always dreamed of a better life, but her hope only brought her agony. But it helped me live. It helped me find my way here. It helped me find my way to him. I didn't believe in happiness, much less happily ever after. But now I know how to hold on to what matters. I'm never letting go.

—Belle Hancock's Diary, October 1870

The crowd assembled at the bar for the election results was spirited indeed. Jessie Jane had never felt so supported. So accepted. Whatever the result tonight, everything was going to be okay. It was.

She tried not to think about Flynn, because that just hurt, and he wasn't here.

His family was, though. Even without him.

She knew they were holding back questions, but they didn't ask them. In fact, no one did, which made her feel alternately irritated and relieved. There were little graphs on the screen, showing the votes being tabulated, and the very niche local elections were coming in more slowly, with the results being shown less frequently, because the state elections were the main thing being covered.

Her brother walked up behind her and squeezed her shoulders. "It's going to be good," he said.

"I hope so."

And she meant that. But she meant more than just the election. Then the door to the bar opened, and in he walked. Flynn Wilder. All six-foot-plus of gorgeous cowboy, a sight that had affected her ever since she was in high school. Chiseled jaw, brilliant green eyes, broad shoulders, and a muscular chest. Washboard abs. Muscular thighs that she wanted to lick. That she had licked. In that blinding moment when he had walked in, it was like the first time she'd seen him. Like all the years combined. Would he always affect her like this?

His eyes locked with hers, and her knees went wobbly. "Flynn Wilder," she said. "Howdy."

"Jessie Jane Hancock. I'd like to speak to you outside."

"Sure," she said.

She cleared her throat and looked at everyone. The room had gone stone-cold silent. "Excuse me."

He put his hand on her lower back and ushered her through the door. She found herself out on the street, staring at the neon sign above The Watering Hole with its curvy cowgirl, just like that night she had first asked him to engage in their charade.

Maybe he was about to shake her hand and tell her it was a job well done. Though it seemed a little weird not to wait until after the election results were announced.

"Well?"

"I just wanted to talk," he said.

And suddenly, with burning conviction, she knew she needed to tell him. She had to put herself out there. She had to open herself up. She couldn't be safe. She couldn't let him walk away. Maybe she would open herself up to rejection. On the same night she might lose an election. She didn't care. Because she loved him. And she needed to know if he loved her too.

"I love you."

It came out at exactly the same time he said it.

His mouth opened just slightly, and he looked dumbfounded. "I love you," he said.

"No," she said. "I love you."

He laughed. That bastard laughed. Like it was hilarious, when she had been marinating in pain for days.

"I . . . What's funny?"

"I knew it," he said. "I just . . . Jessie Jane, I kept thinking that love seemed terrible. That it was hard. Because every time I tried to fit myself into my family, it was like pulling teeth. And I associated love with that feeling. And then my brother Carson got married, and his wife died. And then he and Perry just about took each other apart getting together, and . . . I've just seen love hurt a lot more than I've ever seen it do anything else. At least, that was what I was focusing on. But I realized today, that isn't us. I think sometimes love is just right. And it can be easy. But when it comes into your life, you have to hold on to it."

"Flynn," she said, "that is so . . . I can't believe you said that. Because my mom gave me Belle Hancock's diary. My ancestor who used to be a prostitute in Jacksonville."

His eyebrows shot up. "Oh?"

"It's a good story. But the whole story is going to have to wait. Right now, the important this is that she said something about love. About how love is something you have to learn to hold in your hands. And not let it go. And when you have so many disappointments in your life, or you've been rejected, it's hard to believe that it can be that simple. But I really think it can be. I just needed to be brave. And that was what I needed to tell you, whatever you were going to say to me. I had to tell you not to be afraid of being rejected."

"I'm so sorry I made you afraid. You didn't deserve that. You have been nothing but wonderful. Nothing but a miracle. You understand me in ways no one else does. And you make me understand myself. I just thought love always had to be a fight. And like maybe that was the way it was going to be for me. Because of how I was born, or just . . . But it's not, is it? Not for us. It's not going to be like that for us."

"No."

"Do you know why I never hit on you? Why I fought with you instead of . . ."

"Fucking me?"

"Exactly that."

"Tell me."

"Because it was always going to be this. And I think that scared me most of all. Because I wasn't ready yet. To look at all the things I've been through. To really dig into all the stuff I felt about myself. I just spent my whole life feeling there was something fundamentally wrong with me. Like I wasn't good enough. And that was why I had to fight so hard to be loved. But I've been going over all the things I said to Michael, and some things my mom said to me this morning. It was never me. I didn't put myself in this situation. It was the people around me. And the whole goddamned town. If they didn't make it so hard, it wouldn't be. But we understand each other. And that's why it's easy. We are not trying to protect ourselves or consolidate our power to make ourselves look better. We just want each other. We accept each other. More than that, we really like each other."

She laughed. "I do. I like you so much."

"I like you so much that I love you. We've always been more the same than different, no matter how much we didn't want to admit it. Just two battered and bruised outlaws who want somebody to love them. For who they are." He laughed. "This is not my forte. Austin is a writer. He would do a way better job of professing his love than me."

"What about Carson?"

"By all accounts, Carson kind of made a mess of it. But he seems to be doing okay now."

"Well, good thing I don't care what either of them would do. I only care about you."

"Me too. That's all I care about."

The door to the bar opened just as Flynn leaned in to kiss her, and his lips were hovering over hers when Cassidy shrieked, "Jessie Jane! You won!"

Her eyes flew wide, and her stomach dropped. But then Flynn smiled. "I know I did," she said.

Because she had. Whatever the result of the election, she would've won. So she kissed him instead of cheering. Kissed him, even as the crowd inside the bar went wild.

And when they parted, they both looked into the bar. "You're going to be the first outlaw mayor."

"And you're going to be my first man. But first you have to make an honest woman out of me."

"I don't want to make an honest woman out of you. I want you to stay exactly the way you are. I'll marry you all the same, though."

And right then she knew exactly what she wanted. Flynn Wilder, forever.

She had always thought of herself as a collection of rather toxic traits. But somehow, they had all led her to this moment. To victory, but more importantly, to Flynn.

So maybe there was something just right about her after all.

With that realization, a lifetime of feeling put together wrong just faded away.

Flynn took her hand and led her into The Watering Hole, and the whole town cheered.

"You did it," Cassidy said, bouncing around the room.

Austin shook his head. "I'll be damned."

"You're amazing, sis," West said, clapping her on the back.

"I'm awfully proud of you," her dad said, his eyes shining bright as her mom stood next to him happily.

And then Flynn took her in his arms. "Did you always know that you could do anything?"

"No. I thought I had to pretend to be somebody else to even have a friend. But it turns out, I just needed to be me."

Epilogue

"If you ever want to write a historical romance, Austin, Belle Hancock's life is a pretty great story," Jessie Jane said as they sat down to the second Thanksgiving dinner she and Flynn had attended that week.

Her parents had decided to celebrate the holiday on Monday. "Why not, after all?" her mother had asked.

Why not, indeed.

"I'm not sure I can be moved to write about the Hancocks," Austin said. "No offense. But you're changing your name to Wilder, so I feel like that's a win for us."

"Belle was just Butch's sister-in-law. Her husband Benjamin was a good man. He repaired clocks!"

"Why didn't his legacy trickle down to your family, then?"

"Well, Belle and Benjamin didn't stay in the area. He didn't want her to be forever shunned because of her past. They moved to California and bought a house in San Diego, right on the water. Belle loved it. My mom ended up with all of her old things because she's so great at tracking down collectibles, so now we have her whole story."

"Did Butch leave a diary?" Austin asked.

Jessie shook her head. "Not as far as I know. He didn't keep records. Maybe because being an awful person doesn't make for a great narrative? Who knows. But that's why, in the end, the original Austin Wilder had the last word through you. And Butch just gets to live in infamy."

"But not us," Cassidy said. "Now Austin is a best-selling author, Carson has a respectable business in town, and Flynn is engaged to the mayor. And well, Jessie, you're the mayor."

When she and Flynn were on their way home—she'd moved in with him almost right away, leaving behind the trailer circle, which had been harder than she'd imagined—she was still musing.

"Belle had to leave town so she wouldn't be eternally dogged by her past. Hell really is other people."

"It definitely can be."

"We didn't have to do that, though. This place is actually changing, and we're part of the change. I'm going to remember that whenever I feel that I'm not making much of a difference. We are. All of us. We're changing the story, and I'd like to think changing some of the people around us."

"Because you're a legend, Jessie Jane Hancock, not just an outlaw."

She smiled, and looked out the window, at all the stars overhead. "Jessie Jane *Wilder*."

"Well, you're going to have to change all your political signs next time."

Her heart felt as if it might just burst. "You're worth it, Flynn. You're worth absolutely everything."

Don't miss the final novel in the
Rustler Mountain quartet, *Christmas Valley.*

Chapter 1

Redemption is for men who care. I lost all that a long time ago.

—*Butch Hancock's Diary, June 15, 1867*

Cassidy Wilder had known exactly what she wanted since she was nine years old. To have in this order: a home of her own, a place in the town of Rustler Mountain, and to marry Dalton Wade.

She now had a small home on her brother's ranch—not quite what she was after, but something adjacent. Her brother Austin had turned the tide of public opinion on the reputation of their outlaw family over the last couple of years—which again, wasn't her doing but had given her a sense of belonging she'd been missing.

So really all that was left was marrying Dalton.

The issue was that she might die a vestal virgin waiting for him to ever kiss her.

Dalton was her brother Flynn's best friend, and she knew he was being respectful by not making a move on her. He was being a good friend, a good . . . well, whatever he was to her. Because he was a good guy, and he probably had that weird, wrongheaded idea that sex would corrupt her.

Well, she wouldn't say no to some corruption, but it was becoming clearer and clearer to her that she was going to have to make the first move.

And what better time than now? This season.

The season.

Fa-la-la-la-la-la, fuck me please, cowboy.

That little internal thought made her shiver, just slightly. Whether because she was pondering the meaning of the word, or because she was afraid she'd be struck by a falling Christmas tree for being so irreverent around a holy season, she wasn't sure.

But the season was upon them, nonetheless.

Rustler Mountain was definitely beginning to look like winter was approaching. The trees in front of the town hall had all turned a vibrant red and orange, and Cassidy knew that meant the leaves would wither and drop by next week. The color was vivid, but fleeting, a metaphor, probably, for something she had never experienced.

Every weekend between now and Christmas, there would be festivities on the main street of town. While Cassidy didn't like to betray the fact that she was secretly soft, in her own heart she could admit it. She loved the decorations, the music, the food. Sometimes she thought that if she could immerse herself in Rustler Mountain Christmas, then she would forget all the Christmases that came before, and most crucially, the Christmas when her mother left her stranded on Austin's doorstep, making her a Christmas foundling at the mercy of three older half brothers who had never even known of her existence.

It would not be surprising if she hated Christmas. For a while it had been difficult. But Christmas in Florida had been different. The way the seasons changed—and they did change, contrary to what people who didn't live there believed—was different from the way they changed in Oregon. The air tasted different, the foliage behaved in a different manner. The way fall turned things crisp before winter made the landscape an easily shattered pane of ice was something she had never experienced until she moved here. Christmas had become a new tradition that had new meaning.

Now it reminded her of how lucky she was to have her older brothers. How lucky she was to have this place to call home. And really, how lucky she was to have Dalton. Her entire family was helping with her future sister-in-law's booth. Jessie Jane was doing blacksmithing demonstrations in a station by the courthouse and answering people's questions and concerns as Rustler Mountain's future mayor. Her term would begin in January.

Cassidy was walking toward the booth now, hands in her pockets, a scarf wrapped tightly around her neck to keep the chill at bay. She could hear music, laughter, conversation, could smell cinnamon, apples, and cloves in the air.

There were carolers walking toward her, wearing Victorian costumes, the men in top hats, the women in dark, high-collared dresses with bustled skirts. It was a familiar scene, and yet always different. Always a spectacle.

She quickened her pace as she moved toward the family booth, crossing the street while traffic stopped for her. She waved cheerily at the cars and kept on going.

There was a crowd around Jessie's booth, so she could barely see what was happening, though she could see sparks flying upward and people clapping.

She could see Austin, wearing a black cowboy hat, holding his daughter, Emma. And his wife, Millie, standing beside him holding his arm. The sight made Cassidy ache, but not in a bad way.

One of the things that Cassidy was having a difficult time wrapping her head around was how different everything was this Christmas.

A couple of years ago, Austin and Millie got married; then they had a baby. Then Carson married his best friend Perry, and now Flynn and Jessie Jane were engaged after what seemed to Cassidy to be a whirlwind fling.

She couldn't imagine anything like that.

Because Dalton wasn't a whirlwind.

He was stable and steady. He was everything she valued.

Right. All of the women he'd had casual affairs with would call him stable and steady.

Okay. Maybe they wouldn't.

But she knew him as stable and steady. He was always good to her. Always patient and wonderful and exceptionally kind.

He was everything she could ever want in a man.

The crowd around the booth began to disperse, and that was when she saw him.

Hands moving in broad gestures as he told a story that made Jessie and Perry double over with laughter. Cassidy felt an absurd prick of jealousy. She had nothing to be jealous about. Perry and Jessie weren't single.

She picked up her pace. She cut across the lawn rather than walking around the perimeter and ignored the delicious-smelling treats as she made a beeline for her family.

"Hi," she said.

The conversation broke off, and she became very aware of the fact that she had just crashed in. Not only that, but they had all responded to her appearance by ceasing their conversation.

Her brothers were careful with her. Maybe a little bit too careful, because of the circumstances surrounding her coming to Rustler Mountain. Everyone was so painfully aware of the fact that she'd been abandoned, and while it was really sweet that they worried about her and all, she didn't need to be treated like a charity case. Or like she was tragic.

Though, to be fair, she definitely acted like the youngest, most coddled member of the group. It was a learned habit. And now that everybody was pairing off, getting married, having children, it seemed . . . silly. She felt silly. She wanted things to change.

She looked at Dalton, and her heart jumped. "What's so funny?"

"Oh, I was talking about the time my brother and I were hunting and he got a deer. Then we came up over the mountain, and there was a bear feeding on the deer that he just dropped. Well, then he got the bear, and went running down the hill shouting, 'Two-for-one!'"

She knew this story. Of course she did. It had happened way back when Dalton was a kid, and he got a lot of mileage out of it. But she laughed anyway, because she loved to hear him tell it.

"That's ridiculous," Jessie said, wiping a tear underneath her eye. "What are the chances?"

"They must not be very good, because I've never known another person that it happened to. And it never happened to him again."

"He was just lucky, I guess," Cassidy said, smiling at him.

"I guess so," he responded. "I know I am."

And she tried to pick that apart. To see if there was anything underlying those words. A secret message that was meant only for her. Or something.

Jessie sighed heavily and looked at her phone. "I have to start another round again. Just pounding out a shoe, but look, there's a crowd coming."

"You look tired," Cassidy said, meaning to be helpful.

But Jessie flinched. "Do I?"

"Not in a bad way," Cassidy said hurriedly. "In a way that suggests you're very industrious."

Her older brother Flynn reached over and clapped his hand on her shoulder. "Quit while you're only a little bit behind, Cass."

Cassidy felt her smile falter. "Can I help with anything?"

"You can go gather some people," Jessie said.

"I will," she said, scampering away and finding a knot of teenagers. "There's a blacksmithing demonstration starting over there. Free to watch."

She moved through the group of people, marveling at all the strange faces. So many people drove all the way out to Rustler Mountain around the holidays. It was a local tourist attraction. The kind of place that was worth an hour's drive.

Sometimes Cassidy wondered what it would be like to live close to a movie theater, a chain restaurant, or a Walmart, instead of being well over an hour away. But her ultimate conclusion was that it just wasn't the life for her.

She liked living here. The sense of community, the traditions.

She had no intention of leaving. She liked stability. The familiarity of Rustler Mountain. The sameness of life here.

Well, a lot of things in her life had changed lately, but *she* had no intention of changing.

Except, she did want things to change with Dalton. It was what she had always hoped for.

And if he rejects you, then what?

No. She'd had enough bad things happen to her. She had been over this in her mind before. If you were abandoned by your mother, brought to a town you had never even heard of to live with your father, who died right before you arrived, leaving you totally stranded with three feral older brothers, then you were owed some smooth sailing.

She was convinced of that. Or rather, she wanted to be convinced of that.

She gathered quite a crowd to visit the booth, where she watched her brother admiring Jessie's handiwork.

"She's something," said Flynn.

The way he looked at his fiancée, it was just so obvious he was head over heels in love. It was really something. It brought her back to that earlier interaction with Dalton. What had she seen in his eyes?

She couldn't be sure.

But then, nothing ventured, nothing gained.

She turned her focus on Jessie, who was heating the horseshoe, bringing it out of the forge when it was bright red, and hammering it forcefully, the sound of metal on metal filling the air.

She went on until the shoe was the perfect shape, then doused it in water, cooling it. She gave it to a triumphant little girl in the front row.

"I didn't know girls could do jobs like that," the little girl said.

"Of course we can," said Jessie. "And I'm also going to be the mayor of this town. We can do anything we put our minds to."

Cassidy smiled. Because the exchange was adorable. And honestly, it just made her proud to call Jessie part of the family. Funny, because Jessie was a Hancock, and only two years ago, her older brother Austin would have had a heart attack if he'd been told that a Hancock was going to marry into his family.

Wilder family lore was deep and vast. Well, the lore of this entire town was like that. Founded during the gold rush, Rustler Mountain had been filled with pioneers, both good and bad. When Austin had started doing deep historical research into their family roots, it turned out that the ones who had been touted as heroic for years were somewhat more complex.

For years town lore had been all about the heroes and the villains. The outlaws and the lawmen. And, of course, the Wilder family had been among the outlaws.

Her brother was named after Austin Wilder, who had been a stagecoach and train robber, notorious throughout the state of Oregon for his crimes. He had ridden with his two brothers and a fourth gang member named Butch Hancock. Until Lee Talbot, sheriff of Rustler Mountain, had shot Austin Wilder dead in the street and had the other Wilders hanged for suspicion of murder.

But it turned out that Lee Talbot had colluded with Butch Hancock, agreeing to give him immunity if the sheriff could have the notoriety of taking down Oregon's most notorious gang. The Wilders had been criminals, but they had never committed murder.

Austin had set the record straight in his best-selling book, and Millie had started setting the record straight throughout town, which had led to a lot of historical inaccuracies and half-truths being corrected. Now the true history of the town could be told, not just by the victors—white men who liked to claim ultimate authority— but also through the stories of Chinese immigrants, of Black settlers who had met with hostility and been kept out of the state because of virulently racist laws, and of course the Native tribes whose land had been taken from them.

So maybe things did change. And some of them definitely needed to.

She looked over at Dalton.

And then the atmosphere around the booth changed. Shifted. As if the air itself shivered.

She turned because she was compelled, like steel to a magnet. And not just her apparently, because every head turned.

West Hancock had just arrived. He wasn't dressed seasonally.

He wore a tight black T-shirt, muscular arms on display for no reason. Black ink licked up his forearms, past his biceps, and disappeared beneath the sleeves of the shirt.

He also had a black cowboy hat, black jeans, black boots.

He was, without a doubt, the only man in town with a more dangerous reputation than her brothers.

Visit our website at
KensingtonBooks.com
to sign up for our newsletters, read
more from your favorite authors, see
books by series, view reading group
guides, and more!

BOOK CLUB
BETWEEN THE CHAPTERS

Become a Part of Our
Between the Chapters Book Club
Community and Join the Conversation

Betweenthechapters.net